ONE WAY OUT

Rinker was ready, his hands close to his guns. There was a strange light in the man's eyes, a glowing mix of sadistic joy and the urge to kill that Tyree recognized only too well. He knew right then that this man would not let it go.

Then Dave Rinker went for his gun.

Tyree drew fast from the waistband, and his first bullet hit Rinker square in the chest. Another, a split second later, crashed into the man's forehead.

The big man convulsively triggered a round that thudded into the sod roof. Then his Colt dropped from his hand as he slammed backward onto the table, sending glass flying. Rinker tumbled off the table and fell flat on his back, his stunned eyes wide. The gunman tried to say something but the words wouldn't come. He rattled deep in his throat and blood bubbled scarlet and sudden over his lips. His glazed stare fixed on the glow of the lamp above his head . . . but by then he was seeing only darkness.

Ralph Compton

Guns of the Canyonlands

A Ralph Compton Novel
by Joseph A. West

A SIGNET BOOK

SIGNET
Published by New American Library, a division of
Penguin Group (USA) Inc., 375 Hudson Street,
New York, New York 10014, USA
Penguin Group (Canada), 90 Eglinton Avenue East, Suite 700, Toronto,
Ontario M4P 2Y3, Canada (a division of Pearson Penguin Canada Inc.)
Penguin Books Ltd., 80 Strand, London WC2R 0RL, England
Penguin Ireland, 25 St. Stephen's Green, Dublin 2,
Ireland (a division of Penguin Books Ltd.)
Penguin Group (Australia), 250 Camberwell Road, Camberwell, Victoria
3124, Australia (a division of Pearson Australia Group Pty. Ltd.)
Penguin Books India Pvt. Ltd., 11 Community Centre, Panchsheel Park,
New Delhi - 110 017, India
Penguin Group (NZ), cnr Airborne and Rosedale Roads, Albany,
Auckland 1310, New Zealand (a division of Pearson New Zealand Ltd.)
Penguin Books (South Africa) (Pty.) Ltd., 24 Sturdee Avenue,
Rosebank, Johannesburg 2196, South Africa

Penguin Books Ltd., Registered Offices:
80 Strand, London WC2R 0RL, England

First published by Signet, an imprint of New American Library,
a division of Penguin Group (USA) Inc.

First Printing, February 2006
10 9 8 7 6 5 4 3 2 1

THE IMMORTAL COWBOY

This is respectfully dedicated to the "American Cowboy." His was the saga sparked by the turmoil that followed the Civil War, and the passing of more than a century has by no means diminished the flame.

True, the old days and the old ways are but treasured memories, and the old trails have grown dim with the ravages of time, but the spirit of the cowboy lives on.

In my travels—to Texas, Oklahoma, Kansas, Nebraska, Colorado, Wyoming, New Mexico, and Arizona—I always find something that reminds me of the Old West. While I am walking these plains and mountains for the first time, there is this feeling that a part of me is eternal, that I have known these old trails before. I believe it is the undying spirit of the frontier calling, allowing me, through the mind's eye, to step back into time. What is the appeal of the Old West of the American frontier?

It has been epitomized by some as the dark and bloody period in American history. Its heroes—Crockett, Bowie, Hickok, Earp—have been reviled and criticized. Yet the Old West lives on, larger than life.

It has become a symbol of freedom, when there was always another mountain to climb and another river to cross; when a dispute between two men was settled not with expensive lawyers, but with fists, knives, or guns. Barbaric? Maybe. But some things never change. When the cowboy rode into the pages of American history, he left behind a legacy that lives within the hearts of us all.

—*Ralph Compton*

Chapter 1

Who the hell was Owen Fowler?

As he crossed a broken lava ridge, then rode through high green hills on his way to the three miles of brush flats that would take him to the town of Crooked Creek, the rider on the long-legged zebra dun asked himself that question time and time again.

And with good reason.

Less than four hours before, Owen Fowler, whoever he was, had cost a man his life—and Chance Tyree, now staring moodily beyond the hills to the dusty, sunbaked flats, had killed him.

As they so often did, the gunfight had come up suddenly—and ended with deadly finality.

Tyree reined up in the shade of a post oak, hooked a leg over the saddle horn and built a smoke. He thumbed a match into flame, lit the cigarette, then, dragging deep, brought the shooting to mind, remembering how it had been. . . .

Twenty miles back along the trail, he'd ridden into a settlement, a decaying annex to nowhere built along one bank of a wide, sandy creek. Even as such places went, the town wasn't much—a sod-walled saloon with a sagging timber roof, a general store of sorts, a scattering of tarpaper shacks and a small livery stable fronted by a corral built hit or miss of pine poles. The windmill that pumped water from the creek into an overflowing barrel at one side of the store screeched for oil, and a skinny yellow dog hunting sagebrush lizards nosed around in a clump of bunchgrass near the stable.

The dog lifted its head to look as Tyree swung out of the saddle while he was still a good twenty yards from the saloon. The animal studied the tall young rider for a few speculative moments, decided he was of little interest and went back to its exploring.

Keeping the dun between himself and the saloon, Tyree opened his saddlebags, lifted out a black gun belt and slid a Colt from the leather.

For a few moments the young man studied the worn blue revolver as it lay in the palm of his right hand. In the past, the weapon had seen much of gunfighting and there was within Tyree a growing desire to set the Colt aside, to move into a present clear of powder smoke where all the dying was done and past and the screams that echoed through his dreams at night would finally fade into silence.

There is little a man can do about the past, except forget it. There is, however, a great deal he can do about the present and the future.

With this thought uppermost in his mind, Tyree shoved the Colt into his waistband. A man armed and belted attracts attention. Eyes go to the iron on his hip and other men wonder: Is this just a drifting cowhand who carries a gun only to use the butt to pound nails, the barrel to stretch fence wire? Or is this man of a different stamp, a skilled and sudden fighter who has made his mark and killed his man?

All too often the answers to those questions were written in hot lead. Not wishful of inviting such speculation, Tyree took a hip-length, elk-skin coat from under his blanket roll and quickly shrugged into the garment, pulling it almost closed to cover the walnut handle of the Colt.

The coat was fringed, decorated on the shoulders and front with Kiowa beadwork. A few years back it had cost Tyree a good paint pony and a jug of whiskey. He figured he'd gotten the best of that trade.

Tyree led his horse to the saloon, looped the reins around the hitching post and stepped inside.

The saloon was a single room, built tight and close, but Tyree was grateful for its relative coolness, willing to ignore the pervading stink of tobacco juice, man sweat and stale beer. Dust-specked light from a pair of unglazed windows angled onto the bar—a timber plank laid across a pair of sawhorses. From the ceiling hung an oil lamp, casting a dim orange halo in the gloom. An assortment of bottles stood on a shelf behind the bartender, a big-bellied man wearing a brocaded vest and dirty, collarless shirt. Above the shelf hung a printed sign that asked: HAVE YOU WRITTEN TO MOTHER?

To Tyree's right a small, thin man with the quick, sly eyes of a bunkhouse rat sat at the only table in the place, a bottle and glass in front of him. A couple of men stood at the bar, one middle-aged and nondescript, a puncher by the look of him, the other a tall, wide-shouldered towhead, Colts holstered low on his thighs, wearing his gunman's swashbuckling arrogance like a cloak.

All this Tyree took in at a glance, aware that he had in turn become the object of scrutiny.

The two at the bar and the man at the table were studying him closely, taking in his wide-brimmed Stetson, the Kiowa work on his coat and the jinglebob spurs chiming on the heels of his boots, the rowels cut from Mexican silver pesos. The boots themselves were custom-made, the expensive leather sewn sixty stitches to the inch, using an awl so fine that if it had accidentally pierced the boot maker's hand the wound would have neither hurt nor bled.

Tyree knew that his outfit spoke loudly of Texas, and this was confirmed when the bartender smiled and asked, "Fair piece off your home range, ain't you, Tex?"

"Some," Tyree admitted, prepared to be sociable if that was what it took. He was aware that the towhead's intent gaze was slowly measuring him from the top of his hat to the tip of his boots. The man was on the prod. A combination of belligerence and meanness bunched up hot and eager in his pale eyes.

Tyree had run into his kind before, a would-be hard case, probably with a local reputation as a fast gunman. Such men were not rare in the West. Boot Hills from Texas to Kansas and beyond were full of them.

Tyree, mindful of his decision to leave gun violence behind him, made up his mind right there and then to have no part of him.

"What will it be?" the bartender asked.

"Anything to eat around here?"

The bartender scratched under a thick sideburn, then nodded to a glass-covered dish at the end of the bar. "What you see is what I got. You like cheese? I got cheese and soda crackers." He glanced behind him. "Maybe I got soda crackers."

"It'll do," Tyree answered. "And a cold beer."

"All I got is warm beer."

"Just so long as it's wet."

The bartender found a plate, dusted it off on his apron and moved to the end of the bar. He fingered some chunks of yellow cheese onto the plate, added a handful of soda crackers, then set the plate in front of Tyree. From somewhere at his feet he came up with an amber bottle of beer, thumbed it open and laid it alongside the plate.

Tyree took a sip. It was warm and flat, but it cut the dust of the trail in his throat. The cheese smelled strong and the soda crackers were stale.

The man watched Tyree eat for a few moments, then asked, "Where you headed, Tex?"

Tyree shrugged as he picked a cracker crumb off his bottom lip. "No place in particular. Just passing through."

"That's a damn lie."

The voice had come from behind him, that quick. That raw.

"What did you say, mister?" Tyree asked, his hazel eyes, more green than brown, moving to the towhead who was now standing square to him, straddle-legged, thumbs tucked into his gun belts.

"You heard me plain enough. I called you a damned liar."

There was a vindictive challenge in the towhead's words, the voice of one who had killed his man and was anxious to kill again.

A man can step away from a woman's insult. He may feel that he's all of a sudden shrunk to three feet tall, but he can swallow his pride and walk away from it. An insult from another male is a different matter entirely. There's no walking away from that, not if a man wants to hold his head high and be judged and counted among other men.

This Chance Tyree knew, and he felt a familiar anger burn in his belly. The towhead was a reputation hunter acting out a timeworn ritual Tyree had seen before. This man would not be turned aside by talk, yet Tyree knew he had to make the attempt.

He popped a piece of cheese into his mouth and chewed, looking at the towheaded gunman reflectively, unhurried, seemingly lost in thought, like a man pondering the frailty of human nature. Finally he slowly shook his head, turned to the bartender and made a rubbing motion with his fingers. "Towel? Your cheese must have been feeling the heat because it was sure sweating considerable."

The bartender laid both hands on the counter, his alarmed eyes slanting to the towhead. "Dave, I want no trouble in my place. You heard the stranger. If he says he's passing through, then he's passing through. Hell, he ain't even carrying a gun."

"I don't believe that. He's got one hid away fer

sure." The rat-eyed man at the table stood. He stepped beside the man called Dave. "We know why he's here, don't we, Dave? I say he's tryin' to fool us."

"Sure we know why he's here, Charlie," Dave answered. "But he ain't fooling nobody and that's why he's got two choices—ride on back the way he came or die right where he stands."

Charlie smiled, showing prominent green teeth wet with saliva. "Better make your choice, stranger. This here is Dave Rinker. He's killed more men than you got fingers. He's fast on the draw, mighty fast."

Tyree ignored both men and again turned to the bartender. "Where's that towel?"

The man threw Tyree a scrap of dirty dishrag, then watched as the tall stranger wiped off his hands. He leaned across the bar, his mouth close to Tyree's ear. "Now fork your bronc and ride on out of here, Tex, like the man says," he whispered. "The food and the beer are on the house."

"Much obliged," Tyree said. He turned to face Dave Rinker, a slight smile tugging at his lips. "Now all Mr. Rinker has to do is apologize for that ill-considered remark about my honesty, and I'll be on my way."

To Rinker, this was the grossest kind of affront. He was a man used to bullying lesser men, who spoke and acted respectfully, wary of his low-slung Colts. Tyree's quiet demand had thrown him. The big gunman's jaw almost dropped to his chest and his pale blue eyes popped. "Me, apologize to you? Apologize to a two-bit hired bushwhacker? The hell I will."

"Owen Fowler sent for you, didn't he?" Charlie asked, a taunting note in his voice. "Admit it, Tex. Didn't that no-good preacher killer send for you?"

The other man at the bar, the gray-haired oldster in puncher's clothes, stepped away, opening space between him and Rinker. "I ain't waiting for apologies or otherwise," he said, his wary eyes lifting to Tyree standing cool and ready. "I'm ridin'."

Rinker laughed. "You scared, Tom? Hell, I can shade this saddle tramp."

"Maybe," Tom said. "Maybe not. Either way I don't plan on sticking around to find out."

After the old puncher swung quickly out of the door, Tyree said, "Care to make that apology now, Rinker?"

A tense silence stretched between the two men, the saloon so still that the soft rustling of an exploring rat in the corner was unnaturally loud. Then the bartender spoke, his words dropping into the taut quiet like rocks into an iron bucket. "Maybe he's telling the truth, Dave. Maybe Owen Fowler didn't send for him. He could be just passing through like he says."

"Zack, you shut your trap," Rinker said. "I know why he's here. He's sold his gun to Fowler all right. You know I got no liking for Fowler, so now this is between Texas and me."

"The worst and last mistake you'll ever make in your life, Rinker," Tyree said, his voice suddenly flat and hard as he moved his coat away from his gun, "is to keep pushing me. So go back to your drinking and just let it be." He smiled, forcing himself to relax. He decided to make one final attempt to get this thing to go away. "But just to show there's no hard feelings, I've decided to pass on the apology. I'm going to let bygones be bygones." He nodded toward the door. "Now will you give me the road?"

"Sure," the big gunman said, full lips stretched wide in a cruel grin under his sweeping yellow mustache, "you can go through that door—with four men carrying you by the handles."

Rinker was ready, his hands close to his guns. There was a strange light in the man's eyes, a glowing mix of sadistic joy and the urge to kill that Tyree recognized only too well from past experiences. He knew right then that this man would not let it go.

Then Dave Rinker went for his gun.

Tyree drew fast from the waistband, and his first bullet hit Rinker square in the chest. Another, a split second later, crashed into the man's forehead, just under the rim of his hat.

The big towhead convulsively triggered a round that thudded into the sod roof. Then his Colt dropped from his hand as he slammed backward onto the table, sending Charlie's bottle and glass flying. Rinker tumbled off the table and fell flat on his back, his stunned eyes wide, unable to believe the manner and the fact of his dying. The gunman tried to say something but the words wouldn't come. He rattled deep in his throat and blood bubbled scarlet and sudden over his lips. His glazed stare fixed on the glow of the lamp above his head . . . but by then he was seeing only darkness.

Hammer back, Tyree's gun swung on Charlie. But the little man threw up his hands and screamed, "No! Mother of God, no! Don't shoot! I'm out of this!"

"Shuck that gun belt and step away from it, or I'll drop you right where you stand," Tyree said.

Charlie's trembling fingers quickly unbuckled the gun belt like it had suddenly become red-hot and let it fall. He backed toward the door, looking down at Rinker, a tangle of shocked emotion in his eyes.

"But Dave was fast," the man whispered, shaking his head in disbelief. "He was the fastest around."

"Had he ever been to Texas?" Tyree asked.

"No . . . I mean, I don't think so."

Tyree nodded. "Figures."

From force of long habit, he punched the empty shells out of his Colt, reloaded, then stuck the big revolver back in his waistband. He turned to the bartender.

"You saw what happened. I didn't want this fight and Rinker was notified."

The man opened his mouth to speak, but said nothing, his Adam's apple bobbing like he was trying to swallow a dry chicken bone.

"What's your name, bartender?" Tyree asked.

"Zachary," the man answered finally, his stunned, haunted eyes a mirror image of Charlie's. "They call me Zack Ryan, when they call me anything."

Tyree motioned toward the dead man. "Well, Zack Ryan, will you take care of this?"

The bartender gulped, then nodded. "Sure, sure, Tex, sure. Anything you say."

Tyree dug into the pocket of his pants and chimed three silver dollars onto the bar. "A man should be buried decent," he said. "Lay him out fitting and proper in his best suit, and get a preacher to say the words."

"I'll do it," Ryan said, nodding again, his face gray. "I'll do right by him."

Tyree lifted a hand. "Thanks for the beer and the food."

He turned and stepped toward the door, his spurs ringing like silver bells in the sullen, smoke-streaked silence.

"Wait," Ryan said, his curiosity overcoming his fear. "Did Owen Fowler really send for you?"

Tyree stopped in his tracks. "Who the hell," he asked, a vague anger tugging at him, "is Owen Fowler?"

Chance Tyree ground out his cigarette butt on the heel of his boot, then swung his long leg back into the stirrup. "Well," he said, to no one but himself, as is the habit of men who ride lonely trails, "maybe I'll meet this Owen Fowler one day. Then him and me will have words."

Tyree shook his head and kneed the dun forward in the direction of the flats.

He harbored no illusions about Crooked Creek.

The town would be the same as the last he'd visited, and the ones before that. The warm beer and raw whiskey would taste the same. The same choking yellow dust would cloud the street and the people would be as he'd found them in all the other towns he'd passed through, uncompromising men and women bred hard for a harsh land where nothing came easy.

Tyree was thirty years old that summer of 1883, and behind him lay a decade of gun violence, rake-hell years of blood, fury and sudden death. Many

times he'd walked the line between what was lawful
and what was not. In those days to be young and
brave and full of fight were qualities other men ad-
mired, that fleeting moment of blazing, reckless
youth when the old sat quietly in the shadows and
watched and wondered and said nothing.

His ma had died giving birth to him. His pa had
grieved for a while, then taken a new wife. Tyree
had been raised hard and tough, knowing little of
parental warmth or affection. His pa was too occu-
pied with trying to wrest a living out of a two-by-
twice ranch on a dusty creek south of the Balcones
Escarpment.

When he was thirteen, his pa had given him a
swaybacked grulla horse and four dollars and told
him it was time for him to leave and seek his fortune.
"Things are tough around here, Chance," he'd said,
"what with cattle prices the way they are an' all. I
got your new ma and the three younkers to care of
an' I just don't have the money to feed you and put
clothes on your back no more. So you see how things
are with me here."

Tyree turned his back on the ranch without regret
and spent the next seven years drifting, working in
the hard school of the cow camps and the long, dangerous drives up the trails to Kansas.

During those years he bought his first Colt revolver and learned how to use his fists. By the time
he was eighteen he was counted a man and respected
as a top hand.

He'd just turned twenty, still lacking a man's meat
to his wide shoulders, when he'd first sold his gun.

Tyree had ridden with John Wesley Hardin, the Clements brothers and the rest of the wild DeWitt County crowd in the murderous Sutton-Taylor feud. He'd learned his trade well, patiently tutored by Hardin, a fast, deadly and pitiless gunfighter who had shown him the way of the Samuel Colt's revolver and taught him much of the men who lived by it.

Since then Tyree had hired out his gun in five bitter range wars, worn a town-tamer's tin star twice and for six months had ridden the box as a scatter-gun guard for the Lee-Reynolds Stage Company out of Dodge.

Tyree had been shot once, by a gunman named Cord Bodie, who did not live long enough to boast of it. Three years later he'd taken a strap-iron arrow in the thigh during a running fight with Comanche on the Staked Plains.

He stood three inches over six feet in his socks and weighed a lean two hundred pounds that year, all of it muscle crowded into his shoulders, chest and arms, the tallow long since burned out of him by sun, wind and a thousand trails through the wild country. When circumstances dictated, he'd suffered from the bitter cold of the high mountains like any other man, cursed the sweltering, gasping heat of the desert and gulped at the thick, fetid air of the Louisiana bayous and fervently wished himself somewhere else. But Tyree had the capacity to endure, to reach down deep and draw on a seemingly bottomless reserve of strength and will, and that was what set him apart from lesser men and made him what he was.

If asked, the only reason he would give for riding

into the Utah canyonlands was that he wanted to see
a place he'd never seen before, to stand and wonder
at its beauty and lift his nose to the talking wind.

Like most of his restless breed, he knew that the
iron road, the telegraph and the sodbuster's plow
were changing the vast Western landscape forever.
Soon it would all be gone and there would never be
its like again. Not in his lifetime, nor in any other.

He could not dam the tides of progress, so he
would see the magnificent land, live it . . . and in
later times remember and tell others how it had been.

And maybe, just maybe, he'd find a place out here
where he could flee his reputation as a gunfighter,
and hang up his Colt forever. He could drink his
coffee of an evening from his own front porch, his
face crimsoned by the fire in the sky. And maybe
there would be a pretty woman rocking at his side
and a passel of tall sons to take care of them both
when they grew old.

Tyree rode through blue hills fragrant with the
smell of juniper and sage, the sun hot on his back.
He was still a mile from the flats when he topped a
rock-strewn ridge, then headed down into a narrow
valley where a stream chuckled to itself as it ran over
a pebbled bottom and crickets made their small
sound in the grass. The gulch was a pleasant spot,
shaded from the sun by the leaves of tall cottonwoods, the air smelling of wildflowers. Tyree reined
up and swung out of the saddle.

The day was hot and the brassy ball of sun burned
in a sky the color of faded denim. He decided to let
his tired dun drink and then graze for an hour before
taking to the flats. Crooked Creek could wait. There

was no one there to welcome him, no woman with per-
fumed hair smiling from her doorway, her voice husky
with desire—just strangers wary of other strangers.

Tyree eased the girth on the horse and led the animal to the creek. As the dun drank, so did he,
stretched flat out on his belly on the bank. After
drinking his fill he splashed water on his face and
combed wet fingers through his unruly black hair.
He smoothed his sweeping dragoon mustache with
the back of his hand then settled his hat back on his
head, the lacy tree shadows falling dappled around
him.

The dun had wandered off to graze. Tyree took off
his coat, fetched up against a cottonwood trunk and
rolled a smoke. When he'd finished the cigarette, he
closed his eyes, enjoying the quiet, lulled by the
laughter of the creek and the soft, restless rustle of
the cottonwoods.

He eased his position against the tree as the dun
wandered close to him, cropping grass, and he tilted
his hat further over his face.

Gradually, he drifted . . . his breathing slowed . . .
and he let sleep take him.

A hard kick on the sole of his boot woke Chance
Tyree from slumber.

"Get on your feet, you."

Tyree opened his eyes and saw a bearded man towering above him, the rock-steady gun in his hand pointed
right at his head. He turned and saw another man a few
feet away to his left. That one held a Winchester.

Each wore a lawman's star on his vest. They
looked like grim and determined men.

Moving slowly, his gun hand well away from his body, Tyree rose to his feet. The man with the rifle stepped closer, reached out and yanked the Colt from his waistband.

"Who sent for you?" the rifleman asked. His hair was gray, his eyes tired and washed-out in a thin face lined deep with years and hard living.

Tyree shook his head, cursing himself for letting his guard down. "Nobody sent for me. I'm just passing through."

"Like hell you are," the bearded man said, his black eyes ugly. He was huge, big in the arms and shoulders, and he seemed to have the disposition of a cornered cottonmouth. "Are you kin to Owen Fowler? Or has he hired himself a Texas gunfighter?"

"Mister," Tyree said, a sudden anger flaring in him, "I've no idea who the hell Owen Fowler is. I've never met the man."

"What you think, Clem?" the lawman with the Winchester asked, a moment's doubt fleeting across his face. "You think maybe he's telling the truth?" Without waiting for an answer, he motioned to Tyree with the muzzle of the rifle. "What's your name, boy?"

"Are you asking, or is the law asking?"

"What the hell difference does it make?"

"The difference is I'll answer to the law, but not to you."

"All right," the man said. "I'm Deputy Sheriff Len Dawson. That there is Deputy Clem Daley, and around these parts, we're the law. The only law."

"Then it's Chance Tyree."

Daley scratched his bearded cheek. "Seems to me

I've heard that name afore." He thought for a few moments, scowling in concentration, then nodded. "Hell, now I remember. You were the kid gunfighter out of El Paso. I recollect you rode with John Wesley Hardin and the Clements boys an' them a spell back. You made all the newspapers. They say you rannies played hob and not all of what you done was honest."

"That was a long time ago." Tyree shrugged. "A man changes, and he rides so many trails, he forgets how it was after ten years."

"Strange though," the lawman said. "I mean, you being here the week Owen Fowler gets back, and you being a Texas hired killer an' all."

"Texas and other places," Tyree said. His anger flared. "And I never hired on to kill a man who didn't need killing."

Dawson spoke, his voice ragged with concern. "Clem, maybe we should take Tyree back to town. Best we let Sheriff Tobin decide what to do with him."

The man called Clem shook his great nail keg of a head. "Len, what did Quirt Laytham tell us, huh? He said to get rid of any gun-toting strangers who couldn't give a good account of why they was riding into the canyon country." Clem waved his Colt in Tyree's direction. "Well, he's a gun-toting stranger and he's riding into the canyon country and he's given no good account for being here that I've heard."

"I dunno," Len muttered. "Maybe he's tellin' the truth—just passin' through. Maybe he is. I still say we take him to the sheriff."

"Sheriff!" Clem yelled, disgust heavy in his voice. "I don't take orders from Nick Tobin, that useless, pink-eyed tub of guts. I take my orders from Mr. Laytham and so do you. Laytham told us to get rid of saddle tramps like this 'un who might be riding for Fowler, and when he said get rid of them, he meant permanently."

Chance Tyree knew he had to keep these two talking. So long as they were jawing, they weren't shooting and they might let down their guard long enough to give him an opening.

"Listen, who is this Owen Fowler who's supposed to have hired me?" he asked. "Like I told another feller back on the trail, I don't know the man."

"What feller?" Daley asked, suspicion shading into his eyes.

Tyree shrugged. "A man called Rinker."

"Handsome Dave Rinker?"

"Yeah, I guess that was his name. I never heard the handsome part."

"What happened between you and Rinker?"

"He accused me of being a hired gun for Owen Fowler," Tyree answered. "Then he drew down on me."

"You're here," Dawson said. "Where's Rinker?"

"In hell probably," Tyree answered. He hesitated a heartbeat. "He was notified."

"Dave Rinker was fast on the draw, mighty slick and sudden," Clem said, the suspicion in his eyes replaced by accusation.

"Maybe hereabouts," Tyree said. "Not where I come from." He played for time again. "You didn't tell me about this Owen Fowler feller."

"Him?" Daley said, his mouth twisting into a sneer. "Like you don't know already. Hell, I'll tell it anyway. Fowler murdered Deacon John Kent, the finest, most decent man who ever walked the earth. Deacon Kent was our town preacher, but Fowler shot him in the back anyhow and robbed him of his watch and the few coins in his pockets."

"If he committed murder, why isn't Fowler in prison?" Tyree asked, wondering if Clem Daley would know a decent man if he met one. It seemed the big lawman was parroting words he had heard from others.

"He was in prison," Daley said. "He got twenty-five years at hard labor. That was nine years ago. But this spring cholera broke out in the jail and Fowler helped nurse the sick prisoners. They say he saved the lives of a hundred men, but to my mind that don't count a damn against the thing he done." Daley spat, as though the words he was about to speak tasted bad in his mouth. "Anyhow, the governor pardoned Fowler and now he's come back. He's at his ranch up near Hatch Wash—again like I'm telling you something you don't already know. Well, we burned out that murdering rustler afore, and we'll do it again. Only this time we'll make sure because we're gonna hang him."

Daley smiled like a snake about to strike. "Like I'm fixing to hang you, boy."

Tyree looked into the deputy's burning eyes and found no lie there. On the slenderest thread of evidence, coming upon a stranger who happened to be in the wrong place at the wrong time, the lawman suspected him of being in cahoots with a rustler by the name of Owen Fowler. Daley had set himself up as judge, jury and executioner—and he aimed to do exactly what he'd promised.

Desperately, Chance Tyree tried to get Daley talking again, but the big man shook his head. "Pardner, I'm all through jawing." He turned to Dawson. "Len, bring me your rope."

Dawson hesitated, nervously chewing on the end of his mustache. "Clem, this ain't right. Hangin' is a hell of a way to kill a man. Let's you an' me take him into town. Maybe he can explain hisself to Mr. Laytham."

"His explaining is done," the big deputy answered. "Len, like you said already, you and me is the law in these parts, and the law is gonna hang this hired killer. Why would he ride all the way up here from Texas if it wasn't to sell his gun to Fowler? Huh? Tell me that."

Dawson shook his head. "I dunno. He says he's passin' through."

"In a pig's eye. Quirt Laytham wants us to get rid of gun tramps like this, and that's how it's going to be." Anger flashed red across Daley's cheekbones. His scarlet-veined eyes scorched into Tyree like hot coals. "Now bring that damn rope like I told you."

There was no compromise in Daley and no mercy either, and Tyree knew it. He took his chance and dived for the gun in the lawman's hand. Surprisingly fast and agile for such a big man, Daley danced to his right, swung the Colt and the barrel crashed hard against the side of Tyree's head.

As Tyree fell, he saw the ground rush up to meet him, then open wide and swallow him whole. He plunged, yelling, into the abyss.

Chapter 2

Awareness returned slowly to Chance Tyree and with it came pain, beating inside his skull like a gigantic hammer pounding on an anvil. A green sickness curled in his belly like a living thing and before his eyes he saw only a gray, shifting mist.

He tried to remember, fighting through the agony in his head. It came to him then. He was headed for a town . . . What was its name? Crooked Creek. That was it: He must be riding across the brush flats to Crooked Creek. The big zebra dun danced restlessly between his legs and blew through its nose and he had a mind to pat the horse's neck and settle it down.

But he couldn't move his hands!

Tyree opened his eyes. The valley around him spun wildly, the tumbling creek rocking up and down like a board laid across a log, a thing he'd seen children use for play.

Then he felt the rawhide ring of the honda pressing hard against his skin just under the lobe of his right ear. He tried to move his hands again, but they were tied behind his back.

"You got anything to say, boy, a prayer maybe?"

The voice came from a long distance away, like someone speaking at the end of a tunnel.

Tyree tried to concentrate, struggling to find the words. He knew his time was short. "You got no right to hang me," he croaked finally, looking down at Daley as his vision cleared. "I'm drifting, a stranger passing through."

"I got every right," Daley said, his face tight and hard. "Mr. Laytham is a big man around these parts and it was him who gave me the right. He said to get rid of any low-down buzzard who is kin, friend or hired man to Owen Fowler."

As his eyes began to focus, Tyree saw Dawson standing off to one side, looking gray and sick, and suddenly very old.

"You," Tyree called out to the deputy. "Can you stop this?"

Dawson shook his head, the rifle in his hands quivering. "Clem here wants you dead, son, and so would Mr. Laytham if'n he was here. It ain't up to me to stop this thing. Best you make your peace with God and take your medicine."

"Go to hell," Chance Tyree said, knowing further pleas were useless.

Daley looked up at Tyree. "Hard thing for a man to die with a cuss on his lips." The huge lawman stepped to the back of the dun and slapped the horse on the rump.

Startled, the animal darted forward and Tyree bumped over the high cantle of the Denver saddle and swung free, the noose yanking tight around his neck. A million stars exploded inside his skull and he found himself choking, battling for breath. He kicked his legs, desperately fighting for life as he slowly strangled, the merciless noose mocking his efforts.

There came a noise like thunder as a gunshot trembled loud in the air—then a sudden shock of pain like someone had crashed a sledgehammer into his left side . . . and Chance Tyree knew no more.

He woke to darkness. Floating somewhere above him, a man's face swam into view and he heard a voice ask, "How are you feeling?"

Tyree tried to talk, but found no words, only a raspy croak that quickly died in his throat.

"You take it easy," the man said. "You're hurt real bad. You can talk later."

Mustering his strength, Tyree lifted his head a few inches off the ground. He tried to speak again, and this time managed a feeble, "Who . . . are . . ."

"Who am I?" the man finished for him, and Tyree saw the blurry hint of a smile in a long, melancholy face. "Why, they call me Owen Fowler."

Tyree laid his head back on the grass. "Well, I'll be damned," he whispered.

And he let the darkness take him again.

The night was shading into a pale amber dawn, a solitary star standing sentinel in the sky, when Tyree woke.

For a while he lay still, desperately trying to remember what had happened to him. After a few moments, it began to come back to him, fitting together piece by piece—the fight in the saloon and then his run-in with Clem Daley and Len Dawson. But much of it was still hazy, like a half-remembered dream, faces moving like ghosts through the dim verges of his memory.

He turned his pounding head and looked around him. A tall, lanky man with the face of a martyred saint was squatting over a small fire, a coffeepot smoking on the coals. Beside him lay a Henry rifle and farther away a big buckskin grazed near the stream, a few fallen leaves from the cottonwoods lying on his back.

Tyree struggled to rise, but could not muster the strength and sank back to the ground. He heard the rustle of a man's feet through the grass, looked up and saw Owen Fowler towering over him.

"So you're still with us," Fowler said. "Couple of times during the night I sure thought you wasn't going to make it." The man shrugged. "Your breathing slowed and I felt your heart flutter, like it was giving out finally."

Fowler kneeled beside Tyree. "You're a tough one, all right, and mighty hard to kill. I did what I could for you, cleaned the bullet wounds in your side, then plugged them up with prickly pear pulp. The Indians use it to stop inflammation and infection and I guess they know what they're doing."

Tyree's hand strayed to his neck and Fowler nodded. "Your skin is badly burned by the rope. Couldn't do much for that except boil up some thistle blossom and bathe the burns. Sometimes it works, sometimes it doesn't. I guess we'll find out."

"What happened?" Tyree asked, the two words coming hard and painful from his torn-up throat.

A slight smile touched Fowler's lips. "Well, near

as I can tell, you were half-hung, then shot. I was riding west of here, getting reacquainted with the land on account of how I've been away for a fair spell, and I saw Clem Daley and Len Dawson leading a saddled dun across the flats. Daley was wearing a fancy buckskin coat, Apache maybe—"

"Kiowa. It was my coat."

"Well, anyhoo, it seemed to me them two had been up to no good, so I came looking and that's when I found you. And just in time, I reckon. Another couple of minutes and you'd have been dead as hell in a parson's parlor."

"I'm beholden to you," Tyree said. "You saved my life."

Fowler waved away his thanks. "Think nothing of it. Glad I was close by."

"I'm betting it was Len Dawson who shot me," Tyree managed, the words coming slow in a weak whisper. "I guess he wanted to put me out of my misery, but his hands were shaking so bad, he made a mess of it."

"Oh, he didn't mess up too badly," Fowler said, his voice matter-of-fact. "His bullet hit just above your belt on the left side and exited out your back an inch higher. I don't think any vital organs were hit, but I'm not a doctor so I can't tell for sure."

Fowler was silent for a few moments, then said, "Dawson has killed his share, but he's not the worst of them. Daley now, he's poison mean and good with a gun and his fists. The talk is that he's killed seven men, and I believe it."

Tyree tried to rise again, and Fowler helped him sit up, propping his back against a cottonwood trunk.

After he recovered from the pain caused by the shift of position, Tyree rasped, "Those two said they were acting on orders from a man named Quirt Laytham."

The skin suddenly tightened around Fowler's eyes. "Laytham is the man whose lying testimony got me sentenced to twenty-five years behind bars for murder. He swaggers a wide path around here, owns the biggest ranch for a hundred miles in all directions and is hungry for more, mine included. There are maybe two, three hundred cows on my grass right now, and all of them belong to Quirt Laytham."

"Him and me have a score to settle," Tyree said. He touched the rope burn on his neck. "For this. The two who hung me were acting on Laytham's orders."

"Best you rest your voice for a while," Fowler said. "Keep talking and you may lose it altogether."

Fowler rose and poured coffee into a tin cup. He kneeled behind Tyree and held the cup to his lips. "Careful," he said. "It's hot, but it will do you good."

"I can manage," Tyree said. He took the cup from Fowler and drank. The coffee was strong and bitter, the way he liked it, and it seemed to give him strength.

Fowler watched Tyree drink, then bit his lip as he thought for a few moments. Finally he said, "Mister, I don't know who you are but—"

"Name's Chance Tyree."

Fowler nodded, his eyes suddenly guarded. "Heard of you, prison talk mostly." He was silent for a while, then said, "You being a named Texas gunfighter won't help you none in Crooked Creek.

Go against Laytham and his riders and you'll be bucking a stacked deck. Quirt is fast with a gun, but there are two working for him who are even faster. One is a breed, a natural born killer who calls himself the Arapaho Kid. And the other is Luther Darcy."

If Fowler expected a reaction from Tyree he was disappointed. "There will be a reckoning between Laytham and me," Chance croaked. "Depend on it."

"The name Luther Darcy doesn't mean anything to you?"

Tyree shook his head, a gesture that made pain flare in his throat. "No. Why should it?"

"Then you'd better learn up on him right quick," Fowler said. "There are them who say Darcy is the fastest gun west of the Mississippi and there are others who claim he's the fastest who ever lived, or will ever live, come to that. He killed a named man up in the Montana Territory a while back, then another in Crooked Creek just a few days ago."

Tyree managed a weak smile. "I've come up against a few with that kind of reputation before and I'm still here."

His eyes bleak in his long, melancholy face, Fowler said, "Maybe you're still here on account of how you never come up against Luther Darcy."

Chapter 3

The dawn brightened into morning and the cobalt blue sky was banded by streaks of red and jade. Tyree finished his coffee and built a smoke with unsteady hands. Beyond the hills, toward Crooked Creek, the last shadows had been washed from the brush flats and the wakening jays were already quarreling among the branches of the cottonwoods.

After a while Tyree tried to get to his feet, but the effort drained him and he slumped back to the ground, his head reeling.

Owen Fowler tightened the cinch on his buckskin then stepped beside the wounded man. "We have to ride," he said. "I got the feeling Len Dawson and Clem Daley will come back to check on their handiwork. We don't want them to find us here. Not if we want to keep on breathing, we don't."

A flicker of doubt crossed Fowler's face. "Think you can stay on a horse?"

Tyree nodded. He knew he was very weak and the pain of the bullet wound in his side was a living thing that gnawed at him. His head pounded and his mouth was dry, his torn throat on fire.

"Which way are we headed?" he asked.

Fowler gestured vaguely to the northeast. "That way. Across the brush flats then into the canyonlands. My place, such as it is, is off Hatch Wash, and that's a fair piece away." The man hesitated, then added, "Had me a cabin once, but that's gone. I've been sleeping under the stars since I got back."

Something in Fowler's face told Tyree this wasn't going to be an easy trip. He had heard enough about the canyon country to know he was facing a harsh, unforgiving wilderness of rawboned rock ridges and high-walled mesas, the gorges so deep the rivers were lost below steep cliffs that hid the daylight. Even the Indians had steered clear of the place, visiting it only out of necessity, and seldom at that.

As though reading Tyree's mind, Fowler kneeled beside him. "Where we're headed the country is wild and mighty lonely. The land is broken and raw, all tumbled together, like God grew bored with it and left it unfinished." He smiled. "It's no bargain but considering the alternative, I'd say we've got little choice in the matter."

"I'll ride," Tyree said. He struggled to his feet and the ground suddenly rocked so violently under him that Fowler had to quickly reach out and support him. Blood loss had left Tyree as helpless as a baby, and he cursed himself for his own weakness. He was a proud man who had never in his life asked help or a favor of anyone, and now he was totally dependent for his survival on a man he hardly knew.

"Can you make it?" Fowler asked, concern shading his dark brown eyes.

"I'll make it," Tyree answered. "Let's hit the trail." He looked at Fowler and saw the doubt in the man's homely features. "I told you, I'll make it," he said, a sudden, stubborn anger in him.

Fowler nodded. "Just so you know what you're getting yourself into." A slight smile tugged at his lips. "Right now, Tyree, I'd say your chances of reaching my place are slim to none, and slim is already saddling up to leave town."

Tyree disentangled from Fowler's supporting arm. "Let's ride," he said, his face stiff. "Believe me, I can get there."

Fowler swung into the saddle of the buckskin, then kicked the stirrup loose for Tyree. It took the wounded man several attempts before he summoned the strength to finally get up on the buckskin and settle himself behind the high cantle of Fowler's saddle.

"Ready?" Fowler asked.

"As I'll ever be," Tyree answered.

"Then let's get it done."

When he thought about it later, Tyree could recall little of that ride.

The sun was already hot when they crossed the brush flats then entered the canyon country, but in the gorges between the cliffs and mesas the heat was almost unbearable.

Around them spread an immense, rough-hewn wilderness of sculptured rocks, needles, arches and narrow slot canyons that seemed to stretch away forever in all directions. Stunted spruce grew on the flat tops of immense mesas, desperately struggling for life in an uncaring environment, and the air smelled dry, like the dust of ancient Indian dead.

Only occasionally, mostly along the banks of the creeks, would there be islands of green with trees and grass where fat, white-faced cattle grazed.

"Quirt Laytham's cows," Fowler said, talking over his shoulder as they rode under spreading cottonwoods. "See his Rafter-L brand? Looks like he's pushing his herds into the whole damn country."

Tyree heard but did not answer. The pain in his side hammered at him and the skin of his face and neck felt thin and chafed. His hands were stiff and hard to close.

He knew he needed rest, lots of it, to regain his strength. His revenge on Laytham and the deputies who worked for him would have to wait. For the present, they could enjoy their victory. The reckoning would come later.

It was not in Tyree's nature to back away from what he believed was right. He had been abused, victimized on the orders of a man who didn't even know him, a man who made judgments only in the light of his own greed for wealth and power.

An enduring, sometimes stubborn man, there was in Chance Tyree a fierce determination to live, to fight back and win. He knew of no other way.

He and Fowler rode on. Despite its double load, the man's rawboned buckskin made light of the trail. For miles they traveled in silence, the only sound the soft footfalls of the horse and the high lonesome creak of saddle leather.

The sun climbed in the sky and the day grew hotter. Riding among the canyons was like traveling through a gigantic brick oven. Above them, the sky had been scorched to a pale lemon and the dry dust kicked up by the horse rose around them in veils of swirling tan and yellow.

Tyree dozed, wakening only now and then when Fowler quickly reached back and stopped him from toppling off the horse.

As the daylight began to fall, the cry of a hunting peregrine falcon woke Tyree for the last time. "Hatch Wash just ahead," Fowler said, feeling the younger man stir. "We're almost home. And, as I said before, it sure ain't much."

Tyree blinked his eyes into focus and looked over Fowler's shoulder. They were riding through a narrow gulch that gradually opened up ahead of them, revealing two narrow bands of green on either side of a shallow creek that wound between high canyon walls. Beyond the walls, towering cliffs, mesas, sandstone domes and spires of rock seemed to stretch away forever, here and there rincons, ancient streambeds, showing as yellow streaks high on their steep pink, yellow and red sides.

"The wash runs for twelve miles," Fowler said. "Runs pretty much north and then west. But I guess you'll be glad to hear we're not going that far."

The man kicked his buckskin into an easy lope, and Tyree found himself passing through thick stands of fragrant piñon and juniper. As the trail edged closer to the east bank of the wash, the trees changed to cottonwoods and willow, and cattle lifted their dripping muzzles from the water to watch them as they rode past.

"More of Laytham's cows," Fowler said, his face like stone.

Fowler swung his horse away from the creek, heading for what looked like a break in the canyon wall. The grass played out and the ground they crossed was sandier, covered in a profusion of desert shrubs, mostly sagebrush, greasewood and blackbrush, with tall leaves of yucca spiking among them.

From the trail, the break had looked narrow, but as he got closer Tyree saw that it was maybe two hundred yards wide, carved out of the flat side of a mesa. Fowler entered the break, then rode up a gradual incline onto a flat, open bench. He crossed that bench, then another, the buckskin blowing a little, before riding into a wide, hanging valley shaped like a great, open amphitheater, the thousand-foot walls of the mesa hemming it in on three sides.

"We're here," Fowler said. "This is where I call home." He glanced over his shoulder and grinned without humor. "At least I did, nine years ago."

Tyree glanced around him. The valley was at least nine hundred acres in extent, and had probably been formed when the mesa split and part of it collapsed during some ancient earth shake.

The grass was green and rich, watered by a stream Tyree heard bubble near the far wall. Close to a hundred cows were in the valley, grazing or hunkered down under scattered spruce trees. All of them were sleek Herefords branded with Laytham's Rafter-L.

Fowler kicked the buckskin toward the far parapet

of the canyon and stopped at a wide rock overhang. The sheer wall behind the jutting slab of sandstone was covered in ancient paintings of tall, angular, human figures surrounded by zigzag patterns of red, yellow and blue.

"That's Ute work," Fowler told Tyree. "Sometimes they used this valley as a hunting camp." He swung out of the saddle, and Tyree, not wishful of being helped from the horse, slid off the buckskin's rump. His feet hit the ground and immediately his knees buckled and he fell flat on his back.

"Need some help?" Fowler said, a smile tugging at his mouth as he looked down at the younger man. "Seems to me like you do."

Tyree grimaced. "I can stand on my own feet."

He willed himself to rise, but when he did the canyon bucked wildly around him. His head spun and he staggered against the side of the buckskin.

Fowler nodded. "Heard about the gunfighter's pride—jail talk," he said. "Never seen it in practice until now."

But this time there was no argument from Tyree.

He allowed the man to grab him by the waist and help him into the shelter of the overhang where Fowler made him sit, propping his back against the wall.

"Guess I'm weaker than I thought," Tyree said, lifting his eyes to Fowler, his smile weak and forced. "I'm glad you were here."

It was an apology of sorts and Fowler accepted it as such. "You just sit there tight and I'll rustle us up some grub." He hesitated, his hands on his hips, then

said, "Sorry about the accommodation. My cabin"—
he jerked a thumb over his shoulder—"was over
there. It was a nice one, too. But Quirt Laytham and
his boys burned me out."

Fowler shook his head. "All they left me was ashes
and a few memories."

Easing his back against the hard stone of the wall,
Tyree's eyes lifted to the older man. "Fowler, you
don't look to me like a man who would shoot another man in the back. Someday you have to tell me
what happened between you and that preacher."

"Sure," Fowler answered, the bleakness in his face
suddenly making him look old, "someday." He nodded, his eyes distant. "Yup, maybe someday."

The man walked away and Tyree wondered at
him. Fowler didn't look like a killer, more like a
dreamer than a doer, and he had a gentle, easy way
about him, both with people and horses. Had he
really put a bullet into a preacher's back and then
robbed him? It seemed hard to believe. And what of
all that talk he'd heard from Clem Daley about him
being a rustler? Certainly all the cows in this canyon
bore a Rafter-L brand, but Fowler said Laytham had
put them there and that rang true.

Tyree shook his head. He had much to learn about
Owen Fowler. The question was—did he have anything to fear?

It was full dark, the sky spangled with stars, when
Fowler started a fire and boiled up coffee. From his
meager supplies he sliced salt pork into a pan,
cooked it to a golden brown, then fried thick slices
of sourdough bread in the smoking grease.

"This isn't exactly invalid food," he said, handing Tyree a huge sandwich and a cup of coffee. "But right now it's all I've got."

"It'll do," Tyree answered, suddenly realizing he was ravenously hungry. "My last meal wasn't much, and I been missing the six before that one."

"After prison grub, everything tastes good," Fowler said around a mouthful of food. "They fed us pickled beef that was left over from the War Between the States and biscuit from the war before that." The man shrugged. "The trick with a biscuit is to hammer it on the table so most of the weevils fall out. Then it isn't too bad, if a man has teeth. Army biscuit can be as hard as a chunk of bois d'arc wood. Tastes like it, too."

When they'd eaten, Fowler took up his Henry rifle and nodded toward the entrance to the valley. "Years back, I discovered a game trail on the southern cliff that leads to the top of the mesa. I'll spend the night up there. I don't expect Laytham and his boys to come looking for us in the dark, but you never know. If he does, I want to see him coming." He hesitated a few moments, then added, "At first light I'll come down and change the dressings on your side."

"Thanks," Tyree said. "You really think he'll come?"

Fowler nodded. "He'll come all right. I'd say by this time he knows you wasn't hung all the way. Now he has to kill us both. Me, so he can get clear claim to this valley, and you to shut you up about what happened and what's going to happen in the future. You can bet the Arapaho Kid has picked up our tracks already."

"Fowler," Tyree said urgently, "I need a gun. I mean, I need a gun in the worst way."

"I know you do," the older man said. "But Len Dawson has your guns, so all we got is this here Henry—and about now I'm the only one of us well enough to use it."

"You shoot real good?" Tyree asked, a vague hope rising in him.

"Me?" Fowler answered, grinning. "Hell, no. I shoot real bad."

Chapter 4

Fowler's food, rough and ready as it was, had given Tyree strength. When the man left, Chance unbuttoned his bloodstained shirt and carefully examined his gunshot wound. He had no way of knowing how the one in his back looked, but when he removed the prickly pear plug the entrance wound showed no sign of infection, though it was an angry red and sore to the touch.

As far as he could tell, the bullet had gone through clean and hadn't hit any vital organs. But how long would it be before his strength returned?

Tyree had no answer to that question, but to prove to himself that he was already on the mend, he rose unsteadily to his feet. He would scout the canyon and see how he held up.

The moon was riding high in the sky, touching the rims of a few clouds with silver, when he came on the stone foundation of Fowler's cabin. Judging by the charred beams that were left from the roof, the cabin had been built solid, skillfully crafted to last by a man who knew carpentry and liked to use his hands.

Tyree was puzzled. Fowler had obviously planned to put down roots here, make a home for himself. Why throw it all away by murdering a well-respected preacher for his watch and the few dollars in his pockets?

The killing didn't make any sense, and Tyree decided that when Fowler came down from the mesa come sunup he'd ask him for the whole story.

He stood in the moonlight and looked around him. The cattle had stirred, got to their feet and were now grazing, all of them Quirt Laytham's.

Fowler said the rancher had lied about his role in the preacher's murder. Did someone else kill John Kent, maybe a nameless saddle tramp passing through the canyon country? It could be that Kent's death dropped like a plum into Laytham's lap, a golden opportunity to pin the murder on Fowler and claim his land.

Tyree's eyes lifted to the top of the mesa rising a thousand feet above the valley floor. The moonlight touched the branches of a few juniper growing near the edge and bathed the mesa's pink-and-red walls in a pale glow.

Up there the wind would be blowing and would help Fowler keep alert. Tyree fervently hoped the man's eyesight was better than his shooting skills. If Laytham and his men rode into the valley undetected, he and Fowler would be caught in a death trap.

The canyon grass showed signs of overgrazing, in

some places worn down to bare patches of mud. If Quirt Laytham wanted to expand his empire, he'd have to push constantly for more water and grass, both hard to come by in the barren canyon country.

But there was another way—take away grass and water from those who already owned it. That had been done before in Texas and a lot of other places. From what he'd learned of Quirt Laytham, the man was ambitious enough to be capable of anything.

Tyree allowed himself a wry smile. He'd thought to ride into the canyonlands to find peace and quiet, away from guns and gunfighting men. Instead, he'd kicked over a hornet's nest, and it seemed like every man he'd come in contact with had his stinger out and was spoiling for trouble.

Then so be it. He would give Laytham and the rest all the fight they could handle—and then some.

After making a round of the canyon, Tyree returned to the camp under the rock overhang and studied the colored drawings on the wall. Fowler had said the Utes had occasionally used this place for shelter, and he found small scraps of the finely woven baskets in which they'd stored food. There were also fragments of water jugs, made with coiled ropes of tough yucca or bear grass lined with pine pitch.

Related to the Comanche, the Utes had earned a reputation as mighty warriors with an implacable hatred of the white man. But now, like all the once mighty horse Indians, they were penned up in reservations and the passing of time was already fading the drawings they'd made. Soon those, like the Utes themselves, would be gone forever.

Suddenly weary, the bullet wound in his side seeping blood, Tyree sought his blankets and lay on his back, staring at the moon-splashed sky. The stars looked so close, he felt like he could reach up and grab a handful and let them trickle, shining like silver dollars, through his fingers.

He smiled at the thought; then, the soft cropping sound of the grazing cattle lulling him, he surrendered to sleep.

"Wake up, Tyree! We got to get out of here!"

As is the way of a man who has ridden dangerous trails, Tyree was awake instantly, every sense alert.

"What's happening?" he asked, settling his hat on his head. "Is it Laytham?"

Fowler nodded, his dark eyes revealing his unease. "Probably Laytham. Big dust to the south, coming on fast. We have to move."

Tyree rose to his feet, swaying from weakness and fatigue. The night was dying around him, brightening into dawn, a burnished gold sky showing to the east banded by thin streaks of dark blue cloud. There was a slight chill in the air that would soon be gone, and a faint breeze fanned his cheek.

Fowler was already tightening the cinch on the buckskin when Tyree stepped beside him. "Where are we headed?" he asked.

"North," Fowler answered, "toward Dead Horse Point. Three, maybe four miles this side of the point, there's a slot canyon that branches off to the east off the wash. We'll be safe there"—a faint smile touched Fowler's lips—"at least for a while."

Fowler hurriedly threw what remained of his food

into a sack then swung into the saddle. Tyree slipped a foot into the stirrup and climbed up behind him. He bit back a groan as the wound in his side reopened, suddenly staining his shirt with fresh blood.

"The Arapaho Kid could track a minnow through a Louisiana swamp," Fowler said. "He'll find us eventually and we'll have to move again—unless . . ."

"Unless what?" Tyree asked.

"I just had a thought. But I need time to study on it some. I'll let you know later what I decide."

They left the canyon at a fast trot then looped north along the wash, walls of red rock rising sheer on either side of them. After ten minutes Fowler glanced over his shoulder. "They're riding after us, Tyree. Laytham must have sent that damned Arapaho breed to check the canyon and discovered that we'd lit a shuck. Now he knows we're right in front of him."

Tyree turned and studied their back trail. A dust cloud was rising into the air about a quarter of a mile behind them, and judging by the way it moved, Laytham's riders were coming on at a fast gallop.

At first the buckskin stretched out, setting a good pace. But, carrying a double load and worn out from yesterday's long ride, the horse began to falter, its steady gait slowing.

They'd soon be caught and out here in the open they wouldn't stand a chance.

He looked over Fowler's shoulder to the trail ahead. Like the prow of a great ship, the wall of a dome-topped butte jutted into the wash. At its base were heaps of talus, sandstone rocks that had tumbled down from higher up the slope. The wash rounded the wall then turned sharply to its right, so that what lay beyond was hidden from Tyree's sight.

If they had to make a stand, that was as good a place as any.

"Fowler!" Tyree yelled. "Rein up this side of the butte."

"Why? Man, they're almost on top of us. They'll shoot us all to pieces."

"Don't argue," Tyree snapped. "Damn it, Owen, just do it."

Fowler pulled the buckskin to a ragged halt at the base of the butte, and Tyree clambered awkwardly off the horse's rump. He reached out a hand to Fowler. "Give me the Henry and your canteen."

"But you're in no shape to—"

"The Henry!" Tyree snapped. "And the canteen. Now!"

Fowler looked down at the younger man and read something in his green eyes that chilled him. Without another word he slid the rifle from the boot under his knee and passed it, with the canteen, to Tyree.

"This is my kind of game, Fowler," Tyree said, his drawn, tight face suddenly softened by a smile. "And, unlike you, I shoot pretty good."

"What do you want me to do?" Fowler asked. "I can't leave you here to face Laytham and his men alone."

"Get round the other side of the butte," Tyree said. "When I come a-running, be ready to fog it on out of here."

Fowler's eyes lifted beyond Tyree to the rising plume of dust bearing down on them. He seemed to realize that the younger man's skill as a gunfighter was the only thing that stood between them and death, and he gathered up the reins of the buckskin.

"Tyree," he said, *"buena suerte, mi amigo."*

Tyree's smile grew wider. "Thanks. Something tells me I'm going to need all the luck I can get."

Tyree took up a position among the jumble of talus, his front and sides protected by slabs of sandstone rock, the steep slope of the butte behind him. He looked down the wash, his far-seeing eyes probing the distance.

The dust was much closer now, maybe only a few minutes away. Tyree levered a round into the brass chamber of the Henry and studied the land around him.

Laytham had no way to flank his position. He and his men would have to come at him along the bank of the wash. Apart from a few scattered cottonwoods, to his right there was no cover. Tyree would place his trust in the rapid fire of the Henry to break up their charge.

The sun had just begun its climb into the sky, but the morning coolness was gone and the day was already hot. Tyree felt weak and light-headed, and sweat prickled the grazed skin of his neck. He took off his hat and laid the back of his head on the slope of the butte, his burning, red-rimmed eyes closing. It would be so easy to drift into sleep. . . .

The drum of hammering hooves on the bank of the wash jolted Tyree back to wakefulness. A dozen men were riding toward him at a breakneck gallop, a big, handsome man in a black broadcloth suit and flowered vest in the lead.

Now was not the time for carefully aimed fire. Tyree had to shoot fast to break up Laytham's charge and turn back his oncoming riders.

Rising to his feet, he threw the Henry to his shoulder and cranked off four quick rounds. The results of his firing were devastating.

Hit hard, a man yelled, threw up his arms and toppled backward off his horse. A big sorrel in the lead went down, throwing its rider. Coming on fast, another horse crashed into the fallen animal's flailing hooves and it too tumbled, cartwheeling headfirst into the ground. Its rider, a man in a black hat and black-and-white cowhide vest, screamed as he fell under the horse and the saddle horn crashed into his chest.

Tyree fired at the man in the broadcloth suit, guessing he was Laytham. A miss. Now their trailing dust cloud had caught up with the riders, shrouding them in a shifting, swirling yellow fog.

"Back!" somebody, probably Laytham, yelled. "Damn it, get back!"

His blood up, Tyree fired rapidly into the dust, at the wild tangle of bucking horses and cursing men. He thought he saw another man jerk from the impact of a bullet, then Laytham's riders were heading back the way they'd come, the thick dust that roiled around them making further shooting useless.

Tyree lowered the rifle and a grim smile touched his lips. Quirt Laytham had thought this was going to be easy, twelve against two—one of them wounded and maybe dying, the other a man who couldn't shoot. Instead he'd sure enough grabbed a cougar by the tail.

At least three of his men were dead or wounded, and a third, the man in the cowhide vest, was pinned under his horse, gasping out his life, his face ashen.

As the dust settled, Tyree saw that Laytham and the others had drawn out of rifle range. They were milling around, as though uncertain of what to do next. They'd been badly burned and didn't seem overly anxious to mount another charge.

Tyree turned as Fowler stepped beside him. The man's eyes scanned the destruction Tyree had wrought and he whistled between his teeth. "You sure played hob," he said.

"They'll be back," Tyree said, a sudden weariness in him. "And next time they'll be more careful. From what I've been told about Laytham, he's not a man to quit so easily."

Fowler dug into the pocket of his threadbare coat and gave Tyree a handful of .44 shells. He watched as the younger man fed them into the Henry, then asked, "You think maybe this is a good time for us to make tracks?"

Tyree shook his head. "They'd only take out after us, and if they catch us in the open without cover, we're dead." He smiled and lightly tapped the Henry. "When Laytham makes up his mind to come this way again, I aim to discourage him for good. I want to make damn sure that old dog is done hunting before we fog it on out of here."

"He won't charge us next time," Fowler said, so low and soft it was like he was talking only to himself. "He'll maybe send the Arapaho Kid. That breed can move like a ghost." He turned to Tyree. "You look like hell, by the way."

"Thanks," Tyree said. "And I feel worse than I look. I reckon I'd have to be three days dead before I'd start to feel better."

"You want me to stay close?" Fowler asked.

Tyree shook his head. "No, go back to the horse. Like I told you before, if I come running, just be ready to hightail it out of here."

"Suit yourself," Fowler said. He dug into a pocket again and passed Tyree a chunk of antelope jerky. "It isn't tasty, but it will keep you going."

After Fowler was gone, Tyree chewed on the tough jerky and studied the open ground in front of him. Laytham and his men had drawn off about a half-mile along the wash, taking refuge behind a jutting outcrop of sandstone rock. Judging by all the shouting that was going on, they were arguing among themselves about their next course of action.

Most of these men were the same stamp as Len Dawson and Clem Daley, riders hired for their gun skills, their loyalty stretching only as far as next payday. They'd been badly shot up by a skilled rifleman and no longer seemed eager for the fight.

Tyree smiled as he built himself a smoke. He'd never been a soldier, but he'd learned enough about tactics over the years to know that attacking an entrenched enemy along a narrow front was always a losing proposition.

He calculated that right about now Quirt Laytham must be fuming, and the thought pleased him immensely.

Tyree thumbed a match into flame and lit his ciga-rette. He pushed the Henry out in front of him and waited. When would Laytham renew the attack? That question was answered less than ten minutes later.

A bullet hit a rock near where Tyree was crouched, splattering stinging splinters into his cheek. A second thudded into the butte above his head and a third smashed into the Henry, sending it flying from its place on the rock.

Tyree stretched out and picked up the rifle—and his shocked eyes beheld a disaster. The shot, luckier than most, had badly mangled the magazine tube close to the chamber.

He swore under his breath. The rifle would shoot the round under the hammer, but the chances were that it would not feed a second. Without the Henry, he was as good as dead and Fowler with him. It was not a thought to comfort a man.

Tyree scanned the bank of the wash and saw a flash of metal behind a cottonwood about a hundred yards away. Laytham's men were coming at him on foot, using whatever cover they could find.

Drawing a bead on the cottonwood, Tyree waited. A few slow seconds ticked past, then he saw a man in a blue flannel shirt step out from behind the tree, his Winchester coming up fast.

Tyree fired at the same time as the Laytham rider. The man jerked under the impact of the Henry's .44 bullet and his rifle spun away from him. Clutching a shattered and bloody shoulder he turned and, crouched over, stumbled away, his face white with shock.

Lead whined off a rock in front of Tyree as he worked the lever of the Henry. To his relief, he heard a reassuring *clink-clunk* as the bent and dented loading tube fed a round. But would it feed another?

There was no time to ponder that question. A man was working his way along the canyon wall toward him, a second close behind. Both were carrying Winchesters and were stepping warily, their eyes on Tyree's position.

Tyree sighted on the man in the lead. He took a breath, held it and squeezed the trigger. His bullet hit the tobacco sack tag hanging over the man's shirt pocket dead center. The Laytham rider spun, then slammed against the mesa wall. He slid to a sitting position, his head lolling loose on his shoulders, dead before he hit the ground.

The second man fired a wild shot that split the air above Tyree's head; then he was running, looking back fearfully over his shoulder.

"Five down, seven to go," Tyree whispered to himself, his smile a grim, tight line. He tried to crank the Henry, but the lever jammed halfway on a mangled round.

The damaged rifle was useless.

Weak as he was, the side of his shirt glistening with blood, Tyree knew Laytham and his surviving men were still dangerous and capable of mounting another attack.

He had to find a replacement rifle and fast. The trouble was, the guns were out there . . . with the dead.

Chapter 5

Warily, Tyree rose from his position behind the rocks. Moving on cat feet, he stepped toward the canyon wall. It was very hot and still, the rugged parapets of rock surrounding him a barrier to any passing breeze. Overhead the sky was blue, hemmed in close by the stone ramparts on either side of the wash, a few fluffy white clouds visible now and then. The Laytham rider he'd killed was still slumped over in a sitting position, the front of the man's shirt thick with blood that was already starting to dry.

The rifle he needed was there, and along with it the dead man's revolver. Looking constantly in the direction of Laytham and his riders, Tyree kneeled beside the dead man, knowing that if the rancher decided to attack now he'd be caught out in the open and quickly cut down.

Tyree picked up a .44-.40 Winchester that lay close to the body and stripped the gun belt from the man's waist. The Colt was nickel-plated with hard rubber grips and was in the same caliber as the rifle. Every loop in the cartridge belt was full. Tyree strapped the gun belt around his hips, adjusting the position of the holster to his liking.

There was as yet no sign of another attack, and Tyree took time to look around him. The bay gelding that had earlier collided with the downed sorrel was grazing in the shade of a cottonwood near the creek, apparently unhurt. Tyree took a couple of steps toward the animal and called out softly. The bay lifted its head, the bit jangling, studied the approaching human for a few moments without concern, then went back to grazing.

There was still no sign of Laytham's men, and Tyree decided to take a chance. He needed a horse and what looked to be a good one was standing just a few yards away. Speaking in a reassuring whisper to the animal, he stepped closer. The bay again lifted its head, but this time the horse nickered uneasily and arcs of white showed in its eyes as it pranced backward a few steps.

"Easy, boy," Tyree whispered, still moving toward the horse. "Easy, boy."

The bay retreated further, stepping lightly, its head high, alarmed by the closeness of the tall man and the smell of blood that clung to him.

Tyree made a grab for the trailing reins, but the bay sidestepped, then turned and galloped back in the direction of Laytham and the others.

Cursing under his breath, Tyree watched the horse go, its hammering hooves kicking up a churning cloud of dust. He turned and went back to his position among the rocks, disappointment tugging at him.

He'd badly wanted that horse and now it was well out of his reach.

The day wore on and the shadows cast by the cottonwoods slowly lengthened. The sky shaded to a cobalt blue and now the passing clouds were rimmed with gold. His eyes bloodshot and painful, Tyree kept his gaze on the trail beside the creek, but he saw no sign of activity.

Had Laytham gone, deciding to wait for another day when the odds would be more in his favor?

That question was answered a few minutes later when the rancher himself rode toward Tyree's position, a white rag tied to the barrel of the rifle he carried butt down on his right thigh. Laytham's teeth showed white under his full, black mustache. But he was not smiling. It was the irritated grimace of an angry man.

Laytham was flanked by a big-bellied fat man on a mouse-colored mustang. The man had a lawman's star pinned to his vest and his mouth was concealed by a huge, ragged mustache, the ends drooping over the first of his several chins. Sheriff Nick Tobin wore round, dark glasses and, judging by the white of his hair and mustache, Tyree guessed the man was an albino, his eyes sensitive to the glare of the sun.

There was a pale, unhealthy look to Tobin, like he'd been buried deep in damp ground for a week, then dug up and shoved on a horse. Yet his shoulders and arms were thick, and Tyree realized not all of the man's bulk was fat.

Laytham reined up when he was still a hundred

yards away and he cupped his mouth with his left hand, a plaited leather quirt dangling from his wrist.

Tyree idly wondered if that was how the man had gotten his name.

"Chance Tyree!"

"I hear you, Laytham," Tyree yelled. "What do you want?"

"You killed some of my men, Chance Tyree. That was an ugly thing, mighty ugly."

"They were trying to do the same to me, Laytham."

The big rancher kneed his horse forward and stopped closer to Tyree's position. "I'm carrying a flag of truce, Tyree," he said.

Despite his weakness and the gnawing pain in his side, Tyree laughed. "Don't go thinking that's going to protect you any if I take it into my head to shoot."

Laytham stiffened slightly in the saddle, but not a trace of fear crossed his heavily jowled face with its massive, stubborn chin.

"Chance Tyree, I know you," Laytham called out. "Heard about you being an expert Texas shootist who has killed his share of men. Heard you gunned Handsome Dave Rinker over to—"

"If that's what you heard, you heard right."

Tyree shifted the Winchester to his shoulder, putting his sights squarely on the top button of Laytham's fancy vest. If this was a trap, the big rancher would be the first to die.

"Chance Tyree! Can you hear me? This is Sheriff Tobin."

"I guessed who you were, Tobin."

"Tyree, Mr. Laytham has leveled a very serious accusation. He says Owen Fowler has been rustling his cattle and has taken them back to his canyon. I saw the brands on those cows, Tyree. They're Rafter-L."

"Tobin, Laytham told you a damned lie. His cattle are on Fowler's grass all right, but Laytham put them there."

The following silence stretched into several minutes as Tobin and Laytham, heads together, discussed matters between them. Finally the sheriff kneed his horse a few steps forward and yelled, "Tyree, we have a proposition for you."

"Let's hear it."

"It's Owen Fowler we want, not you. I could arrest you for murdering members of my legally appointed posse. But I won't, not if you come out of them rocks. I'll give you back your horse and guns and you can ride out of the territory free as you please. That's a mighty generous deal Mr. Laytham and me are offering you, Tyree, and I advise you to take it."

Tyree smiled. He knew if he accepted Tobin's offer he'd be playing with a cold deck. The sheriff and Laytham would never let him leave the canyon country alive.

"Forget it, Tobin," Tyree yelled. "I'm not going to bite at that worm." He hesitated a few moments, then yelled, "Laytham, now it's your turn to listen to what I have to say. Acting on your orders, Tobin's deputies hung me for no other reason than I was a stranger passing through. Owen Fowler saved my life and I plan on standing by him."

"Damn you, Tyree!" Laytham yelled. "Damn you and your kind to hell."

The rancher made a move to swing his horse away, but Tyree's shout stopped him. "Laytham, I could shoot you out of the saddle right now. But that would be too easy. I plan on destroying you. You walk a wide path, but I aim to strip you of everything you own. I'll ruin you, Laytham."

Tyree lowered the rifle from his shoulder. "There's a reckoning to come between us. Depend on it."

His face black with rage, Laytham stood in the stirrups and roared, "You talk of reckonings, Tyree, and you're right—there's one to come. But it will end with you and Fowler kicking from the same gallows. You have my word on that."

"Your word means nothing to me, Laytham," Tyree yelled. "Now hightail it out of here before I lose sight of that surrender flag and start shooting."

An anger beyond anger hurtling him into the ragged edge of insanity, Laytham bellowed like a wounded animal and ripped the white rag from his rifle. He threw the Winchester to his shoulder, but Tobin quickly raised his hand and grabbed the barrel. Tyree couldn't hear what the sheriff was saying, but judging by the frantic manner the man was gesticulating, he was pleading with Laytham to let it go and wait for another day.

Tyree rose to his feet and shouldered his own rifle. If Laytham came at him, he'd be forced to drop the man, spoiling the plans he was making for him.

But it seemed that Tobin's frenzied words had gotten through to the rancher. Laytham abruptly turned his horse and galloped back toward his waiting men.

For a few moments the fat sheriff sat his mount, staring in Tyree's direction, the flaming evening sky reflecting bloodred in the lenses of his glasses.

"Tyree," the man yelled, "this was ill done. Mr. Laytham means what he said. He'll see you hang."

"Pick up your dead, Tobin," Tyree called back, suddenly tired, all his talking now done. "Bury them decent for God's sake."

The sheriff made no reply. He turned his mustang and trotted after Laytham, his back stiff. When the lawman was gone, Tyree left his place in the rocks and rounded the butte where Fowler stood beside his buckskin.

"Heard all that," he said. "You've made my enemies your enemies and it seems to me that neither of us stands a chance against them."

Tyree managed a grim smile. "I was a stranger passing through. They had no call to do what they did to me. Count on it, there will be a reckoning."

Fowler shook his head. "Chance, we were lucky today. You killed a few of Laytham's men, but they weren't the best of them. He still has a score of riders left, the Arapaho Kid and Luther Darcy among them." The man stepped closer to Tyree and put his hand on the younger man's shoulder. "Take my horse. Ride north out of here and don't stop until you clear the Utah Territory. This is my fight, not yours."

"No, Owen," Tyree said. "When they hung me, shot me and left me for dead, it also became my fight."

Exasperation showed on Fowler's narrow, lined

face, its gray jailhouse pallor not yet burned away by the sun. "But Quirt Laytham is too big and getting bigger by the day. One man can't declare war on an empire."

Without a trace of false pride or brag in his voice, Tyree looked Fowler in the eye. "This one can."

Fowler, in turn, looked into Tyree's eyes and saw a terrible green fire. He realized with a dawning certainty that hell was coming to the canyonlands.

Chapter 6

Both of them again up on the buckskin, Tyree and Fowler followed Hatch Wash north for several miles as the day faded into evening. Out among the canyons the talking coyotes were filling the night with their sound and a hunting cougar roared once in the distance, then fell silent.

Fowler swung west and splashed across the creek, entering a narrow draw with steep, high walls. Struggling spruce and juniper were just visible in the failing light, clinging to narrow outcroppings of rock high above them. The bottom of the draw was sandy and clumps of mesquite grew here and there, brushing against the legs of the riders with a dry, rasping hiss.

"We're headed due west, toward the Colorado," Fowler said over his shoulder. "But in an hour or so we'll cut north toward where Hatch Wash meets the river. Where we're going we'll be pretty much near level with the peaks of the La Sal Mountains to the east."

"You mean the slot canyon?" Tyree asked.

"Thought it through and changed my mind about that," Fowler said. "You need plenty of bed rest and good grub. We're going to pay a visit on an old friend of mine, a man called Luke Boyd. He'll see us all right."

Now the sun was gone, the night air was turning cool, and Tyree, having lost so much blood, shivered.

Fowler, a perceptive and caring man, turned in the saddle. "Reach behind the cantle, Chance. I've got me a mackinaw inside my bedroll."

Tyree found the coat and quickly shrugged into it, grateful for the warmth of the wool, thin and threadbare though it was.

After thirty minutes the draw widened out into a patch of open, flatter country, less hemmed in by the surrounding bastions of rock. Mesquite and clumps of rabbit bush covered the ground, and the night air smelled of cedar and juniper.

As they cleared the confining walls of the draw, Tyree looked up and saw a sky full of stars. The moon was not yet visible, but already its diffused glow was painting the land around them the color of tarnished silver.

Weak as he was, Tyree nodded in the saddle, lulled by the rocking motion of the buckskin and the sound of its soft footfalls on the sand.

Fowler's voice woke him. "Almost there, Chance, but from now on we ride real careful. Ol' Luke Boyd has a Sharps fifty-seventy ranged at a hundred yards and he's never been bashful about using it."

"Must be a real good friend of yours, huh?" Tyree asked, the smile in his voice evident.

"He was, before I was sent to prison. I guess he

still is, but in the dark a Sharps sometimes can't tell the difference between friend and foe, so I plan on making sure he knows it's me that's a-coming at him."

"What's he do, this Luke Boyd with the Sharps ranged at a hundred yards?"

"He runs a one-loop spread a couple of miles east of the Colorado. He also does some gold prospecting around here from time to time. Between one thing and another, he's always gotten by. Has himself a right lovely daughter called Lorena. I guess she must be about twenty-five by now. Luke says she was the child of his old age." An edge of bitterness crept into Fowler's voice. "Quirt Laytham is sweet on her. He says he wants to marry her, and last I heard, Lorena hasn't said yes, but she hasn't said no."

As the moon swung into the sky, Fowler urged the buckskin up a steep rise crested by jumbled rocks of all sizes, dark clumps of mesquite and juniper growing among them. Once there he reined in the horse and pointed to a narrow valley below them.

"See the light beyond the creek? That's Luke's cabin. I'd say we're in good time for supper."

Tyree looked over Fowler's shoulder. The bright moonlight reflected on the creek, turning it into a ribbon of silver flanked on both sides by grass and cottonwoods, and farther out, scattered stands of piñon pine and spruce. The cabin was built on the far side of the creek, backing up to the massive rampart of a flat-topped mesa that rose in a series of pink-and-yellow ledges to a height of more than six thousand feet. A ribbon of gray smoke tying bowknots in the still air, lifted from the cabin's chimney, and even at a distance Tyree smelled burning cedar.

The dark bulk of a barn loomed a distance to the left of the cabin, beside it a pole corral and a windmill. A small bunkhouse, its single window darkened, stood off a ways, closer to the creek.

It was a wild, beautiful place, but one that echoed of isolation and aching loneliness, located as it was between earth and sky in the midst of a hard land where life was a daily struggle and everything came at a price, paid in sweat or blood—or both.

It was, Tyree decided, no place for a lovely woman. The thought surprised him. He only had Fowler's word for it that Lorena was lovely . . . but somehow he knew, perhaps from the music of her name, that she was.

"Once we get onto the flat, I'll hail the cabin," Fowler said. "Let me do the talking and show as little of that Winchester as you can. Then we ride in real slow and easy, and do nothing sudden. Luke Boyd isn't a trusting man."

"You're the boss," Tyree said. "I'm willing to risk the Sharps to get off of this buckskin for a spell."

Fowler urged the horse down the slope, then crossed the flat to the near bank of the creek. There he reined up and cupped his hands to his mouth. "Hello the cabin!"

Immediately a lamp inside was doused, the door opened a crack and a man's harsh voice yelled, "What do you want? I got me a Sharps big fifty here and I ain't a-settin' on my gun hand."

"Luke, it's me. It's Owen Fowler."

A few moments of silence, then, "Owen, it's you? Why in tarnation didn't you say so in the first place instead of settin' out there gabbing? Come on in."

Fowler kicked the buckskin into motion and splashed across the creek. The cabin door opened wider and a squat, heavily bearded man who was somewhere in his midsixties stepped into the yard, a rifle in his hands.

Smiling to himself, Tyree decided that Fowler had been right—Luke Boyd wasn't a trusting man.

Fowler reined up when he was close to Boyd and jerked a thumb over his shoulder. "Got me a friend with me. He's been half-hung and shot up pretty bad."

"Then light, Owen, and bring both of you inside."

Tyree climbed off the buckskin, staggered a little, then glanced beyond Boyd to the cabin where a shadow was standing in the doorway. He looked closer, his eyes trying to penetrate the gloom . . . and beheld an angel.

Lorena Boyd stepped quickly to Tyree's side, her lovely brown eyes dark with concern. "I saw you stagger. Are you all right? You seem very weak."

Tyree managed a tired smile. "I'm fine. Tired is all."

"Then let me help you inside."

Lorena put her arm around Tyree's waist and helped him step up onto the porch and into the cabin. He was very aware of the woman's warm closeness and the firmness of her breast against his side. She was, he decided, the most beautiful creature he'd ever seen in his life.

Her thick mass of auburn hair was drawn back from her face and tied at her neck with a pink ribbon. Her cheekbones were wide and high, her mouth full, the lips generous and voluptuous. When she smiled her teeth were even and very white. Hers was a mysterious, haunting beauty, the kind that lingers long in the memory of a man, and Tyree felt his breath catch in his throat as she lit a lamp in the cabin and the light fell across her face and body.

Lorena was dressed in a severely tailored white shirt open at the neck, showing a triangle of flawless, lightly tanned skin. Her straight, canvas skirt was split for riding. Neither garment did anything to conceal the generous curves of her body.

She pulled out a chair and said, "Sit here, mister. . . . Sorry, I didn't catch your name."

"There's no mister." Tyree smiled. "The name is Chance Tyree."

Lorena tasted the name on her tongue, then said, "Chance Tyree, I like that. It has a ring to it."

Luke Boyd stepped into the cabin and froze in his tracks when he heard Lorena speak. "Chance Tyree," he said. "Would that be the Chance Tyree out of Texas? DeWitt County maybe?"

"There's unlikely to be another," Tyree said, his eyes guarded as he studied the stocky rancher. "DeWitt County and other places."

"Heard of you," Boyd said. "Heard a lot about you over the years." The rancher was silent for a few moments as though making his mind up about something. Finally he set his rifle down on the table and held out his hand. "Luke Boyd."

Tyree shook the man's hand; then Boyd said, "I

don't hold a man's past against him. What's done is done. But when you're well enough to ride, I'd consider it as a favor if you'd move on."

It was in Tyree's mind to say, "Old man, there's nothing to keep me here." But when he looked at Lorena, the woman he'd all of a sudden made up his mind to marry, the words died stillborn in his throat. Instead he managed, "I don't aim to be a burden on you, Mr. Boyd. At first light tomorrow I'll leave."

"No need for that," Boyd said. "You can stay here for a few days, a few weeks if need be, at least until you're well enough to ride. But then you got to be going." The older man smiled, his teeth flashing white under his beard. "No hard feelings I hope, Chance. And mister don't set right with me any more than it does with you. The name's Luke."

The old rancher had offered the peace pipe, and Tyree took it. "I'm obliged to you, Luke," he said, matching Boyd's smile with one of his own. "But I figure I can ride in a couple of days—that is, if you can sell me a horse."

Boyd nodded. "We'll talk about that when the time comes." His eyes lifted to his daughter. "Lorena, can't you see this young feller is wounded? Judging by the amount of blood on his shirt, it's bad, so see to him, child." Without waiting for a reply he turned to Fowler. "Now, Owen, what the hell are you doing out of jail?"

In as few words as possible, Fowler told Boyd about the jail's cholera outbreak that won him his freedom, his finding Tyree south of Crooked Creek hanging more dead than alive, then their fight with

Quirt Laytham and his riders along the bank of Hatch Wash. He also mentioned Sheriff Tobin parroting Laytham's accusation that he'd been rustling his stock.

Lorena, who had been listening intently as she gently bathed Tyree's wounds with warm water then bound them up with a bandage, gave an audible gasp at the mention of Laytham's name.

"That doesn't sound like the Quirt Laytham I know," she said. "For heaven's sake, Owen, why would Quirt accuse you of rustling his cattle and then attack you?"

"He wants my land, Lorena," Fowler said evenly. "His cows are already grazing in my canyon."

Lorena's chin lifted in a stubborn tilt. "Quirt told me about that. He said he mixed his stuff in with yours and that he planned to give you a share of the profits when you got out of jail. He was doing you a favor, Owen. Can't you see that?"

"And was Laytham doing me a favor when he told Sheriff Tobin's deputies to hang me?" Tyree asked, annoyance starting to niggle at him. Lorena seemed so sure of Laytham's innocence, and that burned him.

"That was obviously a case of mistaken identity," the girl flared in return. "The canyonlands are infested with rustlers. Quirt is trying to run them clean out of the country. Just ask Pa. He's lost cattle and he's losing more by the day."

Boyd nodded. "Can't argue with that, Chance. I don't quite know how many head I've lost, but it's a passel. That's why I graze my Hereford bull close to the cabin."

"Lorena," Tyree said, keeping his voice level despite his growing irritation, "Laytham knew who he was shooting at along Hatch Wash. He called Owen and me by name."

The girl bit her lip, then shook her head defiantly. "I'll ask Quirt about this. I know there's been some kind of terrible misunderstanding." She hesitated a moment, then said, "However, cattle are being stolen from the range and you are a stranger in these parts, Chance. And . . ."

Lorena swallowed hard, as if what she was about to say was not coming easy. "Owen, you've known me since I was a little girl in pigtails, but you are a convicted murderer." She waved her hands help-lessly. "Oh, I'm messing this up completely, aren't I? But what I'm trying to say is that you can understand how Quirt might have jumped to certain conclusions, wrong as they might be."

Tyree lifted his eyes to Lorena's flushed face. The cabin was very quiet, the only movement a tiny silver moth that fluttered around the oil lamp above the table.

The girl was obviously sweet on Laytham and was determined to defend him to the bitter end. Did that mean she was in love with him? Did I, Tyree thought bitterly, jump to my own wrong conclusion that I could make her my wife?

Boyd's voice, gently chiding, cut across Tyree's thoughts. "Lorena, I've told you often that I didn't think Owen was capable of murder. I believe some-one else killed and robbed John Kent."

For a few moments Lorena stood still, her eyes revealing a knot of different emotions. Finally she walked swiftly across the cabin and threw her arms around Fowler's neck. "Owen, I know you're not a killer," she said. "You're a gentle, loving man. When I was young, I used to marvel at how animals came to you, especially when they were sick or injured. Animals have an instinct about people—they can sense goodness in them, just as I have always sensed the goodness in you."

She kissed Fowler on the cheek, then stepped back and brushed away a stray lock of hair that had tumbled onto her forehead. "It's just . . . just that when I heard you and Chance say all those terrible things about Quirt I got quite angry." Her eyes moved from Fowler to Tyree. "I can't explain it, but when I'm with him, I also sense a goodness in Quirt."

Tyree thought about Laytham, with his handsome, brutal face, his expensive clothes and his cattle and blood horses. He was a suitor of wealth and power, the kind to turn any young woman's head. Lorena had not yet learned that it's fine to judge a wildflower or a butterfly by its appearance, but not a man.

He was about to say so, when Boyd interrupted him. The rancher slapped his hands together and grinned. "Well, I don't know about the rest of you folks, but I'm getting real hungry for supper." He turned to Lorena. "What are we having, daughter?"

Later, as Lorena busied herself at the stove and Owen and Luke talked and smoked their pipes outside, Tyree stepped beside the girl and lightly touched her shoulder. "Lorena, I've got something to say to you. The first is yes, I've ridden a few owl-hoot trails in my life, but I'm no rustler and neither is Owen Fowler. The second is that someday I plan to make you forget all about Quirt Laytham and take you as my wife."

The woman's back stiffened; then she slowly turned to face him. "Mr. Tyree," she said, her beautiful eyes blazing, "I certainly wouldn't count on that if I was you."

Chapter 7

A week drifted by and Tyree's strength grew as his wounds began to heal. He moved his gear into the bunkhouse, no longer wishing to crowd Lorena and her father in the cabin.

Lorena still bathed and bandaged him every day. She even washed and mended his shirt, but she was frosty and distant, polite to a fault, the looming shadow of Quirt Laytham lying between them.

Tyree was yet to tell Lorena that he planned on destroying Laytham, wiping out even his memory from the canyonlands. He would have to let her know soon, but he feared how she would react. There was a distinct probability she'd run into Laytham's arms and he would lose her forever.

His frustration growing, Tyree considered another possibility—he could step away from his showdown with Laytham and ask Lorena to leave with him. But even as he mulled over this option, he soon dismissed it. A devil was driving him and it would not let up until justice was done. He had been a stranger passing through, but Crooked Creek lawmen, men

Laytham kept in his pocket, had seen fit to hang him. There could be no going back from that. Tyree was a man who measured things only in the light of his own experience, a seasoning he had gained among tough, uncompromising men. He had no other yardstick. He knew he had been badly wronged and for that, there must be a reckoning. It was a principle as old as the Bible—an eye for an eye, a tooth for a tooth. Even his growing love for Lorena, coldly distant as she was, would not sidetrack him from his purpose.

On the morning of the eighth day of his stay at Luke's ranch, Tyree stepped out of the bunkhouse door after breakfast and saw the old rancher and Fowler saddling their horses in the barn.

He strolled over and Boyd answered his unasked question. "It's high time I made a tally of my herd, Chance. I've been prospecting some this past three months and during that time they've scattered to hell and gone, them that haven't been rustled. I'll drive them out of the canyons toward the creek and count them there."

Interested, Tyree asked, "You planning on making a drive, Luke?"

The old rancher nodded. "I figure come spring I'll hire me a couple of men and push a herd to the Union Pacific railhead at Salt Lake City." He shrugged. "Money's been tight for a spell, and I want Lorena to be able to afford some nice things, women's fixin's and the like."

"I was once pretty handy with a rope," Tyree said. "Mind if I tag along today?"

"You up for it, boy?" Luke asked. "That bullet

wound in your side has some healing to do yet and you still look a mite peaked."

"I'll be all right," Tyree said. "I'll need a good cutting horse, though."

Luke thought the younger man's offer through for a few moments, then said, "We could sure use another hand. Glad to have you along." He nodded toward the corral. "Throw a saddle on that steeldust. He'll buck a time or two just to keep you honest, but after that he'll settle down. He's a first-rate cow pony."

The old rancher's eyes moved to Tyree's waist. "Better wear your gun."

Tyree smiled. "I thought we were rounding up your cows, not shooting them."

"Wear your gun just the same," Boyd said, his face solemn. "Back in seventy-eight, Governor George W. Emery told the legislature that the Utah Territory had more rustlers to the square mile than any other place in the country. It was the only damn thing I ever agreed with him on." Boyd's eyes met Tyree's. "Wear your iron, boy. I'm not saying we'll run into shooting trouble, but out there among the canyons a man never knows."

Tyree saw the logic in what Boyd was saying. He went back inside the bunkhouse, retrieved the gun belt from the peg and strapped it around his hips, then lifted his Winchester from the rack. When he passed the cabin the door was open. Lorena had her back to him, putting away dishes, and she didn't turn.

"We're heading out to make a tally of your pa's cows," Tyree said. "Will you be all right here alone?"

"I can use the Sharps about as well as Pa," the girl answered, still without turning. "I'll be just fine."

Tyree pulled his canvas suspenders over his shoulders and settled his hat on his head. He was about to step toward the barn again, but Lorena's voice stopped him.

"Be careful out there, Chance," she said. "Those canyons can be treacherous."

Lorena still had her back to him as Tyree said, "Worried about me, Lorena?"

The girl turned to face him. "Yes, you and Pa and Owen. All of you."

Tyree could not read Lorena's eyes. But was there something there, real concern, maybe? Was it something he might hold on to, to give him hope? He had no time to ponder those questions. The girl turned away again, her back straight and stiff.

He stepped through the bright light of the morning, confused, feeling no closer to Lorena now than he had for the past eight days.

Luke Boyd had been right about the steeldust. The horse bucked a few times, enough to justify his reputation, then settled down and seemed eager for the trail.

"We'll head east along the creek and search the canyons," Boyd said. He wore a battered black hat, a plaid shirt and corduroy pants tucked into mule-eared boots. An old cap-and-ball Remington rode on his hip and, like Tyree, he had a Winchester under his knee.

His Henry shattered and inoperable, Fowler had Luke's Greener scattergun tied to the back of his saddle with piggin strings, and he wore a Green River knife on his belt. A copy of Thomas Carlyle's *History of Frederick the Great* was stuffed into a back pocket of his pants. Seeing the book, Tyree smiled. It seemed Owen planned to do more reading than cowboying.

Lorena stood at the door of the cabin as Tyree and the others rode out, and he waved to her. She waved back, but whether to him or her pa he did not know.

Under a flaming sky streaked with banners of dark blue cloud, the riders followed the creek south. Around them spread a desolate, silent land of high, serrated ridges, great flat-topped mesas, rocky basins and slender spires and pinnacles of pink, red and yellow sandstone. Sparse growths of Douglas fir, mountain mahogany, scrub oak, sagebrush and mountain shrub grew high up the canyon walls, piñon and juniper at the lower levels.

It was still early, but the morning was already hot, the steep, rocky crags on all sides beginning their shimmering dance in the heat. Dust devils spiraled ahead of the riders and sand began to work its way inside their clothes and make their eyes red and gritty. Among the canyons phantom blue lakes glittered, mirages formed by the strengthening sunlight and the clear, dry air.

Along the creek, grazing in the shade of cottonwoods or standing knee high in the cool water, they counted eighty Herefords, all carrying Boyd's LB brand. The cattle were fat and sleek, wary and wild as deer.

But as they rode Boyd's eyes were shadowed with concern. He had yet to cut sign of his bull, and that bothered him.

Now the easy part of the tally was over. It was time for the three men to fan out and begin their search of the canyons and draws for the rest of Boyd's cows.

Tyree took a sandy switchback cattle trail up a sloping ridge and rode down the other side into a narrow gorge. The trail showed signs of recent use, the cattle tracks overlaid with those of deer and antelope. Because of the canyon's steep walls, little light penetrated to the bottom and Tyree found himself riding in a strange, violet gloaming. Here, away from the sun, the air was much cooler—one reason cattle were so attracted to canyons, including the slots that were just narrow, twisting fissures in the rock.

Tyree found half a dozen cows lying around a shallow seep on the canyon floor where grew a few stunted willows and scattered clumps of sagebrush. The Herefords were reluctant to move back to the heat and flies, but the steeldust knew his business and soon had them up and headed for the canyon mouth.

Tyree hazed the cattle toward the creek and saw Fowler driving another small herd. Boyd, looking grouchy, had ridden into a canyon to the east and had returned empty-handed.

"Damn it all," the old rancher growled, the heat and dust making his patience wear thin. "I haven't seen hide nor hair of my bull. Now where in hell has he wandered off to? He always liked to stay close to them cows."

Tyree took off his hat and wiped sweat from his forehead with the back of his hand. "Still a lot of canyons and draws to search, Luke." He settled his hat back on his head. "We'll find him."

"I sure hope so," Boyd said. "And I'll rest a lot easier when we do. I set store by that bull. A time back I read that John Slaughter down in Texas had paid five thousand dollars for a prize Hereford bull. Well, a fool and his money are soon parted I guess, because I guarantee that I bought a better animal for less than half that price."

By eleven, after four hours of sweaty, grueling work in the growing heat of the day, Tyree and the others had counted over two hundred head. But there was as yet no sign of the bull and that rankled them all, especially Boyd.

At noon, they camped in the shade of a cotton-wood by the creek, boiled coffee and broiled slices of salt pork over the fire. Lorena had packed a round of yellow cornbread and a small pot of honey. They spread the corn pone thick with honey, then ate it with the pork.

"Good vittles," Fowler commented as he brushed crumbs from the front of his shirt. "Stick to a man's ribs."

Tyree nodded, smiling. "You're right about that. Salt pork does stay with a man and it keeps on repeating itself."

"And Lorena put a good scald on the corn pone—that's fer sure," Boyd said. He turned to Tyree. "How you holding up, boy?"

"My side is punishing me some, but I reckon I'll stick."

"Good, I'm glad you're feeling spry, because next

we start on the slot canyons. Maybe my bull is in one of them."

"How are we going to get the cows out of the slots, Luke?" Fowler asked, laying down his book. "Those canyons are so darned narrow there's no room for a pony to turn and not enough space to swing a cat, let alone a loop."

Boyd answered Fowler's question with one of his own. "How long were you in the cattle business before you was sent to the hoosegow, Owen?"

"Not long—a twelvemonth, I guess." He thought about it. "No more'n a twelvemonth."

Tyree built a smoke and studied Fowler. The man had the long, melancholy face and sad brown eyes of a poet, and his hands were slender, like a woman's. He was high-shouldered, his chest narrow and sunken.

Fowler was, Tyree decided, nobody's idea of a cattleman.

"I was working as a bank clerk over to Crooked Creek when a feller rode in with twenty head of Herefords and a Red Angus bull he was trying to sell," Fowler said, as though his start in the ranching business needed some explanation. "Well, I was getting mighty tired of the bank, so I withdrew my savings, asked for my time and bought the herd. Cost me just about every cent I owned. Then I pushed them up Hatch Wash, looking for a place to start a ranch, and by and by, I found my canyon. Built my cabin, then had it pretty good for three, four months, until Quirt Laytham moved into the territory with his herd." Fowler shrugged. "After that, well, you know what followed."

"I don't, Owen," Tyree said. "You never did tell

me what happened." He smiled. "And feel free to tell me it's none of my damn business."

"Since you've made an enemy of Quirt Laytham on my account I guess you're entitled to know," Fowler said. The leaves of the cottonwood cast shifting shadows on the man's face and his eyes lost their light, fading to a dull, expressionless black.

"We had a preacher in Crooked Creek by the name of John Kent. He was a good man, cared about folks and not only his own flock. John was a sociable man and he rode up the wash to visit with me from time to time, and we'd drink coffee and talk cattle prices and books we'd read and stuff like that.

"Then one morning, nigh on nine years ago, I woke up and found John's body near my cabin. I knew he'd been shot in the back at close range, because his coat had caught on fire. And he'd been robbed. I was leaning over John's body when Quirt Laytham rode in along with Nick Tobin, Len Dawson, Clem Daley and a few others.

"Tobin said they'd been out looking for John since he'd failed to return home last night after visiting with me. Then he pulled his gun on me, accused me of murder and told Dawson to go search my cabin. When Dawson came back out he was holding John's watch and some money. Said he'd found it piled up on my table where I'd left it.

"I looked up at Laytham and he was grinning, something mighty akin to triumph in his eyes. 'We got him, boys,' he said. 'We got us that man who murdered John Kent.'" Fowler shrugged. "You know the rest. I was found guilty and sentenced to twenty-five years at hard labor."

"Who do you think killed Deacon Kent, Owen?" Boyd asked.

Fowler shook his head at him. "I don't know. A drifter maybe. All I know is that it wasn't me. I liked and respected John. He was a good man. I had no reason to murder him."

While Fowler spoke, Luke Boyd had been whittling on a piece of fallen tree branch. He tossed the branch away, folded his knife and said, "That's quite a story, Owen. First time I've heard the whole thing." He rose to his feet. "Time to mount up, boys. We've a passel of slot canyons to search before nightfall."

"You still haven't told us how you plan on doing it, Luke," Fowler said, also standing, carefully putting Carlyle in his back pocket.

Boyd smiled. "Owen, I knowed you hadn't been ranching long enough to learn about slot canyons and God apples."

"God apples are a new one on me, too, Luke," Tyree said.

The old rancher nodded. "All right, since neither of you know, I'll tell you about them. A few years back a puncher had himself a one-eyed hoss for sale up in the Bradshaws in the Arizona Territory. This Easterner dude asks him why the pony has only one eye. 'Well, sir,' the puncher says, 'that don't bother him none. He's still the best cow pony in these parts.' But the dude wouldn't let it go. 'What happened to his eye?' he asks, all curious like. 'God did it,' the puncher says. 'How?' asks the dude. 'One time that there hoss wouldn't go in the corral an' I cut him down with a God apple,' says the puncher. 'A what?' asks the dude, real buffaloed. 'A rock, you eejit,' says the puncher. 'God left them around to help us poor cowboys.' "

Boyd grinned. "And that's how come that ever since punchers call rocks God apples."

Tyree and Fowler exchanged looks, then the younger man asked, "Luke, what's all that to do with the slot canyons?"

The rancher smiled, bent over and extended a hand to Tyree, who took it. With surprising strength, Boyd pulled the younger man to his feet. "This is how we're going to do it, Chance. Since you're the youngest atween us and feeling right spry again, you're gonna get an armload of God apples and get up on the rims of those canyons. Toss your rocks into the slots and when the cattle come hightailing it out of there, me and Owen will count them." He nodded to Fowler. "All except my bull, Owen. I plan to dab a loop on him and lead him closer to the cabin."

Tyree grinned. "Then I guess I'd better start searching for God apples."

"Plenty of them around, son," Boyd said, throwing that last of the coffee on the fire. "God provides us with every blessing in abundance, the Good Book says. So get to gathering."

Chapter 8

Getting up to the rim of a slot canyon was no simple task, as Tyree soon discovered when he studied his first climb. He had to make it to the summit of a massive pink-and-yellow mesa that rose in a series of narrow benches to a height of about a thousand feet above the flat.

He decided his best route was to follow one of the many deep runoffs that scarred the mesa's eroded surface where, he hoped, the going would be easier.

Tyree clambered upward along a stony, slanting streambed, then across a sandbank that held captive the skeletal white trunk of a dead juniper. The way was made even more difficult by massive boulders and a series of steep, treacherous dry falls. The searing, relentless heat was an added misery along with the weight of the rocks in his pockets.

Boyd had given Tyree a pair of work gloves for the climb that protected his hands, but cactus spines, especially those of the tiny claret cup that hid behind boulders and laid traps for the unwary, soon lacerated his knees and elbows.

Halfway up, he stopped to catch his breath on a bench, flat purple-colored rocks and clumps of sagebrush scattered along its length and breadth.

Tyree took off his hat and wiped sweat from the band with his gloved fingers, the blazing sun hammering at him mercilessly. He was about to replace his hat but stopped in midmotion, frozen in place by a sudden, angry rattle.

He turned slowly. Ten feet away a huge sidewinder that had been basking on a rock raised its head, tongue flickering, warning him to keep his distance.

Tyree took a step backward, then another, his hand dropping to the gun on his hip. But the snake, its point made, slithered into a cluster of boulders shot through with bunchgrass and disappeared.

Swallowing hard, Tyree settled his hat back on his head and began to climb again.

The slot canyon itself was a deep gash in the sandstone rock, sculpted over millions of years into fantastic twists and turns by raging floodwaters. Judging by the closeness of the walls in some places, parts of it were so narrow a wide-shouldered man would have been forced to turn sideways to get through.

When Tyree stood on the rim and looked down into the canyon's depths, he could see twenty or thirty feet of wall bathed in a dim amber light, and below that only darkness.

There was no telling if there were actually cows down there, but if there were, the God apples would hopefully get them moving.

One by one Tyree tossed his rocks into the canyon and listened to them bounce off the walls. A few moments later there was a thud of hooves as spooked cattle ran in panic along the sandy bottom.

Tyree grinned, let out a wild whoop and tossed down a few more rocks. Luke had been right—it was actually working.

But after four hours and as many slot canyons, Boyd and Fowler had counted only a handful of cows, and the Hereford bull was not among them.

After throwing the last of his rocks, Tyree decided this fourth canyon, carved into the side of a high, flat-topped butte, was his last. He was scraped and bruised all over from climbing, and his knees and elbows were bleeding from cactus spines. He was yet to regain all of his strength, and he felt hot, irritable and completely worn-out. Making his way through scattered boulders, Tyree reached the meager shade of a stunted juniper and built a cigarette, the smoke tasting hot, dry and acrid on his tongue.

Tyree finished his cigarette and ground out the butt under his heel. He walked back toward the run-off and had just begun his hazardous descent when a brownish-yellow smudge in the sky far to the north stopped him in his tracks.

He used his hat to shade his eyes against the glare of the sun, scanning the hazy distance. But there was no mistaking what he'd seen, a dust cloud hanging in the still air, thick enough to have been kicked up by several riders.

Tyree studied the dust, wondering at its meaning. Fowler had told him there was a settlement to the north called Moab, a farming and ranching community run by Mormons. It could be the dust was being raised by punchers from there, though it was a fair piece off their home range.

But Tyree immediately dismissed the thought. Dust to the north coupled with Boyd's missing bull was too much of a coincidence—or at least enough of a coincidence to justify an investigation.

He came off the butte in a hurry, sliding on his rump most of the way. When he reached the bottom he jumped to his feet and yelled, waving his hat to Boyd and Fowler, who were some distance off by the creek.

The two men loped toward Tyree, Boyd leading the steeldust.

"What's all the fuss, boy?" the old rancher asked, reining up beside the younger man. "You seen my bull?"

Tyree shook his head at him. "There's dust to the north, Luke: three, maybe four riders. It could be that your bull is with them."

A frown gathering between his eyes, the rancher sat his saddle for a few moments, thinking it through. He glanced at the sun, as though seeking the answer to a question he'd just asked himself.

"How far?" he asked finally.

"Four, five miles."

Again Boyd sat lost in thought. Then he said, "That bull wouldn't have wandered far from the cows. We've searched high and low for him and he ain't here, so he's someplace else." He glanced at the sun again. "We still have a couple of hours of daylight left, time enough to catch up with the rustlers if that's what they are." He tossed the reins of the steeldust to Tyree. "Mount up, boy. Slip the thong off your

Colt, and let's go talk to those gents and see what they're about."

It did not occur to Tyree, for even an instant, to refuse. He had enjoyed Boyd's hospitality and he was therefore expected to ride for the brand if the need arose. Among Western men, to do otherwise would have marked him as a man of low character and, even worse, a coward.

The three men rode north, working their way through narrow, sandy canyons and wider draws, a few of them with grass and water. Whenever possible they kept to the grass or rode through stands of cedar to settle their own dust.

After an hour, at the mouth of a canyon between high, heavily corroded bluffs, Tyree cut sign. The tracks of three horses led into the gulch and among them what could only be the wide, split-toed prints of Luke Boyd's bull.

"I reckon they're planning to head all the way north to Salt Lake City," the rancher said, his face grim. "They'll sell my bull cheap, but even so, the money will keep them in whiskey and women for a long time."

"Could be Salt Lake, Luke," Fowler allowed. "Unless they make a turn east and head for Colorado."

Boyd shook his head in irritation. "North, east, it don't matter a damn. I'm going after them." He turned in the saddle and looked at Fowler. "Owen, you're not a gunfighting man. I wouldn't think any less of you if'n you was to ride back to the cabin."

Fowler shook his head. "I reckon I'll stick."

Boyd's smile was slight but genuine. "Good man. Then let's get it done."

The advancing dusk was starting to crowd out the light as the three riders entered the canyon and followed its twists and turns for several miles. Some places were so narrow their stirrups scraped along the walls. At other points the canyon widened around shallow, water-filled basins surrounded by willow and cottonwoods, the gound muddied by the tracks of deer, elk and cattle.

In the falling darkness, Boyd led Tyree and Fowler out of the canyon and then up a steep, hogback rise formed by the slanting talus slopes of a pair of dome-topped mesas, the way made treacherous by loose rock and gravel. The air smelled stale and old, the dusty odor of sandstone not yet cooled from the blazing heat of the day.

Before they reached the crest of the rise, Tyree told Boyd to hold up. "The way I see it, those boys will soon camp for the night," he said. "Judging by their tracks, I'd say they're not hustling any, so they don't know they're being followed and they won't want to run too much beef off that bull."

"What's on your mind, son?" Boyd asked.

"I suggest you and Owen stay here. I'm going on ahead to scout for the camp. When I find it, I'll come back and get you." Tyree shrugged. "Less chance of being seen if we know exactly where those rustlers are holed up. Last thing we want to do is go wandering around in the dark."

Boyd thought that through, then turned to Fowler. "How does Chance's notion set with you, Owen?"

"Makes sense," Fowler answered. "We go stumbling around hunting for their camp they could hear us coming and kill all three of us quicker'n scat."

Boyd turned back to Tyree. "All right, go do it, boy, but when you find the camp come hightailing it back here, mind. There's too many of them for one man to handle."

His face revealing nothing, Tyree touched the brim of his hat then swung the steeldust toward the top of the hogback. He crested the rise and rode down the other side, dropping four hundred feet, his horse sliding most of the way on its haunches. He crossed an area of sandy, open ground, dotted here and there with patches of prickly pear cactus and mesquite, and rode into a shallow arroyo.

The moon came up, silvering the night, and out among the canyons the coyotes were talking.

Tyree thought he smelled smoke, but with no wind to carry the scent the odor was faint and fleeting. He reined up the tired steeldust, stood in the stirrups, and lifted his nose, testing the air.

There it was again, just a fragile whiff of burning cedar that seemed to come from right ahead of him. And there was something else, another smell intertwined with the cedar—the tantalizing aroma of frying bacon.

The steeldust, mountain bred and as sensitive to the nearness of danger as any wild creature, suddenly tensed and tossed up his head, the bit jangling loud in the silence. The horse let out a low, soft whinny. Tyree whispered, "Easy, boy, easy."

He swung out of the saddle, yanked his rifle from the scabbard, then went ahead on foot, leaving the steeldust with its reins trailing.

His boots shuffling softly in the sand, Tyree crouched low and worked his way out of the arroyo, then across flat ground, stepping quietly through cactus, clumps of mesquite and scattered rock toward the source of the smoke. He had no illusions about what he was facing. Rustling was a dangerous, rakehell business and these young men would be as tough as rawhide, hard and good with guns, and willing to fight like wolves to escape the consequences of their misdeeds.

There would be no backup in them. Chances were they'd be fast and deadly as striking rattlesnakes. They would not give mercy—or ask for it.

His face grim, his jaw set and stubborn, Tyree took a moment to ask himself if his falsehood back there at the hogback had been justified. But he knew full well it had. Owen Fowler was no gunfighter and would only be in the way. Luke Boyd was slowed by age, good with a Spencer at a distance, but up close and sudden as this fight would be, he'd lack the flashing speed to make his gun count.

There had been no other way, Tyree decided. He might survive this fight, but the chances were that Owen and Luke would not, and they were men he liked and respected.

Moving with care, Tyree inched his way forward. In the distance, near a stand of trees he could not identify, he caught the flicker of a campfire. Fearing no pursuit, the rustlers had built the fire large against the desert cold of the night.

And it was getting cooler. Tyree shivered slightly as he worked his way toward the camp. In the distance the coyotes were calling louder as their hunger grew, their noses lifted to the rising full moon . . . a rustler's moon.

Carefully, making no sound, Tyree moved closer. In the moonlight the bare, white rocks around him stood out clearly and the green branches of the brush were frosted with silver.

When he was still a ways from the camp, Tyree shifted the Winchester to his left hand. If the outlaws chose not to surrender and made a fight of it, he'd be faster with the Colt.

He stopped in the shadows when he was just a dozen yards from the camp. Water chuckled somewhere close, probably one of the numerous streams that ran into the canyon country off the Colorado a few miles to the west, and the snap and crack of the fire was loud in the silence.

Tyree carefully studied the camp and marked the locations of the rustlers. One man lay on his back while smoking a cigarette, his head on a saddle. Another was concentrating on the fry pan he held over the fire, and a third was rubbing down a horse with a handful of bunchgrass.

Most cowboys held their mustang ponies in slight regard and seldom worried about them. But gunmen, gamblers and outlaws took excellent and constant care of their mounts, since a fast horse could mean the difference between life and death.

It seemed this bunch was no exception.

Now it was time to make his move.

Tyree rose to his feet and stepped into the camp, careful to avert his eyes from the blazing fire to keep his vision unclouded.

"Evenin', boys," he drawled, smiling, "any of you seen a prize Hereford bull hereabouts?"

Chapter 9

The man who'd been lying down sprang quickly to his feet. He threw his cigarette butt into the fire and faced Tyree, his eyes wary. The cook, his bacon sputtering, carefully placed the fry pan at the edge of the coals and began to rise. He was a tall, lanky man who unraveled like a piece of string, coming together only when he was upright. The third man dropped the grass he'd been using and stayed right where he was, his hand close to his gun.

"Well, Lordy me." Tyree grinned, looking past the outlaws to where the bull was grazing. "And there he is." He let his grin grow wider. "Thanks for finding him, boys. My boss surely sets store by that bull."

For a few moments nobody spoke. The flames of the campfire cast flickering scarlet shadows on the faces of the men across from Tyree. Three pairs of eyes were fixed on him, glittering like ice in the dark hollows of their sockets.

The man who'd been grooming the horse stepped closer. He was of medium height, a redhead, dressed in dusty range clothes. He wore two guns in crossed belts, a showy mode of carry that was seldom seen.

"Mister," he said, "we've laid claim to that bull. Now, if you want to keep on living, you just turn and walk on out of here."

Tyree did not allow his grin to slip. "Sorry, boys, but you seem to have made a mistake. See, that's my boss's Hereford and he told me I had to bring him home right quick. So, if it's all the same to you, I'll just dab a loop on him and be on my way."

Again a tense silence stretched between the four men, taut as a fiddle string.

The three rustlers were sizing up Tyree, taking his measure, and he knew what they were seeing. There was nothing in Tyree's appearance to intimidate these three, and the contempt in their eyes told him they'd summed him up and had found him wanting.

The redhead turned to the man who'd been frying the bacon. "Jed, what do you think?"

"I think we kill him and be done." The man called Jed grinned, a sudden recklessness in the look he threw at Tyree. "Hell, the bacon is burning, so it's high time we ate."

Then he went for his gun.

Jed had barely cleared leather when two of Tyree's bullets smashed dead center into his chest. Jed staggered, his lips peeled back in an ugly, defiant snarl. His gun dropped from his hand and he turned away, out of the fight.

Tyree ignored the dying outlaw and concentrated on the redhead who had shucked both guns and was firing, streaks of orange-red flame slashing across the darkness. A bullet burned across Tyree's right cheek as he slammed a shot at the redhead, then another. Hit hard, the man screamed and went down, blood blossoming scarlet on the front of his shirt.

A bullet tugged viciously at Tyree's sleeve. The third outlaw steadied himself for another shot and both men fired at once. The rustler's bullet spitefully split the air next to Tyree's ear, but Tyree's own Colt bucked and the round smashed into the man's right shoulder. The rustler cursed and took a couple of steps back, his gun hanging loose in an arm that no longer had the power to lift it.

"Don't even think about trying," Tyree snapped as the outlaw tried to throw his Colt to his left hand. "Make the shift and I'll drill you square."

It was over.

The wounded outlaw swore savagely, his face a twisted mask of disbelief and hate. He dropped the gun and stepped away from it. "Damn you," he yelled, pain hacking at his voice. "Who the hell are you?"

"Name's Chance Tyree."

Recognition dawned in the outlaw's face and his stunned jaw hung slack. "Heard that name plenty of times. They say Clay Allison once backed off from you."

Tyree nodded. "That's what they say."

"We never stood a chance agin' you, did we?"

His face bleak, Tyree answered, "There were three of you and you were ready and I reckon you could have done better. But as soon as you drawed down on me, you were bucking a losing game."

"My name is Roy Will, and that's my brother Jed lying there with two of your bullets in his chest," the rustler said. "Is he dead?"

"As he'll ever be."

"Then I swear to God I'll kill you for this, Tyree. One day I'll catch up with you and kill you, even if it takes me the rest of my life."

"Which won't be long, boy," Luke Boyd said, stepping from the shadows into the circle of the firelight. "On account of how I plan to hang you right here and now from the nearest tree."

"No, Luke." Tyree's words were soft spoken, but they cut like a knife across the silence that followed Boyd's statement. "Seems to me, there's been enough hanging around here already."

The old rancher looked shocked. "But, Chance, that's what we do with no-good rustlers in the canyonlands."

Tyree was suddenly tired, sick of all the dying that lay around him. "Luke, Lorena told us that Quirt Laytham and Sheriff Tobin have declared open season on rustlers. Take him into Crooked Creek and let those two deal with him."

Boyd seemed uncertain, but when he met Tyree's eyes and saw their hard, determined light he let it go. "Well, if you say so, but I'd rather string him up my ownself." He glanced around the camp. "I heard this one say his name was Roy Will. Who are the other two?"

"The man by the fire is Jed Will, this one's brother. The redhead over there, I don't know his name."

"Trace Henderson," the man called Roy said. "Out of Blanco County, Texas. Ran with Jesse Evans for a spell and killed his share."

"Well, his killin' is done," Boyd said. "And good riddance I say."

Owen Fowler led the horses into camp and looked around him, his face pale with shock. "Are they . . . are they . . . ?"

"Yup, Owen, both of them are dead as rotten stumps," Boyd said, rising from where he'd been kneeling beside Henderson.

"Then we have to bury them," Fowler said, a man who couldn't come to terms with the destruction around him desperately latching on to something he did understand.

"Need a shovel for that, and we don't have one," Boyd said. "I saw a cave back in the arroyo. We'll lay 'em in there. Good a place for their kind as any."

Tyree kneeled by the fire and placed the fry pan back on the coals and shook the bacon. "Let's eat first," he said. "No point in letting good grub go to waste."

Tyree and the others rode back to the cabin with their prisoner under a moonlit sky ablaze with stars.

When he was a ways off, Boyd yelled to Lorena that he was coming in, and the door swung open a moment later, throwing a rectangle of light onto the porch. The girl ran into the yard.

When her father dismounted, Lorena threw herself into his arms. "Pa, where were you? I've been so worried."

"Later, child. I've got a wounded man here."

"Who?"

Lorena's alarmed eyes went directly to Tyree, but he smiled and jerked his thumb at Roy Will. "Not me, him."

Had he seen real concern in Lorena's face? Why,

when her father said someone was wounded, had she looked for him first? It could, Tyree decided, mean nothing. Or everything.

Fowler volunteered to unsaddle and feed the horses. Tyree followed Lorena and her father into the cabin. As the girl began to wash blood from the outlaw's shoulder, Boyd told her what had happened, sparing none of the details.

Lorena stopped what she was doing and looked at Tyree, an expression of horror crossing her lovely face. "You killed two of them?" She glanced at Will's shattered shoulder. "And you did this?"

Tyree nodded. "It was either them or me. It was a mighty sudden thing and I didn't have time to study on it."

Lorena continued to look at Tyree for a long moment, a tangle of confused emotion in her eyes. She'd been born and raised in the West, and she knew well what happened to rustlers when they were caught. But now, seeing it up close in all its bloody reality, she was obviously struggling to come to terms with what had happened.

"Chance did what he had to do, Lorena," Boyd said mildly. He pointed at Will, who was sitting with his head bowed, sullen and silent. "Him and the others were taking my bull and they were willing to fight to keep it."

Lorena struggled to regain her composure. "Is this what it means to be a named gunfighter, Chance? Am I seeing the true, cruel reality behind all the dime novels? In a single instant to have the ability to cut down two men and smash another's shoulder to pieces?"

Though aware of the barb, Tyree smiled. "Yes, that's what it means. That and other things."

The girl lifted her head high. "Then I hope to God I never meet another gunfighter. There isn't a Hereford bull in the world that's worth the lives of two men."

"I'm with you there," Tyree said, nodding toward Will. "But maybe him and the other two should have thought of that before they stole it."

"That's what I say, boy," Boyd agreed. The rancher put his hand on Tyree's shoulder. "Do you recollect my telling you to ride on once you were well enough? Well, that don't go no more. You played the man's part today, Chance, and I'm beholden to you. Stay on here as long as you want."

Whatever Tyree was about to answer was lost as the door opened and Fowler stepped inside. "I rubbed down the horses and fed them," he said. "Turned the rustlers' mounts into the corral. Rubbed down your paint too, Lorena. He was lathered up some."

The girl nodded. "I went riding just before sundown. I was about to go see to him when you all came back."

Fowler nodded toward Will. "How is he?"

"His shoulder is bad," Lorena said. "I think the bullet is still in there. I've done all I can, but he needs a doctor."

"He'll see one tomorrow," Boyd said. "At first light I'm leaving with him for Crooked Creek."

"And I'm coming with you," Fowler said.

Tyree looked at the man, his face alarmed. "Owen, do you think that's wise? Quirt Laytham means to kill you, and Sheriff Tobin won't lift a finger to save you. Those two are in cahoots, tighter than Dick's hatband." Ignoring Lorena's annoyed frown, he added, "Owen, you stay here. I'll ride into town with Luke."

Fowler shook his head. "No, Chance, this has been going on for too long and it's got to stop. Tobin is a sorry excuse for a lawman, I admit, but I'm going to demand he bring in the United States Marshal. Let the marshal investigate Laytham's claim that I'm rustling his cattle."

"Owen," Lorena said quickly, "I'll talk to Quirt. I'll get this whole sorry mess cleared up. I'm still sure there's been some kind of misunderstanding."

Fowler's smile was slight. "Thanks for the offer, Lorena, but I still think I'll put my trust in the U.S. marshal."

Tyree was about to object again, but Boyd cut him off. "Chance, I'll be with Owen in Crooked Creek. People know me in town; they've known me for years. Nothing will happen to Owen so long so I'm with him."

Despite his misgivings, Tyree conceded to himself that Boyd had a point. He'd been in the canyon country for over twenty years and by Fowler's account was well liked and respected. It was unlikely Laytham would try to kill Owen while Luke was with him.

"Besides, Chance," Boyd was saying, "if Lorena is wrong about Laytham and everything you and Owen have been telling me is a natural fact, you're a marked man your ownself."

"I'm not wrong, Pa," Lorena flared. "I just know I'm not wrong about Quirt."

"Well, anyhow, it's settled," Boyd said. "Come first light, Owen and me will ride this bull-stealing varmint to Sheriff Tobin and have him telegraph the marshal."

"What are we going to do with him until then, Pa?" Lorena asked. "He's in bad shape."

Boyd drew his gun. "I'll take him to the barn and tie him up good. He'll be comfortable enough."

Roy Will, who had been sitting through all this in a hurting silence, stood and turned to Lorena. He gestured at his bandaged shoulder and with the Western man's inherent respect for decent women said, "I'm much obliged to you, ma'am."

As Boyd prodded the rustler toward the door, Will's eyes slanted to Tyree and flashed him a look of implacable, burning hatred. Then he was gone.

Tyree followed Boyd outside, glanced at the night sky and what he saw stopped him dead in his tracks.

The moon was covered in blood.

Chapter 10

Boyd and Fowler rode out with their prisoner at first light. For the rest of the morning Tyree kept himself busy with chores that badly needed to be done around the ranch.

He spent a couple of hours cutting hay against the coming winter. He had just straightened up and hammered in place a sagging partition between two of the stalls in the barn when Lorena stepped inside.

Despite the heat of the day she looked cool and lovely in a green velvet riding skirt topped by a butterfly yellow shirt, her hair drawn back from her face with a ribbon of the same color.

Tyree, feeling sweaty and dirty, tossed his hammer into the tool chest and smiled. "You look wonderful today, like a meadow of wild flowers."

Lorena dropped a little curtsy. "Well, thank you, kind sir." She turned and nodded to her saddled horse, a basket tied behind the saddle. "I wondered if you would like to join me for a picnic."

"I'd love to," Tyree said, delighted at the prospect. "Just as soon as I wash up some."

He stepped outside to a barrel topped up by water from the creek, loosened the red bandana around his neck, then splashed his face and neck. He ran wet fingers through his thick, unruly hair and combed it into place as best he could, then did the same for his mustache. That done he retied the bandana and settled his hat on his head.

"You look very handsome," Lorena said, smiling. "Quite the dashing gentleman."

Tyree felt himself flush under Lorena's amused scrutiny. He mumbled a hasty thank-you, then glad to make his escape, said, "I'll go saddle the steeldust."

A few minutes later he and Lorena rode away from the cabin, then turned east in the direction of Hatch Wash.

"Where are we headed?" Tyree asked.

"It's a secret place of mine," Lorena answered. "I found it when I was a little girl and I used to go there when I wanted to be alone." She looked at Tyree from under the dark fans of her eyelashes. "I still do sometimes."

Lorena seemed to have forgotten the events of last night, making polite small talk as they splashed across the wash. They saw plenty of Laytham cattle, then quartered to the northeast. The girl's paint set a good pace as she led the way in the direction of looming Abajo Peak, a dome-shaped mountain rising more than eleven thousand feet above the level, its slopes covered in fir, maple and aspen.

Just when Tyree was convinced they were riding all the way to the mountain, Lorena turned into a narrow side canyon that opened up gradually around a massive boulder three times the height of a man on horseback. The huge rock had toppled from the canyon rim in ancient times and a third of its bulk was now buried in sand. They rounded the obstacle and rode through patches of sagebrush and mesquite, the ground under them rising steeply until, after a mile, it leveled off at a clear and beautiful lake.

Tyree reined up beside Lorena and smiled. "You must have been a brave little girl to have found this place by yourself."

"I was." She smiled in return. "I guess it was the way Pa raised me after my mother died. He always wanted a son, but when I came along he made do and turned me into a tomboy." Lorena laughed, a small, lovely sound in the silence of the canyon. "I explored everywhere by myself, as far north as Moab and all the way south to Black Mesa." She turned and patted the basket behind her. "Shall we?"

Lorena had packed roast beef sandwiches, a yellow cake dotted with poppy seeds, and a bottle of wine. They sat in the shade of a willow that trailed branches into the lake and ate in silence for a while, enjoying the play of the sun on the water and the small sound made by crickets in the bushes.

"Why did you bring me here, Lorena?" Tyree finally asked the question he'd been turning over in his mind since they'd left the ranch. "Last night you did everything but accuse me of being a cold-blooded killer, and now we're having a picnic together."

The girl shook her head. "I don't know. Maybe I just wanted to share my secret place with you. The lake is small, but it is lovely, isn't it?"

Tyree nodded. "It sure is, but the lake isn't the reason you brought me here."

Lorena turned to him, her troubled eyes finding his. "You're right. It's not the reason. Chance, I wanted to talk to you about Quirt Laytham."

Tyree stiffened. "What about him?"

"I want you and Quirt to be friends." She held up her hand. "I know, I know, mistakes were made, but nothing that can't be undone."

A small anger flared in Tyree. "You're blinded by him, aren't you, Lorena? You can't see past the good looks and flashy clothes to the man underneath. I was a stranger passing through, but I was hung by men acting on Laytham's orders. I'd have strangled to death if Owen hadn't found me. And what about him? What about Owen? Laytham wants him dead so he can claim his few acres of grass. Tell me, what kind of a man thinks that way? How can greed and the desire for power possess a man so badly that he'll kill everybody in his path to get what he wants?"

Tyree dropped the piece of cake he'd been eating and wiped his fingers on his jeans. "How many must he kill to get you, Lorena?"

"That's a terrible thing to say," the girl snapped, color flooding into her cheeks. "The trouble is you're jealous of Quirt because he's rich and successful, and you'll stop at nothing to discredit him."

The day that had begun so full of promise was going downhill fast, the shadows once again gathering between them.

"I'm not jealous of Quirt Laytham, Lorena," Tyree said. "In my entire life I've never wanted anything badly enough to envy the man that had it." He hesitated a moment, then added, "That is, until I met you."

"No one has me."

"Does that include Laytham?"

"Quirt asked me to marry him, and he believes we've reached an understanding. For right now at least, I'm content to let matters rest where they are."

"Laytham isn't the man for you, Lorena," Tyree said.

"And you are?"

Tyree nodded. "Yes, Lorena, I am."

Maybe it was the sincerity in Tyree's voice that made the girl hesitate. She opened her mouth to speak, then closed it again and for a few moments sat lost in thought. Finally she turned to Tyree. "Chance, no matter what, I won't be the wife of a gunfighter. I'd sit at home, dreading the knock on the door. And, sooner or later, it would come. I couldn't live like that."

Tyree slid the Colt from the holster and held it in the palm of his hand. "Lorena, this is the Colt Frontier revolver, model of 1873, and a long time ago I accepted its ways and I've lived by its code most all of my adult life. But a man can change. Recently I've been thinking that it's time to put this away and never pick it up again." He shoved the gun back into the leather. "I'm thirty years old and it's time I was moving on."

"What would you do?" Lorena asked.

Tyree looked at the woman, at the sunlight tangled in her hair and the green fire in her eyes, and he thought her achingly lovely. "Ranch maybe," he said after he'd collected his thoughts. "I've always had a yen to raise Percheron horses. Percherons are fine animals and they have a long history. Back in the Middle Ages, they carried armored knights into battle, and today they can drag a plow across rough land that would bring oxen to their knees. One time in Denver I even saw a team pull a carriage and look mighty good doing it. It seems to me that just about every farm and ranch in the country needs a pair of Percherons, so the market is there."

Lorena smiled. "Chance, your whole face lights up when you talk about those horses."

Tyree nodded. "I was fourteen when I went up the trail to Kansas for the first time. The chuck wagon was pulled by a Percheron team, grays they were, standing over sixteen hands, and I never forgot them."

A frown gathered between Lorena's eyebrows. "Raising horses takes money. I know Pa wants you to stay on and help him. He couldn't pay much, but it might help."

"I'll work it out," Tyree said, sidestepping the girl's suggestion. "There's always a way."

"There is a way," Lorena said uneasily, as though she was wary of widening the already yawning gulf between them.

Tyree smiled. "And what's that?"

"You could make your peace with Quirt. He'd be willing to help you get started. I know he would."

It took a few moments for the full impact of what the girl had said to hit Tyree. And when it came, it was like a punch in the gut.

"Lorena," he said, rising to his feet, "the only thing I want from Quirt Laytham is six feet of ground between us and a gun in my hand." It had been direct, almost brutal, and Tyree felt the hurt of it as much as Lorena.

The girl looked like she'd been slapped. She slammed the lid shut on the picnic basket, the noise adding the final period to their conversation.

"Let's go," she said. Her face looked like it was carved from pale marble. "It's getting late."

As the light began to fade, they rode home in silence under a lemon sky, tinged with thin brushstrokes of crimson.

Lorena went directly into the cabin, her head held high, while Tyree led the horses to the barn. He rubbed both animals down with a piece of sacking, then tossed them some hay and a bait of oats.

When he stepped outside again into a pale blue twilight, a single, sentinel star glimmered high over his head. Tyree was reluctant to enter the cabin, so he sat on the tree trunk that served as a seat beside the barn door and built a smoke.

The chasm between him and Lorena had widened so much that it could well nigh be impossible to bridge. She could not understand the depth of his hatred and bitterness toward Laytham, the wrong he felt had been done him. Tyree knew that only the man's complete destruction could loose the bonds of revenge that gripped his heart, an emotion Lorena found alien and disturbing.

The pain in his side and the rope burn that was still red and raw on his neck were constant reminders that he had yet to bring about the reckoning. Defeated and baffled though he was, he knew there was no other way.

He could not walk away from Laytham—not now, not ever. If he did, he'd be spitting on every principle that made him what he was.

But in gaining his revenge he would lose Lorena. That was the price that had to be paid and there would be no bargaining.

A deep sense of loss in him, Tyree ground the butt of his cigarette under his heel and began to build another. But his hands stilled on papers and tobacco as the clarion clang of a cowbell echoed its clamor among the canyons, a mournful tolling that was growing closer.

Had Boyd belled one of his cows?

Tyree rose to his feet, puzzled, and listened as the ringing became louder. A couple of minutes passed and a rider trailing a horse emerged through the gathering dusk at the other side of the creek. The bell in the rider's right hand clanged constantly, and he was yelling the same unintelligible words over and over again.

Tyree was aware of the cabin door opening, then Lorena was at his side. "It's Pa," she said. "And he's leading Owen's buckskin."

Luke Boyd splashed across the creek, his horse stepping high, throwing tall sprays of water into the air. He kept right on ringing the cowbell, yelling something above its insistent clangor.

Behind him, a man was hanging facedown over the saddle of the buckskin, his falling hair moving with the motion of the horse.

Then both Tyree and Lorena heard the old rancher clearly.

"Owen is dead!" Boyd cried. "Shot down like a dog in the street!"

When he rode up to the cabin, Boyd reined up his horse and dropped the buckskin's trailing reins. He rang his bell and called out again, "Owen Fowler is dead. . . . Owen Fowler is dead. . . ."

Tyree reached up and gently held Boyd's arm, the bell clinking into silence. Boyd looked down at him with wounded eyes. "I bought this in town after Owen was killed. I rang it all the way here. I wanted everyone to hear me and know what had happened."

As Lorena ran to help her father from the saddle, Tyree eased Fowler from the buckskin and laid him on his back on the ground. The front of the man's shirt was covered in blood, but the two bullet holes in the center of his chest were easy to see.

Tyree looked up from the dead man. "Luke," he asked, "who did this?"

"The Arapaho Kid," Boyd answered. He stood close to Lorena, as though needing her strength and support. "He gunned Owen down in the street like a—"

"How did it happen?" Tyree interrupted, an ice-cold, killing rage building in him.

Boyd rubbed his hand across his face as though to erase a painful memory. "We couldn't find Sheriff Tobin, so I dragged that no-good rustler into Bradley's saloon to ask around for him. I told Owen to stay close, but he said he was crossing the street to talk to the gunsmith about repairing his rifle. Then somebody ran into the saloon and said the Arapaho Kid was outside, bracing Owen Fowler.

"I left the saloon to see what was happening, just in time to hear the Kid call Owen a back-shooting lowlife. Then the Kid said to Owen, 'You've got a rifle. Use it.' Owen tried to show the Kid that his Henry was damaged, but as soon as he done that, the Kid drew and fired."

The old rancher shook his head. "I couldn't stop it, Chance. I think the Kid would have killed me too. As Owen lay there dying, the Kid stood over him and grinned. He said now there was one less preacher killer in the territory."

"Where was Tobin?" Tyree asked.

"He showed up later. Three men swore Owen had tried to level his rifle at the Kid and that the killing was self-defense. I told Tobin otherwise, but he wouldn't listen to me. He said too many reliable witnesses stated that Owen Fowler tried to kill the Kid." Boyd shrugged, his face haunted. "And that's how it stands." His baleful eyes sought Tyree's. "Tobin locked up my prisoner and he says he plans to hang him directly."

"Was Laytham there during all this?"

"No," Boyd said. "I didn't see him."

"Quirt would have nothing to do with a cold-blooded murder," Lorena snapped, sudden tears filling her eyes.

"The Arapaho Kid works for him, doesn't he?" Tyree asked.

"I don't know," the girl said. "But if he does, Quirt will send him packing, I can promise you that."

"Who were the three witnesses, Luke?" Tyree asked.

"Tobin's deputies, Len Dawson and Clem Daley. The third was a gunfighter out of Missouri, dresses like a preacher his ownself. Calls himself . . ." Boyd shook his head. "Everything was happening so fast I don't recollect his name."

"Luther Darcy?" Tyree prompted.

"Yes. That was it. Luther Darcy. How did you know?"

"Owen told me about him," Tyree said. His eye slanted to Lorena. "He said Darcy draws gun wages from Quirt Laytham."

Tyree saw confusion in the girl's face, but she made no attempt to defend Laytham again. Instead she kneeled by Fowler's body and tenderly lifted a strand of hair off his forehead. "Poor Owen," she whispered, her voice breaking. "You were a mild-mannered man, never cut out to live in the West. You should have gone back home to Boston and worked in a bank." Her tearstained eyes lifted to her father. "Pa, we have a burying to do."

"Not here," Tyree said. "We'll bury him in his own ground, at his canyon. He loved that place and that's where he'd want to rest."

Neither Lorena nor her father voiced an objection, understanding that Tyree had the right of the thing.

"Chance, let's lay Owen in the barn for the night," Boyd said. "We'll move out at sunup."

"You'll do nothing of the kind!" Lorena snapped, her eyes flaring. "Bring him inside and let me wash his poor body. I won't send Owen to his Maker looking the way he does."

For the first time, Tyree was aware of the steel in
Lorena Boyd, the metal tempered by the hard men
among whom she'd lived and by the land itself. She
was no shallow, bustled belle reluctant to touch a
bloody corpse. She was a woman of the frontier—
she'd swallow her revulsion and do what had to be
done without complaint.

"So be it, Lorena," Tyree said. "And you're right.
A man should be buried decent."

There were just three mourners at Owen Fowler's
funeral when they laid him to rest in his canyon
amid the first of the morning light, but in the end, it
was enough for any man.

Lorena wet the black earth with her tears and Boyd
said the words from the Book. When they were done,
Tyree whispered his last farewell and walked quickly
toward his horse.

"Chance, where are you going?" Boyd asked, closing his Bible.

Tyree stopped beside the steeldust and turned.
"You know where I'm going, Luke. Where can I
find him?"

The rancher looked into Tyree's green eyes and
shivered, as though their coldness had reached out
to him. This was not the time for argument, he knew.
Owen Fowler had saved Tyree's life and now he
would do right by him. Revenge was a harsh, unforgiving code, but men like Chance Tyree lived by it,
and he would not be turned aside.

"The Kid works for Laytham," Boyd said, "but
he's never used a rope or handled a branding iron
in his life. He says he has to keep his hands soft for

gun work. You'll find him in Crooked Creek, most likely holdin' court at Bradley's."

"No, Chance," Lorena said, stepping toward him, her agitation evident by the way she waved her hands at him. "I've heard about the Arapaho Kid, and he's a killer. He's shot down a dozen men, and maybe more. You're no match for him."

Tyree swung into the saddle. "Look around you, Lorena," he said. "There's nobody else. Your pa isn't a gunfighter, so I've got it to do."

"Owen wouldn't want this, Chance," the girl said. "He wouldn't demand blood for blood."

The girl's eyes were wet with tears, but for him or Fowler, Tyree couldn't guess.

"Maybe so," he said. "But Owen had his way and I have mine. Maybe I was wrong when we spoke of ranches and Percherons at the lake. It seems no matter how he tries, a man can't turn his back on what he is."

Tyree swung his horse toward the mouth of the canyon, but Boyd's voice stopped him. "Chance, the Kid carries a gun on his hip and another in a crossdraw rig on his belt. He favors the crossdraw."

"A thing to remember," Tyree said. He touched his hat brim to Lorena and spurred the steeldust out of the canyon, swinging south along the bank of Hatch Wash.

He didn't look back.

Chapter 11

Crooked Creek was a sprawling collection of shacks, saloons and houses scattered along the base of a high yellow mesa. The town had a raw frontier look to it, yet, like a penniless but genteel dowager, it had pretensions to grandeur. White-painted gingerbread houses huddled together on the outskirts of town and the place boasted a church, school and fire station.

It was not yet noon when Tyree, his hat pulled low over his face, rode along the main street and tied up his horse outside Bradley's Saloon.

He stepped onto the boardwalk, but instead of entering the saloon walked to his right and stopped at a restaurant with a weather-beaten sign outside that said simply: EATS.

He was hungry and, at least for now, the Arapaho Kid could wait.

Tyree stepped inside, grateful for the coolness of the place, and found a table facing the door. At this time of the day, the restaurant was quiet. A couple of men who looked like bank clerks sat at another table, lingering long over their coffee.

The two had studied Tyree closely when he entered, taking in his gun and the hard glint in his eyes, then had turned quickly away, wanting no part of him.

A young, pretty waitress took his order for steak and eggs and filled his coffee cup. He ate with an appetite, ordered more coffee and built a smoke. More people came into the restaurant, mostly the town's respectable businessmen and their wives, then a couple of grinning young punchers in dusty range clothes who talked pretties to the waitress and made her giggle.

Tyree paid his bill and stepped to the door, his chiming spurs attracting the attention of the punchers. "Hey, Tex, you lookin' for a ridin' job?" one of them called out to him.

Tyree turned and shook his head. "Just passing through."

"Too bad," the man said. "We could use an extry hand or three."

It was hot outside and a dust devil danced in the street before collapsing in a puff of yellow near the Overland Stage depot where passengers made small talk and tried not to think about the hours of jolting, sweating misery that lay ahead for them. Outside the firehouse, a man in suspenders and collarless shirt was polishing the brass of a red steam engine, arcs of dark sweat under his arms.

Including his steeldust, six horses now stood at the saloon hitching rail. Tyree stepped along the boardwalk and checked the brands. The five ponies bore Laytham's Rafter-L on their shoulders. It was an easy brand to alter with a running iron, Tyree decided, but by now rustlers had probably learned to ride wide around the big rancher's herds.

The horses' necks were lathered where the reins had rubbed, so Tyree knew they had just arrived. Was the Arapaho Kid among them?

There was only one way to find out, and Tyree figured it was high time he did what he'd come to do. He stepped inside the saloon, letting the doors swing shut behind him.

Five men stood at the long, mahogany bar, one of them the huge Clem Daley, wearing Tyree's buckskin coat. A smaller man stood at the deputy's side, a smoking black cigar clenched in his teeth. This man was grinning as he held aloft a shining new double eagle. "The drinks are on me, boys," he said. "We're celebrating today and there's more gold where this one came from."

Laughter and cheers went up from Daley and the others, and a few men who were sitting around the saloon at tables joined in with enthusiasm.

The bartender, a thick-shouldered man with a broken nose, set up drinks, then stepped to where Tyree stood at the bar. "What will it be, stranger?" he asked. "You heard the man. He's buying."

"Rye," Tyree said. "But I buy my own drinks."

"Now that ain't real neighborly of you—" the bartender began. But Daley's booming roar cut him off in midsentence.

"What in the blue blazes are you doing in town,

Tyree?" he yelled. "You must be hell-bent on committing suicide because you must know you ain't leaving Crooked Creek alive."

Tyree ignored the question. "Your time will come, Daley," he said, "but not today. Right now I'm looking for a yellow-bellied snake who goes by the name of the Arapaho Kid."

The man who'd been smoking the cigar took a puff, laid the stogie carefully in the ashtray in front of him then stepped away from the bar. "They call me the Arapaho Kid," he said, his hands hanging loose and ready at his side. "You hunting trouble with me?"

The Kid was not much above medium height, black hair hanging loose and greasy over his shoulders under a low-crowned hat with a flat brim. He had the wide, heavy cheekbones of an Indian, but his eyes were blue, the heritage of his mixed blood. He looked confident and poised and eager to kill.

"You murdered a friend of mine yesterday, Kid," Tyree said. "I'm here to do right by him."

"You mean that back-shooting scum Owen Fowler." The Kid smiled. "He was heeled."

"He was carrying a broken rifle that couldn't shoot," Tyree said. He stepped closer to the Kid and saw the man's eyes widen in alarm. Sharing a trait common to all gunmen, the Kid liked distance between himself and his victim. Too close, and even a dying, badly frightened sodbuster might get off a lucky shot.

From off to his left, Tyree heard the bartender say, "Mister, you best let it be. You don't want to mess with the Kid. He'll kill you for sure."

Tyree ignored the man. "Kid, Owen Fowler was a

kind, decent man, a better man than you'll ever be. But you gunned him down like a dog in the street. For that there has to be a reckoning."

"Reckoning my ass," Daley said, a grin stretching his cruel, thick lips. "You want to take him, Kid, or will I do it?"

"I told you, Daley," Tyree said. "This is not your day. But if you want to take a hand in this, shuck off my coat. I don't want your blood all over it."

"Damn you, Tyree. I'll—"

"Leave it be, Clem," the Kid said, his smile razor thin. He reached out, retrieved his cigar and stuck it in the corner of his mouth. His right hand, slender and well manicured as a woman's, hovered near his belt buckle. "This one's all mine. I enjoy killing a man for breakfast."

The Arapaho Kid grabbed for the Colt in his cross-draw holster—but Tyree, expecting the move, did the last thing the gunman expected. He made no attempt to draw.

Shifting position fast, he stepped into the Kid and pinned the man's gun hand with his left as it closed on the butt of his gun. His right fist crashed into the Kid's face and Tyree felt the man's nose smash under his knuckles. The Kid dropped his gun and let out a bubbling scream, but Tyree was merciless. He back-handed the gunman across the face then held him upright to take a hard left. The Kid's lips pulped against his teeth, and his knees buckled. Tyree took a half step back and as the man fell he slammed a powerful uppercut to the Kid's chin. The gunman staggered back, then crashed to the floor. He lay on his back, his left leg twitching, and did not get up.

For a few moments the other men at the bar froze, trying to make sense of what they'd just witnessed. Then Daley hurled a wild curse at Tyree and went for his gun. He still hadn't cleared leather when he found himself looking into the muzzle of Tyree's Colt.

"That's it. I'm done!" Daley screamed, his eyes popping out of his head. He let his gun drop and it thudded onto the floor.

The three others at the bar, bad actors all, had the wild, reckless look of men who were thinking about auditioning for parts in the play.

But Tyree's cold command stopped them. "Call off your dogs, Daley, or I'll gut shoot you right where you stand."

"You heard the man. Back off!" Daley shrieked. The big deputy was almost frantic with fear, knowing how close he stood to a bullet in the belly.

The others reluctantly lifted their hands clear of their guns, and one of them, a lantern-jawed man in a butternut shirt, asked, "Clem, you sure this is how you want it?"

"Yes, damn it," Daley yelped. "Step away from it."

"Daley," Tyree said, no give in him, "take off my coat and lay it on the bar."

The deputy hesitated and Tyree yelled, "Do it now!"

His face gray, Daley quickly peeled off the coat and did as he was told.

"Take me a month to get your stink out of that," Tyree said. He leaned down and grabbed the Kid by the back of his shirt collar; then his eyes lifted to

Daley again. "Where's my dun?" he asked. "And my Colt."

"They ain't here, honest," Daley said. "I took your hoss and the guns to the Rafter-L."

"Daley, I plan on staying in town tonight," Tyree said. "Come first light tomorrow morning I want to see that dun standing outside the hotel. I want my gun and belt hanging from the saddle horn. You got that?"

The big deputy touched his tongue to dry lips. He was badly frightened. With the Arapaho Kid out of it, no longer there to back his play, he felt naked and alone.

"Sure, anything you say," Daley said.

"Now you and the others get on your ponies and ride out of here," Tyree said. "I don't want to have to be always watching my back."

Tyree strolled outside the saloon door until Daley and the other Laytham riders mounted up and left town, the big deputy in the lead, slapping his horse with the reins until it stretched its neck and its legs blurred into a flat-out run.

When Tyree stepped back inside, the bartender asked, nodding toward the still unconscious Arapaho Kid, "What about him?"

"He killed a friend of mine," Tyree said. "But I reckon his days as a shooter of unarmed men are about to come to a permanent close."

"You gonna kill the Kid?" the bartender asked, his face shocked.

Tyree nodded. "Something like that."

"Mister," the bartender protested, "there ain't nothing like that."

"Maybe so," Tyree said. "But there's worse."

He hauled the Kid outside and, as a curious crowd gathered, dragged him by the collar of his shirt to the horse trough near the hitching rail. Tyree repeatedly dunked the gunman's head into the water, each time leaving it there until the man began to frantically kick and struggle and bubbles rose to the surface.

Finally Tyree forced the Kid to his knees. Then he bent and looked into his face, their noses only inches apart. "You awake now, Kid?" he asked through gritted teeth. "I want you to know exactly what's happening to you, every last part of it."

Blood ran in watery fingers from the gunman's nose over his mouth and chin, but his face was dark and ugly with anger. "I'll kill you for this, Tyree," he snarled. "By God, I'll gun you first chance I get."

Tyree smiled and shook his head. "Kid, your killing days ended when you murdered Owen Fowler." Tyree pulled the gunman to his feet and spun him around. He shoved his hand into the Kid's pocket and found what he'd been looking for—four shiny new double eagles.

Tyree turned the man again and shoved the coins under the Kid's smashed nose. "Four of these in your pocket and one on the bar in the saloon," he said, his eyes hard, each breath short and harsh. "Is that what Laytham considered Owen Fowler's life was worth, huh? A lousy hundred dollars?"

"You go to hell!" the Kid snapped.

Tyree viciously backhanded the gunman across the face. "Was it?" he yelled. "Was Owen worth only a hundred dollars?"

The Kid's face was a bloody mess and he was

struggling to breathe. "A bonus," he gasped. "It was a bonus."

"For murdering Owen Fowler?"

"Yeah, yeah, for Fowler."

The Arapaho Kid's right hand dropped for the gun on his hip. But Tyree saw it coming and slapped the hand aside. He yanked the Kid's Colt from the holster and shoved it into his own waistband.

"You're a sorry piece of low-life trash, Kid," Tyree said, his voice suddenly level and chillingly calm. "Now I'm going to make sure you never kill another unarmed man."

Judged by the standards of a later era, what followed next was brutal, savage and merciless. But it is wise for a man to hesitate to judge the conduct of Western men lest he fall into the common error of condemning what he does not understand. Chance Tyree lived at a violent time in a violent land and justice as he understood it was swift, certain and tailored to fit the crime.

Tyree dragged the kicking, yelling Arapaho Kid to the hitching rail and laid the gunman's manicured, pampered right hand on the rough pine of the cross post. He pulled the Kid's Colt from his waistband, held it by the barrel and, with the butt, smashed the hand into a pulp of blood, gristle and splintered bone.

Ignoring the Kid's screams and the cries of the crowd for Sheriff Tobin, he did the same thing with the Kid's left. And when it was over, he stepped back and looked down with cold eyes at the whimpering gunman, who was bent over on his knees, his ruined hands held close to his belly, rocking back and forth.

No backup in him, and no compassion either, Tyree said, "You'd best find yourself another line of work, Kid. I'd say your days as a hired gun are over."

He grabbed the Kid by the back of his collar and pushed him toward his horse. "Now ride, and if I ever see you in the canyon country again, I'll kill you."

The Kid staggered to his horse, his pain-filled face ashen and scared. He wanted to get away from here, as far away as possible from the tall, relentless man with eyes the color of cold green death.

After several attempts, the Kid finally swung into the saddle and he kneed his horse forward. The big bartender from Bradley's stood on the boardwalk. He threw Tyree a look of hatred, and called out to the Kid, "Hey, Kid, you want my shotgun?"

The Arapaho Kid gave the bartender a sidelong glance and gasped, "You go to hell."

He kicked his horse into a lope and headed out of town. Tyree watched him leave until horse and rider were swallowed up by dust and distance.

"What's going on here?"

Tyree turned and watched as Sheriff Tobin, pulling a suspender over the shoulder of his dirty red vest, bellied his way through the crowd.

"Can't a man get any sleep around here?" he demanded, his eyes hidden behind his round, dark glasses. The hair that showed under the lawman's hat was pure white and his face was pasty, like the skin on the belly of a dead fish.

"Sheriff, this man just done for the Kid," someone in the crowd yelled. "Smashed both his hands to pulp."

Then it seemed everybody was talking at once, trying to get in their two cents' worth about what they'd just witnessed. Many voices were raised, but Tyree heard none that were friendly.

"Where is the Kid now?" Tobin asked, his uplifted hands quieting the crowd.

"He's gone, Sheriff," Tyree said. "And he won't be coming back."

He looked into Tobin's face but could not read the man's eyes, hidden as they were behind their circles of darkness.

Tobin turned and saw the bartender on the board-walk. "Benny, what happened?"

The bartender stepped off the walk and pointed to Tyree. "This man braced the Kid in the saloon. Then he dragged him out here and smashed up both his hands, just like you was told, Sheriff." The man called Benny turned and extended his arms to the crowd. "I think it's a crying shame that an honest citizen can't enjoy a little celebration in the saloon without being attacked and manhandled."

A murmur of agreement ran through the crowd. A few were the respectable townspeople of Crooked Creek, but most were drifters and the assorted riffraff of the frontier, anxious for any kind of excitement, especially a possible lynching.

Tyree was an outsider here, and all the town's sympathies were with the Arapaho Kid.

"Honest citizen, huh?" Tyree asked Tobin. He stepped closer to the big lawman. "Hold out your hand, Tobin."

"Why?"

"Just do it."

Tobin extended his powerful white paw and Tyree

dropped the four double eagles into his palm. "You'll find another one on the bar in the saloon. The Kid told me Quirt Laytham gave him these—a bonus for murdering Owen Fowler."

Some of the respectable element in the crowd exchanged puzzled looks, wondering about what Tyree had just said, trying to gauge the truth or falsity of it.

Tobin felt, rather than saw, the shift in attitude and stepped quickly into the breach. "Maybe that's what the Kid said, Tyree, and maybe it wasn't. But in any case I wouldn't take the word of a damn breed on anything."

A tall, thin man who looked like a merchant in a broadcloth suit and a high celluloid collar, said, "Hear, hear." Tobin pressed home his advantage. "You people break it up now," he said. "Be about your business." He turned to Tyree. "You come with me. I want to talk to you."

"You arresting me, Sheriff?" Tyree asked, his voice hard-edged.

"No, though I could for what you did back at the wash. Cost us some good men."

"They were coming at me shooting," Tyree said. "I was defending myself."

Tobin rubbed a hand across his unshaven cheeks then glanced at the blazing sun. "I don't care to stand here in the street and talk. I burn up real easy. Come with me to my office."

"What do you want to talk about, Tobin?" Tyree asked.

The big lawman stepped closer, so close Tyree could smell him, and his voice dropped to a confidential whisper. "I've got another proposition for you, and this one you'd be well-advised to take."

Chapter 12

The sheriff's office was a low log cabin with a timber roof, sandwiched between the telegraph office and a hardware store. It had a narrow porch and an awning held up by slender poles, a rocking chair set to one side of the door.

Inside, the place smelled like Tobin himself, a heavy mix of stale sweat, tobacco juice and smoke from the kerosene lantern that hung from a ceiling beam, its orange flame guttering. Black canvas shades were pulled down across the cabin's two windows, blocking out every glimpse of sunlight, and the air was thick, cloying and close, hard to breathe.

A door at the rear of the office hung ajar on rawhide hinges and beyond was a single cell. The front wall of the cell was of red brick, a barred, iron door to the right. The rustler Roy Will lay on his back on a bunk in the half-light, staring at the ceiling, his shoulder heavily bandaged.

Tobin closed the office door leading to the cell. "I plan on hanging him the day after tomorrow, but, even so, it's best he doesn't hear our talk." The lawman sat at his desk, opened a drawer and took out a bottle of whiskey. "Drink?" he asked.

Tyree shook his head. "Cut to the chase, Tobin. What's your proposition?"

Tobin lifted the bottle to his mouth, took a gulping swallow that made his throat bob, then wiped the back of his hand across his mouth. He sat in silence for a few moments, studying the tall younger man, then said, "Tyree, now that Fowler is dead, this thing is over and it's time you was riding on. There's no point in your staying around and causing all kinds of trouble for everybody. Which brings me to this. . . ."

Tobin slid open another drawer, rooted around for a few moments, then came up with a thick stack of greenbacks. He threw the money on the desk in front of Tyree. "That's a thousand dollars, more money than you'll ever see in one place at one time in your whole life. All you got to do is lean over, pick it up and then be on your way. Ride out of the territory, Tyree. Go to Denver maybe and spend the money on women and whiskey. Hell, man, have yourself a time."

Tyree made no attempt to pick up the money. He tilted his head to one side, smiling. "I'd say Quirt Laytham must be mighty scared of me."

"Mr. Laytham isn't scared of anybody," Tobin scoffed, "especially not you."

"Then why did he tell you to bribe me with a thousand dollars?"

The lamplight accentuated the pockmarks that cratered the sheriff's white cheeks, picking out the beads of sweat on his forehead and nose. It was unbearably hot in the office. Tyree felt his shirt sticking to him, the fetid, feral stench of the fat lawman assailing his nostrils.

"You're so smart, ain't you, Tyree?" Tobin said. "So damned smart." He leaned forward and propped his elbows on the desk. "Get this through your thick skull: Quirt Laytham doesn't need to bribe you to leave anywhere. Step in his way again and he'll crush you like a bug." The sheriff shook his head. "No, this money was give me by somebody else, somebody who wants you long gone from here. For your own good, you understand."

Tobin shifted his bulk in the chair and it squeaked in protest, sending a frightened rat scuttling across the floor. "After that . . . ah . . . shall we say, unpleasantness at Hatch Wash, Mr. Laytham and me figured Fowler would head for Luke Boyd's place, seeing as how him and the old man were real close at one time. Me, I was gonna ride out there with the money today and talk to you private, like. But now there's no need because there you stand as bold as brass and on the prod as ever was."

"Who put up the money?" Tyree asked, intrigued despite himself.

Tobin grinned, saliva stranding between his small, pegged teeth. He tapped the side of his nose with a forefinger. "That's between me and the snubbin' post, boy, or maybe I should say between me and the party of the third." As though suddenly bored with the whole business, Tobin pushed the pile of bills toward Tyree. "Now take that and you git. If Mr. Laytham or Luther Darcy happen to ride into town, you're a dead man."

"No, it's your turn to listen, Tobin," Tyree said.

"Hand that money back to whoever gave it to you and tell him I'm staying right here until I settle a score with Quirt Laytham. On his orders, his men, your deputies, hung and then shot me and me just a stranger—"

"I know, I know," Tobin interrupted, his irritation evident. "Just a stranger passing through. I've heard all that afore. See, it was an honest mistake and Mr. Laytham surely regrets it. Clem Daley and Len Dawson took ye for a friend of Fowler's, another damned rustler like the one I got locked up here." Tobin waved his pudgy hands. "Well, what's past is past. Let bygones be bygones, I always say. Forgive and forget. After Fowler came back and started to rustle Mr. Laytham's cows, everything was topsy-turvy, all kinds of regrettable things were happening. But now Fowler is gone and the rustling ended, we'll get back to normal pretty damn quick."

A hot anger flaring in him, Tyree placed his hands on the desk and leaned toward the sheriff. "Tobin, I believe you had nothing to do with what happened to me back there at the brush flats. If I thought you did, I'd have put a bullet into your fat gut by this time."

Tobin opened his mouth to interrupt, but Tyree waved him into silence. "I want you to give a message to Laytham from me. Tell him I expect him to leave the territory, taking only what he can carry on a horse. Tell him if he doesn't go, I'll come after him and destroy him."

The sheriff shook his head. "Hard talk, Tyree, mighty hard talk. But Mr. Laytham isn't going anywhere. He's backed by twenty guns and one of them is Luther Darcy. You won't find Darcy as easy to handle as you did the Arapaho Kid. He's good—the best there is."

Tyree straightened up and looked down at the sweating lawman. "Tobin, I'm all through talking. You take my message to Laytham and tell him to be gone by the end of the week. You tell him that and make it real clear."

"I'll tell him." Tobin shrugged. "It's your funeral."

He picked up the money from his desk and tossed it back in the drawer. "The party of the third," he said, "is going to be powerful disappointed in you."

Tyree booked a room in the Regal Hotel, wondering why he was doing that instead of riding back to Boyd's place. Then the answer came to him—he was doing it to avoid Lorena, unable to take the hurt, accusing looks she threw at him when he talked about Quirt Laytham.

He needed some time to himself, to think the thing through. He didn't believe that Lorena was in love with Laytham, but she did seem attracted to the man, and she had not given the big rancher an outright refusal when he'd asked her to marry him.

And what about himself? If he succeeded in destroying Laytham as he planned, would Lorena ever forgive him? More to the point, would she forgive him enough to fall in love with him? Only time would answer those questions.

Yet there was another question, and this one demanded an immediate answer—was he really in love with Lorena?

Surprising himself, Tyree admitted that he did not know.

Lorena was so beautiful, sometimes it hurt him just to look at her. And she had sand. She'd proved that when she washed and cared for poor Fowler's body back at the cabin.

But was it enough? Was beauty and grit a solid basis for love?

As he led the steeldust away from the hotel hitching rail to the livery stable, Tyree told himself that he didn't know and gloomily admitted that he was more confused than ever.

He ate at the restaurant again that night, aware of the stares of the other diners, some curious, others frankly horrified, then went directly back to the hotel.

Wary of being bushwhacked, he kept away from the windows and placed the back of a chair under the doorknob. He had shamed Clem Daley in front of other men and, unlike Tobin, the big deputy was not the kind to forgive and forget.

Tyree stripped, gave himself a cold sponge bath from the pitcher and basin on the dresser, then turned down the oil lamp and got between the sheets. He laid his gun close to hand on the bedside table and closed his eyes, willing sleep to come.

The wound in his side was healing well, but it still pained him, and his run-in with the Arapaho Kid had taken more out of him than he realized. But gradually he relaxed, his breathing slowed and he drifted into the healthy young man's deep slumber. . . .

A single revolver shot woke Tyree, blasting apart the fabric of his sleep, hurling him into wakefulness. He grabbed the Colt from the bedside table and stepped quickly to the window. His room was at the back of the hotel and looked out on the flats where the dawn light was lacing the branches of the sage and antelope bitterbrush. In the distance the buttes, mesas and broken rocky ridges of the canyon country were fantastic blue silhouettes against a pale lemon sky.

Nothing moved out there. The landscape was serene and peaceful.

Tyree eased his thumb off the hammer of the Colt and smiled to himself. "Getting jumpy in your old age, Chance," he said aloud. "That was just some rooster coming home drunk and letting off steam."

But a few moments later, running feet pounded on the stairs outside, and from somewhere, a woman's voice rose in a stifled shriek.

What was going on?

Tyree put on his hat, then dressed quickly and buckled his gun belt around his hips. He opened the door and went to the top of the stairs, passing a man wearing a red velvet robe on the way. "What happened?" Tyree asked.

The man—a drummer by the look of him—shrugged and brushed past. "Go see for yourself," he said.

Tyree ran downstairs and elbowed his way through a clump of hotel guests who were standing at the door, looking out into the street. He stepped onto the porch then stopped in his tracks, scarcely able to believe what his eyes were telling him.

His zebra dun lay sprawled in death at the hitching rail, a bullet hole in its forehead oozing a trickle of blood. A white scrap of paper was tied to the horse's mane, fluttering slightly in the morning breeze.

Tyree undid the paper and read. The note was short, scrawled on a page torn from a tally book.

HEERES YOUR HOSS
—ENJOY THE RIDE

Clem Daley had kept his promise. He had delivered the dun.

The man had obviously regained his confidence after talking to Quirt Laytham. Tyree's own cartridge belt and holstered Colt hung over the top rail of the hitching post.

By returning the gun, Laytham was sending him a message.

He was telling Tyree that he wasn't afraid of him.

Chapter 13

Tyree decided there was nothing to be gained by remaining in Crooked Creek where every man's hand was turned against him and he was friend to none. It was time to head back to Boyd's ranch—and Lorena.

Laytham had until the end of the week, three more days, to leave the territory. Of course he wouldn't, that much was clear. But what then?

Tyree had no plan of action, not even a vague idea sketched out in his mind. He only knew that when the time came he would act.

After picking up his saddlebags from the hotel, Tyree walked to the livery stable, on the way passing the firehouse volunteers who were busy removing the dead horse from the street, dragging it with chains behind a mule-drawn pump wagon.

The loss of his horse tugging at him, he saddled the steeldust and was walking him toward the barn door when his toe accidentally hit an upturned iron bucket and sent it clanking across the floor.

Immediately an angry voice bellowed from the hayloft. "Hey, you!"

Tyree looked up and saw bloodshot eyes in an annoyed, freckled face, glaring at him. "Do you need to make all that damned noise?" It was a girl's voice and when he looked closer, Tyree saw a pert, upturned nose and a tangled mass of corn yellow hair. "Ooh," the girl groaned. "I shouldn't have hollered like that." She clutched her head and rocked back and forth, obviously in the throes of a massive hangover.

"Sorry." Tyree grinned. "I'll be more careful next time."

"Well, see you are. First there was all that shooting. Then you start kicking buckets around." The girl shook her head. "Ah, the hell with it. I'll never get back to sleep now. I need a whiskey. Do you have any?"

"What you need," Tyree said, "is a gallon of coffee and some bacon and eggs."

"Mister, I asked you if you had whiskey. Do you?"

"No."

"Then why the hell am I wasting my time talking to you?"

Tyree's grin widened. "I don't know. I kinda figured you liked my company."

"Yeah, that will be the day."

Tyree waved to the girl. "Well, since you don't care for my company, I guess I'll be on my way."

"Wait!"

The girl's feet thudded on the boards of the loft then Tyree watched her climb down the ladder. At the bottom she stood for a few moments, her hand on a rung, and clutched her head, groaning. "What kind of who-hit-John rotgut," she asked herself, "did that damned bartender at Bradley's serve me last night?"

She was dressed in striped pants three sizes too large for her, tucked into down-at-heel, rough-out boots. She wore a man's canvas coat, and under that a blue gingham shirt open at the neck. Despite her baggy clothes, her taut, well-curved figure was very obvious, and her eyes were brown, shot through with tiny flecks of gold. Her hair, tangled with wisps of straw, fell in loose curls from under a battered black hat and her lips were full, pale pink and inviting.

"What you looking at, mister?" she asked. "Ain't you never seen a woman before?"

"Not one that just fell out of a hayloft." Tyree smiled. "Besides, you're a girl, not a woman."

"The hell I'm not. I turned nineteen in the spring."

"You're sixteen, maybe seventeen," Tyree said. "And that's giving you the benefit of the doubt."

The girl opened her mouth to speak, thought better of it, then said finally, "Look, mister, I need a drink real bad. Could you loan me a dollar?"

Tyree shook his head. "The last thing you need is more whiskey. Tell you what. I was going to be on my way, but I'll take the time to buy you breakfast."

Whatever the girl was about to reply died on her lips. Her eyes, widening in surprise, slid over Tyree's shoulder to the door of the barn.

Tyree turned. A man stood straddle-legged in the doorway, a black flat-brimmed hat with a low crown pulled low over his eyes. He wore an ivory-handled Remington on each side of his chest in ornately carved shoulder holsters. The morning was already hot and he wore no coat, just a frilled white shirt, string tie, brocaded red vest and black pants tucked into expensive boots of the same color. His cold blue eyes slanted slightly and his skin had a yellowish tinge, giving him the look of an ancient Mongol conqueror who expected lesser men to grovel at his feet.

The man's chin jutted arrogantly toward Tyree. "You the one they call Chance Tyree?"

"Who wants to know?"

The man ignored the question, his icy eyes searching Tyree's face, measuring him. "Nick Tobin told me you have a message for Quirt Laytham. You want to give it to me?"

"Like I asked you already," Tyree answered, suddenly tense and ready, "who are you?"

"Name's Luther Darcy. If the name don't mean anything to you, it should." Beside him, Tyree heard the girl shriek, not a cry of fear but one of raw anger.

"You son of a bitch, that name means something to me," she screamed. The girl turned and ran back to a stall where a paint pony was penned. A saddle with a booted Winchester hung over the stall partition and she grabbed the rifle and racked a round into the chamber, striding toward Darcy, her eyes blazing.

Using a movement too fast to follow, the gunman crossed his arms and drew his Remingtons, the big revolvers coming level in a single, flashing instant.

"No!" Tyree yelled. He quickly stepped in front of the girl and wrenched the rifle from her hands. "You little fool, he'll kill you!"

For a few seconds, the girl fought him like a tiger;

then she gave up, realizing the futility of her struggles.

"Darcy," she yelled, jumping to look over Tyree's shoulder, "remember this—I'm coming after you and I'm going to kill you one day."

The gunman's lips stretched in a grin under his sweeping black mustache. "Now that really scares me. Hell, I could gun both of you right now, then go eat breakfast."

One arm holding the girl back, Tyree turned on Darcy. "Then why don't you try?"

The man waved a negligent hand. "Now is not the time." His eyes again wandered over Tyree from boots to hat, summing him up in his own mind. "Heard about you, Tyree," he said. "Heard some wild stuff about when you were running with Wes Hardin and them, and later. They say you're good with a gun, mighty slick and sudden. Don't know if that's the truth or not. But anyhow, I'm letting you live, at least for the time being. Call it"—he thought for a few moments—"call it professional courtesy."

"Darcy, did you kill my horse?" Tyree asked, his voice level and cold.

The gunman shook his head. "Tut, tut and tut, Tyree. You ought to know that's not my style. Clem Daley shot your horse. Him and a couple of others."

"I know what your style is, you damned murderer," the girl snapped. "Shooting down poor cowboys in the street."

"Now what cowboys would that be?" Darcy asked, his voice a soft, menacing hiss. "There have been so many."

"My brother for one," the girl said. "His name was

Tom Brennan and you killed him in Cheyenne a year ago. He was all I had in the world and you murdered him.''

Darcy nodded. "Ah, yes, I remember now, a towhead, wasn't he? Had freckles all over his face like you, like he'd swallowed a dollar and broke out in pennies. In my capacity as range detective, I caught him riding a horse that wasn't his and he went for his gun. Now, all things considered, that was very foolish of him, wasn't it?''

"Tom had a bill of sale for that horse, and you know it!" the girl yelled.

Darcy shook his head. "This grows tiresome. What's one damn saddle tramp more or less?" He spun his guns and they thudded solidly back into their holsters.

"Hear this, both of you. I want you out of town and out of the territory—today. Tyree, if I see you in Crooked Creek tomorrow, or anyplace else for that matter, I'll forget all about professional courtesies and gun you." He smiled, his teeth very white, the long canines prominent and wet, like fangs. "This I promise.''

Anger flared in Tyree. "You want to try it right now, Darcy?''

"No, not right now. If I gunned you now, it would set just fine with Mr. Laytham, but there is someone else who would take it hard. And for that reason, I was told to give you only a sternly delivered warning." Darcy smiled. "For this day at least.''

"Well, you've told me. Now let me tell you something. I won't leave this territory until my business with Laytham is over.''

Darcy nodded. "Of course, I knew you'd say that. So, from this moment on, Tyree, consider yourself a walking dead man." The gunman smiled again, touched his hat to the girl, and was gone.

The girl rounded on Tyree, her face dark with anger. "Why the hell didn't you draw down on him?"

"Because"—Tyree grinned—"it would have spoiled my appetite for breakfast."

"You're scared of him, aren't you? You're a scaredy cat."

Tyree shook his head. "No, I'm not scared of him, but maybe I should be."

"How come?"

"Because he's good. I think maybe the best with a gun I've ever seen and I've seen plenty."

The girl stuck out her tongue. "Scaredy cat."

Tyree grinned. "Say, what's your name anyway?"

"Sally. Sally Brennan."

"Well, Sally Brennan, now I'm taking you to breakfast."

Despite her hangover, the girl ate hungrily, demolishing two plates of flapjacks and bacon before she sighed and slumped back in her chair.

"When did you last eat?" Tyree asked, an amused smile touching his lips.

Sally shrugged. "I don't recollect. It was a spell back."

She watched Tyree build a smoke and asked, "Will you make me one of those?"

Tyree shook his head. "No. Tobacco will stunt your growth."

"Didn't do that to you."

"Maybe I was lucky."

Since the morning was well advanced, there were no other diners in the restaurant. Tyree leaned closer to the girl. "How long have you been hunting Luther Darcy?"

"A year, maybe a little more."

"How did it happen? With your brother, I mean."

Sally dipped the tip of her middle finger into a small puddle of molasses syrup on her plate and licked the finger clean. "My folks had a hardscrabble ranch just south of the Platte in the Wyoming Territory, but when I was six years old they were both took by the cholera. My brother, Tom, was barely twelve at the time, but he kept the place going and he raised me—well, him and an old hired hand who passed on a couple of years ago."

The girl leaned forward in her chair. "Mister, you sure you want to hear all this? It ain't like we're kin or anything."

Tyree smiled. "The name's Chance, and, yes, I want to hear about it. It seems to me we share a common enemy, and that's kin enough."

"Well, Chance, about eighteen months ago there was a sight of rustling along the Platte and the local cattleman's association hired Darcy as a range detective—just a fancy name for a hired killer.

"About then, Tom rode into Cheyenne trying to get a bank loan to tide us over until we sold our herd. Tom had just bought a paint pony from the Rocking J ranch, off a man called Bill Hardesty, a mighty important member of the association. Darcy

saw Tom in the street and accused him of stealing
the horse and pushed him into going for his gun.
Tom hadn't even cleared leather when Darcy shot
him." Small tears reddened Sally's eyes. "I was told
my brother died a few minutes later, cursing Darcy
and all he stood for."

"And you've been tracking Darcy ever since?"

"Uh-huh. I sold the ranch for what I could get,
and that was little enough, then tracked Darcy all
over the territory but never got close enough to get
a shot at him. Then I heard he'd moved south to Salt
Lake City. I followed him there but lost him again.
Finally a couple of punchers in Moab told me a gun-
slinger by the name of Darcy was working for a big
rancher near Crooked Creek.

"I followed him here, got in yesterday. And you
know the rest."

Tyree crushed out his cigarette butt in the ashtray
and refilled Sally's coffee cup. "How come you tied
one on last night?"

"I was hurting and it eased the pain."

"Of your brother's death?"

Sally shook her head. Suddenly her eyes were old
and her voice dropped to a husky whisper. "No, that
pain I'll have always. This is another pain, sharper
and a lot more agonizing, a pain I've had spiking at
me for a twelvemonth because I want to kill Luther
Darcy so bad. I plan to look into his eyes as he dies
and laugh and see the fear in them. I hate him and
I want revenge and that's a festering sore no doctor
can heal. With all the hatred that's inside me, my life
has become a hell. For every hour I hate, I lose sixty

minutes of happiness, but there's no going back from it." The girl tried to smile. "With Tom gone, there's only me, so I have it to do."

Sally picked up her coffee cup with both hands and held it close to her lips. "And what about you, Chance Tyree. Who is this Quirt Laytham? And do you have a pain inside you?"

"I never thought about it in those terms," Tyree answered, his face troubled. "But, yes, I guess I do."

Tyree told Sally about being hanged and shot, then about Owen Fowler and finally Luke Boyd and Lorena.

When he finished speaking, the girl leaned back in her chair and smiled. "We're a pair then, aren't we? We live with hate and it's eating away at us like a cancer. How about this girl, Lorena Boyd? Is she beautiful?"

"Very."

"Do you love her?"

Tyree hesitated for just a moment, surprised at the girl's question. But, with a woman's perception, Sally read his face. "You're unsure, aren't you?"

"Yes, maybe I am. Quirt Laytham stands between us."

"And when you kill him?"

"Then his ghost will stand between us."

Sally rose. "I'd say that's a no-win situation, Chance Tyree. Well, it's been nice talking with you, but I have to be going."

"Where?"

The girl shrugged. "I don't know. Around I guess."

"You'd better come back with me to Luke Boyd's place. I'm sure you'll be made welcome."

Sally hesitated, uncertain, and Tyree said: "I can't leave you here with Luther Darcy in town. Now he knows you're after him he'll be on his guard and he'll kill you any way he can."

"Darcy doesn't want to kill me," the girl said. "At least not right away. I saw that much in his eyes back at the livery stable. He wants something else. Maybe he nurses a sick fantasy about ravishing the sister of a man he murdered. I don't know."

"That settles it then, Sally," Tyree said. "We'll get your horse. You're coming with me."

The girl nodded. "I'll go along with that at least for now. But just so you know, Chance—if I come with you you'll be borrowing my trouble. Big trouble."

Tyree smiled. "I guess I can handle it."

"Just so you know," Sally said.

Chapter 14

The day was shading into evening when Tyree rode up to Boyd's cabin. The old rancher immediately burst through the door and seemed genuinely pleased to see him. He looked at Sally, taking in her shabby clothes and the rifle under her knee. "And who might this young lady be?"

Tyree smiled. "Just a maverick passing through. Her name's Sally Brennan. She's flat broke and needs a place to stay and I thought about you."

"Of course she can stay!"

Lorena stepped out of the cabin and gave the girl a dazzling smile. "You can stay here as long as you like, Sally. It's been ages since I had another woman to talk to."

Sally smiled in return and swung out of the saddle. "Thank you. I could sure use a bath and somewhere soft to sleep. I've been lying on rocks or straw for months."

For a brief moment Lorena's eyes caught and held Tyree's, both of them aware of the uneasy truce that lay between them. She had not asked him how he'd met the girl, but he knew that would come later.

Lorena fussed over Sally and led her into the cabin. When they were gone, a grinning Boyd studied Tyree, his left eyebrow rising in a question.

"It's not what you think, Luke. Like I said, she's passing through and needed help."

Boyd nodded, but seemed unconvinced. "Whatever you say, Chance." The grin died on his lips and his face became somber. "You catch up with the Arapaho Kid?"

"Yes, I did."

Tyree swung off the steeldust and Boyd said, "Well?"

A few moments passed before Tyree answered, the old rancher's question dangling in the air. Finally he said, "The Kid won't be murdering anyone else."

Boyd grinned. "You kill him?"

"No," Tyree answered. "I smashed up his hands. As long as he lives he'll never be able to shuck a gun again."

"You . . . you broke his hands?"

"Yes, that's exactly what I did. Killing him would have been too easy. I wanted him to pay for what he did to Owen—pay for it every single day of his life."

Tyree saw Boyd struggling to come to terms with what had he'd told him. Killing a man he understood, but maiming him and then letting him go was beyond his comprehension.

"Luke, I made the punishment to fit the crime," Tyree said. "It was a reckoning. And in the end, the Kid knew it and the memory of what happened will stay with him."

Boyd opened his mouth to speak again, but Tyree turned, gathering up the reins of his horse and doing the same to Sally's pony. He was about to walk the animals to the barn, when a man's voice called out from across the creek. "Hello the cabin!"

Boyd's eyes screwed up against the falling darkness as he scanned the far bank. "Hell, that's Steve Lassiter. He's got a spread north of here. Now, what does he want?" Boyd cupped his hands to his mouth and yelled, "Come on in, Steve."

Steve Lassiter was a solemn, long-faced man with the eyes of a bereaved bloodhound. He sat round-shouldered and ungainly in the saddle of his bay mustang.

"Light and set a while, Steve," Boyd said. "Take a load off yourself."

The rancher shook his head. "I'm obliged, but I can't stay, Luke. Jean will have supper on the table and she gets a mite testy if'n I'm late for meals." Lassiter groaned softly and eased his position in the saddle. "Got news, Luke. Big news."

"Well, let's hear it."

"I was in Crooked Creek buying pipe tobacco and some pins for Jean at the general store." Lassiter shrugged his skinny shoulders. "I'm forever running out of tobacco. Then I heard shots being fired and all kinds of commotion going on in the street outside."

Lassiter, a dour, taciturn man by nature, nodded. "Yup, that's what I heard all right. Darnedest thing."

"And?" Boyd prompted, a hint of irritation in his eyes.

"Well, it seems that rustler you caught . . . what's his name—"

"Roy Will."

"Yeah, him. Well, anyhoo, he escaped. Got himself a gun and a good pony from somewheres and skedaddled."

"Tobin, that fat useless . . ." Boyd began angrily.

"The sheriff took a few shots at him," Lassiter interrupted, "but there are them who say he was holding his gun mighty high, like he was shooting at the moon."

Lassiter sat in silence for a few moments, then said, "Just thought you'd like to know, Luke. Best you keep that prize bull of your'n right close until Will is caught again or kilt."

The rancher's hound dog eyes slid to Tyree, widening in surprise. "By them that described you in town, I'd say you must be Chance Tyree. Heard about you this morning, you and the Arapaho Kid." Lassiter shrugged. "Can't say as I approve of what you done. Best just to kill a man like that and be finished with it. Don't see much point in taking a man's soul besides." He touched his hat to Boyd. "Well, I'll be on my way now, Luke. We're having fried chicken for supper."

After Lassiter had gone, Tyree tended to the horses, then rejoined Boyd who was sitting on the cabin stoop, thoughtfully smoking his pipe.

"Come first light tomorrow, I'll go haze the bull back toward the cabin," Tyree said. "Just in case."

"You think Will plans on coming after you, Chance?"

"Certain of it. I believe that's why Tobin let him escape. He figures Will can do Laytham's dirty work for him."

"You sure Laytham is behind it?"

"If I was a gambling man, I'd bet the farm on it."

"Why does Laytham want you out of the way so bad?"

"Because I'm a thorn in his side. He knows Clem Daley and Len Dawson told me they were acting on his orders when they hung me. And he's learned by this time that I found out about the Arapaho Kid getting paid a hundred dollar bonus for killing Owen." Tyree shrugged. "Add to that the fact that I warned him through Tobin to leave the territory, taking only what he can carry on a horse, and he's got reason enough to want me dead. Plenty of men have been killed for a lot less."

Boyd smiled. "Leave the territory. Hell, I doubt ol' Quirt will do that."

"He has a couple more days. And if he doesn't leave, I'll go after him."

The old rancher shook his head. "You're not a forgiving man, are you, Chance?"

Tyree turned and looked into Boyd's eyes. "Owen Fowler was a forgiving man, but it didn't do him much good. He was still shot down in the street like a dog. I won't repeat that same mistake."

Boyd sat in silence for a while, then said, "Tomorrow, you be careful. Don't make yourself a target for Roy Will. He's a bad one."

Tyree grinned. "Luke, I reckon I'm already a target for Roy Will."

As the two men sat and smoked, the darkness gathered around them and the night sky became bright with stars. A cooling breeze had picked up from the north, rippling the surface of the creek, stirring the branches of the cottonwoods to a restless rustling.

Good smells wafted from the cabin—the tantalizing odors of frying beef and coffee—and Tyree felt his stomach rumble.

"Come and get it, you two," Lorena said, her head popping out of the open doorway.

Tyree and Boyd stepped inside and Lorena bade them sit at the table. "Now," she said, "I want both of you to close your eyes. Don't peek."

Boyd turned to Tyree, a long-suffering look on his face. "Best do as she says, Chance, or we'll never get to eat."

Tyree closed his eyes. Then, after a few moments, Lorena called out, "Ta-da!"

When Tyree opened his eyes again, Sally stood at the end of the table in a blue gingham dress with a lacy white front. She had washed her hair and it cascaded over her shoulders in loose, shining curls.

"Lorena gave me this," she said. "I've never had a dress this pretty before in my whole life." She smiled at Tyree. "It's good to feel like a girl again."

Sally had none of Lorena's classic beauty, but to Tyree she looked fresh and lovely with a childlike innocence. It was hard to believe this was the same girl, smelling of horses and cheap whiskey, he'd met in the barn at Crooked Creek.

It was even harder to believe that she'd tracked a man all the way from Wyoming for the sole purpose of watching him die.

Tyree rose and gallantly pulled out Sally's chair for her, while Boyd did the same for Lorena. "Why, thank you, Mr. Tyree," the girl said as she sat.

"You are quite welcome, Miss Brennan," Tyree said.

And they laughed, all four of them.

Tyree left the Boyd place before the sun was up, while the sleepless coyotes were still talking. He rode east along the creek, casually eyeing the darkened canyons as he passed. He saw no sign of Boyd's elusive bull, but that didn't really matter because it was not the reason he was here.

He knew Roy Will would come back to try and make good on his vow to kill him, and Tyree wanted the man well away from the cabin, where there was no chance a stray bullet might hit Lorena or Sally.

Just as the darkness was giving way to the dawn, Tyree stopped in a wide dry wash beside the creek and lit a fire. He built the fire big, with plenty of smoke, a beacon that would attract Will to this place.

Tyree filled his coffeepot at the creek, threw in a handful of Arbuckle's Best and placed the pot on the coals to boil. Like smoke, coffee could be smelled for a long distance and would be further bait for the rustler.

When the coffee boiled, Tyree poured himself a cup, then rolled a cigarette. Around him the new day was brightening into morning. The light was chasing the shadows from the canyons, adding color to the surrounding mesas and rocky crags, painting them in muted hues of pink, tan and dusty yellow. Green splashes of spruce and juniper were becoming visible and along the creek trout jumped at the first flies.

Tyree hitched up his gun belt, slipped the thong off the hammer of his Colt and waited, every sense alert, knowing what must inevitably come—the gun violence that was probably even now headed his way.

There seemed to be no end to his years of living by the Colt, years of watchfulness, the constant keen awareness of everything and everyone around him. He had spent most of his life looking into the eyes of other men, measuring them, wondering if this was a man he'd have to kill—or would this be the one, faster, surer, that killed him.

For a while now, he'd been thinking of finding a place right here among the canyons, where the name Chance Tyree and what it stood for might be forgotten. He had thought to hang his gun from a nail on the wall and live without trouble.

But that dream seemed more remote than ever.

If he survived his encounter with Roy Will, there would still be Quirt Laytham—and Tyree's desire for revenge on Laytham was a living thing that ate at him and gave him no peace. It was an open wound that his hate kept festering, a wound that otherwise would have healed and done well.

But that was the hard way of the gunfighter, the only way Chance Tyree knew, and perhaps he had no chance of ever stepping back from it.

It was a gloomy thought, not one to bring much comfort to a man.

The morning wore on, and by the time Tyree had drained the coffeepot to the grounds, the sun had climbed high into the sky above the canyons, scorching the hot, dusty land into drowsy silence.

Tyree threw another branch on the fire and watched a foot-long leopard lizard panting on a rock close to him. From nearby he heard the stealthy slither of a snake through the long grass. He rose, stretched, then froze into immobility as a pair of startled ravens burst from the branches of a juniper growing close to the sandy base of a mesa opposite him, near the dark entrance to a canyon.

An animal instinct taking over, he immediately hurled himself to the ground, drawing his gun as he hit flat on his belly behind a low hummock of sand and sagebrush. The flat statement of a rifle shot echoed through the canyons and a bullet *spaaanged!* viciously off the rock where the lizard had been basking. A second kicked up a startled exclamation point of dirt close to Tyree's head.

A drift of smoke rose from a jumble of talus rock to the right of the juniper, and Tyree thumbed off a couple of fast shots in that direction. He had seen no target, but he hoped to keep the hidden rifleman's head down.

Tyree turned onto his back, punched out the empty shells from his Colt, then, thumbing cartridges from his belt, filled all six chambers. He rolled on his belly again and lifted his head, trying to see better. Immediately a bullet kicked a stinging spurt of sand into his face.

He was pinned down where he was and it was only a matter of time before the rifleman found the range and nailed him. Somehow or other he had to outflank the man and get a clear shot at him.

Tyree hammered a fast, offhand shot at the rifleman and heard his bullet clip a rock, whining wickedly. A couple of rifle shots probed for him, one thudding into the roots of the bunchgrass an inch from his head.

He couldn't stay where he was.

Slowly Tyree inched his way back from the hummock and regained the comparative shelter of the dry wash. Crouching low, he followed the wash to the creek and dived into the shelter of thick brush growing around the roots of a stand of cottonwoods. A bullet rattled through the branches above him, then another.

Tyree worked his way to the creek and rolled off the bank into the water, a drop of several feet. Here he was shielded from the rifleman by a high dirt embankment crowned with tall grass and scattered white and pink wildflowers. His boots slipping and sliding on the rocky bottom, he followed the creek east for twenty yards, the embankment slowly diminishing in height until he had to bend over to stay hidden.

Now and then a bullet split the air near him, but mostly the rifleman's probing shots went well wide, behind and in front of him.

Ahead of Tyree the creek took a sharp bend to the left, around a high, jutting sandbank crested by coarse bunchgrass and a stunted willow that trailed drooping branches into the water. Between Tyree and the tree lay thirty yards of open ground where the creekbank was broken down and trampled flat by the hooves of cattle. Before he reached the cover of the willow, he'd be exposed to the rifleman's fire for four or five seconds. The risk was great, but it was a chance he'd have to take. He couldn't stay where he was. To go back would mean taking up a position behind the high embankment. He'd be out of danger but would have no hope of getting a clear shot at his bushwhacker. If the man left his position and came at him he wouldn't see him until the last moment and by then it could be too late.

Tyree made up his mind.

He straightened, then made a dash for the willow. Immediately he heard the crash of the rifle and felt a bullet tug at the back of his shirt. He ran on . . . twenty yards to go. Running flat out, awkward in spurs and high-heeled boots, he covered another few yards, then his foot rolled on a loose rock and he stumbled and fell flat on his face in the water. A bullet spurted a small fountain near his head, then a second burned across the back of his right thigh. Tyree got to his feet and ran, thumbing off wild shots toward the rocks where the rifleman was hidden.

The sandbank was very close now and he dived for its shelter as bullets whapped into the water or creased the air around him. Tyree splashed into the creek, throwing up a cascade of water, rolled, and came up against the bank, a four foot high ledge of soft yellow sand tangled with willow roots.

For a few moments, he leaned against the bank, breathing hard, his chest heaving. Then he took off his hat, filled it with creek water and poured the water over his head, enjoying its welcome coolness.

It was time to move again.

After several attempts, his boots slipping on the loose sand, Tyree managed to get a toehold on a thick root and clambered up the bank. Heavy clumps of Indian grass grew around the base of the willow, and he worked his way through those until he had a clear view of the rocks where the rifleman was hidden.

There had been no time to grab his own rifle, and Tyree was keenly aware of the uncertainty of his Colt at this distance. Between him and the bushwhacker lay fifty yards of open ground, too far for accurate revolver work.

But he couldn't get any closer without exposing himself to the hidden marksman's rifle, so for better or worse, here he had to stay.

There was no movement among the rocks, and Tyree took the time to reload his gun. The day's heat was building and the sun was hot on his damp back, steaming off the creek water.

He waited, scanning the rocks with eyes that missed nothing.

There it was, a movement, just a flash of blue cloth against the drab dun of the rocks!

Tyree pushed the Colt straight out in front of him, holding the handle of the gun with both hands. He thumbed back the hammer, the metallic triple click loud in the quiet, and sighted on the rocks.

A few slow minutes inched by as beads of sweat gathered on Tyree's forehead and his mouth ran dry. Around him the rugged land lay still, silent and unchanging, except in the far distance where the buttes, crags and mesas were already shimmering, shifting shape in the growing heat.

Another fleeting glimpse of blue. And another. More of it that time.

Slowly, looking around him like a wild thing, a man emerged from the rocks, a rifle slanted across his chest. Tyree recognized the yellow hair under the man's hat and the bloodstained bandage on his shoulder. It was Roy Will. As he'd expected, the outlaw had wasted no time on making good his promise to avenge his brother's death.

Will took a few steps toward the creek, then stopped, his head turning, checking the land around him. Warily, he angled toward the spot where Tyree was hidden, advanced three or four yards, then stopped again, his eyes speculatively scanning the willow.

Tyree laid the front sight of his Colt on Will's chest and his forefinger took up the sixteenth of an inch of slack on the trigger. He held his breath, gripped the gun rock steady—and fired.

Will jerked as the bullet burned across his left arm. He threw the rifle to his damaged shoulder and hammered off three fast shots in Tyree's direction, all of them crashing into the branches of the willow well above his head.

The man was close enough that Tyree saw him wince as the recoiling rifle pounded against his broken shoulder.

Tyree fired again. A clean miss. But it was enough. It seemed Will was an outlaw who clearly understood his limitations and he had decided this was not his day. The man ran back to the shelter of the rocks and a few moments later Tyree heard the echoing clatter of a horse's hooves in the canyon.

Quickly Tyree sprang to his feet and ran to the dry wash where the steeldust was grazing. He caught up the reins and swung into the saddle, then galloped toward the canyon mouth.

He had no intention of letting Will escape to bush-whack him another day when his shooting shoulder was better healed and his aim surer.

Ahead of Tyree the canyon entrance yawned open, a clean-cut cleft in the rock not a whole lot wider than a slot, its sheer sides climbing six or seven hundred feet to the flat top of the mesa. Will was obviously gambling that the canyon had an outlet on the other side of the mesa, an uncertain thing since so many of them were boxes, ending in an impassible barrier of rock.

Tyree reined in the steeldust and entered the canyon at a walk, his Winchester ready to hand across the saddle horn. There was a thin trickle of water along the canyon bottom and a few deer and cattle tracks. The light was thin, picking up an amber tint from the walls, and the sandy bottom was broken in places by clumps of prickly pear and ocotillo. The canyon smelled of cows and the dust kicked up by Will's horse.

Down here it was very quiet, the only sound the creak of Tyree's saddle leather and the soft thud of the steeldust's hooves on the sand. His stirrups scraping against the walls, Tyree rode around a tight bend and then entered a rock passageway about fifty yards wide with smooth, curved walls. Here the water had pooled in a long, shallow tank but was only a couple of inches deep.

Ahead of him, its top hidden from sight by an outcropping of rock, a shallow trough rose from the canyon floor and slanted upward, following an unexpected, gradual slope in the wall. The basin had been gouged out in ancient times by the fall of heavy boul-

ders, and later by rain erosion. Tyree guessed it went
clear to the top of the mesa.

He rode around the outcropping and immediately
reined in the steeldust. Roy Will, probably fearful
that he'd ridden into a box, was urging his horse up
the trough. The rustler rode to his left, then turned
right again, creating his own switchback trail up the
slope. He was attempting to reach the summit of the
mesa, trusting to luck that he'd find a way back onto
the flat.

But Will wasn't going to make it.

The rustler fought his horse as it faltered, its
hooves skidding on loose sand and talus, frightened
arcs of white showing in its eyes.

"Will!" Tyree yelled. "Throw down your gun and
get down from there."

"Damn you, Tyree!" the man cried, surprised, his
face twisted in fury. "I'll see you in hell first!"

Will savagely swung his struggling horse around
and headed down the slope, his mount sliding most
of the way on its haunches. The rustler had booted
his rifle, but the Colt in his hand barked. The bullet
missed Tyree's head by inches, caromed off the canyon wall then ricocheted wildly, the whining lead
bouncing back and forth from rock to rock, dangerous and lethal.

Will had almost reached the bottom of the canyon
and was firing as he came. His plunging horse was
an unstable platform for accurate shooting, but his
bullets rebounded from the rock walls and Tyree was
aware of the peril of all that wildly flying lead.

Tyree fired his Winchester from the hip, working
the lever fast, hammering bullets into Will. Sudden

red roses bloomed on the rustler's blue shirt and the man screamed, threw up his arms and fell backward out of the saddle, hitting the sandy floor with a thud.

The hollow echoes of his gunshots were still reverberating through the smoke-streaked canyon as Tyree swung out of the saddle and stepped to the fallen rustler.

Will's eyes were wide open, but he was seeing nothing. The man had been already dead when he hit the ground.

The rustler's horse was also down, its right leg shattered by a ricocheting bullet. Tyree put the animal out of its misery with one well-aimed shot, then holstered his gun.

Suddenly he was tired, tired beyond belief, the wound in his side a dull, relentless ache that pounded at him. He stepped into the saddle once more and turned his horse toward the mouth of the canyon.

For some reason he could scarcely fathom, he badly wanted to see Sally again.

Chapter 15

Tyree was still a mile from the cabin when he met Luke Boyd on the trail alongside the creek. The old rancher rode up to him and his eyes searched the younger man's face, a question forming on his lips.

"Yes, Luke," Tyree said, beating him to it, "I ran into Roy Will."

"He dead?"

Tyree nodded. "Back in a canyon. He didn't give me any choice."

"Heard guns. Noise travels far in these canyons. I was on my way to help." He looked Tyree over. "You hurt any?"

"Shallow bullet burn across the back of my leg is all." Tyree smiled. "Nothing to speak about."

"You look all used up, boy. Tell you what. Why don't you come back to the cabin and let's you and me share a jug?"

"Best offer I've had all day, Luke." Tyree grinned.

The day was hot, and Lorena and Sally were sitting in chairs outside, under the shade of a spruce growing near the cabin. Despite the heat, both women looked cool and lovely, and Tyree's breath caught in his throat, like a man who'd unexpectedly come across a pair of blooming prairie roses in the desert.

"Chance," Lorena said, jumping to her feet as Tyree swung out of the saddle, "we heard shooting. We've been so worried."

Tyree held the reins of the steeldust and nodded. "It was Roy Will. He bushwhacked me, or at least he tried to."

"Is he . . . ?"

"Yes, he's dead."

Sally, looking crisp and pretty in another of Lorena's dresses, took the reins from Tyree's hand. "Chance, you look exhausted. Best you sit for a while and I'll see to your horse."

"Sally, you don't have to do that."

"I know I don't have to." The girl smiled. "But I want to."

Later, Boyd brought out his jug. He and Tyree passed it back and forth, and Tyree was pleased when Sally refused a drink. Maybe her heavy drinking had been a onetime thing and it was over.

Rustler or no, the killing of Roy Will seemed to cast a pall over everybody, and even Sally didn't talk much. Lorena seemed oddly withdrawn, as though she was busy with her own thoughts. As to what those thoughts might be, Tyree could not hazard a guess.

As the long day shaded into a warm, starlit evening, Boyd brought a couple of lanterns outside and set them up, their flickering flames casting dancing circles of orange light on the hard-packed dirt of the yard. A few moments later he produced a fiddle and said, "We're all of us sitting with long faces and I reckon it's time I livened things up around here."

Grinning wide, he tucked the fiddle under his chin and played. It was immediately clear that Boyd was a fine musician and he performed an excellent rendition of "Ducks in the Pond," followed by a lively version of "Old Joe Clark."

"Let's have some dancing," Boyd yelled, the music and the whiskey taking ahold of him. "Here, Chance, let's see you and Sally step it out."

Taking his cue from Boyd and caught up in the moment himself, Tyree grinned, walked to where Sally was sitting and bowed. "May I have the honor of this dance, Miss Brennan?"

"Why, of course, Mr. Tyree." Sally beamed, extending her hand.

Tyree was a fair dancer, as was Sally, and together they made an attractive couple as they went through the complex circles, promenades and allemandes of the "Virginia Reel" and then "Money in Both Pockets."

Lorena joined in the fun, her dancing both enthusiastic and elegant. For a few hours she, Sally and Tyree forgot their troubles and the dark shadows that lay between them, letting the music lift them to a different, happier place.

It was well after midnight when Tyree sought his bunk. He lay on his back, smiling into the darkness, and conceded that he had just spent one of the most pleasant nights of his life.

But that mood vanished come the dawn, when he rose and went down to the creek to wash . . . and Luke Boyd told him that Sally was gone.

*   *   *

"She laid the two dresses I gave her out on her bed and left me a little thank-you note," Lorena said, as Tyree and Boyd drank coffee in the cabin.

"Anything else?" Tyree asked. "Did she say where she was headed?"

"No," Lorena answered. "Just a thank-you and nothing more."

Tyree gazed into his coffee cup, feeling a knot of emotion in his belly. He had grown to like Sally, and now he feared for her. She would try to track down Luther Darcy and kill him. But she was no match for the gunman, either in skill or in cunning.

Lorena broke into Tyree's thoughts. "Women don't keep secrets from each other for long, Chance," she said. "I know why Sally came to the canyonlands."

Tyree's head jerked up in surprise. "She told you?"

"Yes, she told me about her brother's death and her hunt for Luther Darcy."

Tyree was not anxious to reopen unhealed wounds, but what had to be said had to be said. "Did Sally tell you that Darcy works for Quirt Laytham?"

Lorena's chin lifted defiantly. "Yes, yes, she did, and that's why I'm going to talk to Quirt today. I'm going to demand that he give Darcy his time and send him packing."

"And if he doesn't?"

Lorena shook her head. "That won't happen. Quirt wants to marry me and he'll do anything I ask."

"Lorena has a point, Chance," Boyd said. "Ol' Quirt sure is sweet on her. It isn't likely he'll refuse her anything."

Tyree rose to his feet. "You do as you please, Lorena. But in the meantime I'm going to look for Sally and try to keep her away from Darcy."

"Chance, I'm also going to do something else. I'll ask Quirt to talk to you and see if we can get rid of the bad blood between you two."

A small sadness in him, Tyree looked at the girl, her beauty so dazzling it caused him a sweet pain. "Don't waste your efforts, Lorena," he said. "I'll deal with Laytham in my own way and my own time."

Anger flared in the girl. "Oh, for heaven's sake, then why don't you just leave? You've caused nothing but trouble since Owen Fowler brought you here."

"Lorena," Boyd said mildly, his eyes lifting to his daughter, "Chance is my guest. I'll be the one to tell him to leave, not you."

Slowly the angry red stain drained from Lorena's cheeks. "I'm sorry, Pa. It's just that some people around here are so . . . so pigheaded." She grabbed her hat and riding crop from the rack. "I'm going to talk to Quirt. At least *he* will listen to reason."

The girl stormed outside, and a few moments later Tyree heard the hammer of her horse's galloping hooves recede into the distance.

Tyree's mood of last night had now totally gone, the memory of it extinguished, and cold gray ashes of regret were all that remained. He turned to Boyd. "Luke, you think Lorena really loves Laytham?"

The old rancher shrugged, his face unreadable. "Son, I don't know who Lorena really loves."

                    *   *   *

The way Tyree figured it, Sally Brennan could be in one of two places—Crooked Creek, or staking out Quirt Laytham's ranch. At either location she had a good chance of running into Luther Darcy.

He made a decision and headed the steeldust toward Crooked Creek. By what he'd heard from others, Darcy was work shy, a trait shared by most hired guns, and by all accounts spent more time in Bradley's saloon than he did at the Rafter-L.

Laytham's cows were spread out along both sides of Hatch Wash, even farther north than before, and all were in excellent shape. On a whim, Tyree turned into Owen Fowler's canyon, and saw more of Laytham's Herefords.

It seemed like the man was moving herds into the entire country and Tyree wondered how long it would be before small ranchers like Luke Boyd and Steve Lassiter were pushed out as Laytham expanded all the way north to Moab, and maybe beyond. Grass and water were at a premium in this magnificent but barren country. Laytham needed grass—and both Boyd and Lassiter were sitting on a lot of it.

Crooked Creek lay drowsing in the afternoon heat when Tyree rode to the livery stable. An old-timer in denim overalls and a straw hat was sitting on a bench outside the stable and Tyree reined up close to him.

"Howdy," Tyree said. "You new here?"

The man lifted faded brown eyes to the young rider then spat a string of tobacco juice. "Right back at ya, howdy your ownself. And, no, I'm not new here. I been laid up for a few weeks with the rheumatism, is all. Couldn't leave my cabin, an' that was surely hard on me on account of I'm what you might call a watching man."

"Well, watching man, I'm looking for a girl, maybe seventeen years old, yellow hair, stands a couple of inches over five feet."

"Hell, mister, ain't we all," the old man said.

Tyree smiled. "She might be sleeping in your hayloft."

The old-timer shook his head. "Ain't nobody like that up there. Trust me, I'd know if a gal like the one you're asking about was sleeping here."

"You seen Luther Darcy in town?" Tyree asked, taking a different tack.

"No, I haven't seen him and I don't want to see him either," the old man answered. "That one is pure pizen."

Tyree touched fingers to his hat and swung the steeldust away. "Obliged to you."

"Stop by anytime," the oldster said. "I don't get much comp'ny around here, yellow-haired females or otherwise."

There were a couple of cow ponies outside Bradley's, both with Rafter-L brands, and Tyree slipped the thong off his Colt before he stepped inside.

At first the bartender, the man Tobin had called Benny, seemed surprised to see him, but then his face screwed into an ugly scowl. "What the hell are you doing here?" he asked. "Luther Darcy told you to stay away."

Tyree ignored the man and studied the two Laytham riders who were propping up the bar. Both were young, and had a wild, reckless look about them, their guns worn low on the thigh, handy to get at and not for show. Both were dressed in worn range clothes. The taller of the two wore a long, canvas duster.

Satisfied that the men presented no immediate threat, Tyree turned to the bartender again. "I'm looking for a girl who was in here drinking a few nights ago. Blond gal, name's Sally Brennan."

"Haven't seen her since," the bartender said. "Whores like that come and go."

Tyree smiled. He was still smiling when he reached across the bar, grabbed the man by the front of his shirt and backhanded him hard across the face.

"Mister," Tyree said, his voice level, without a trace of anger, "I don't know where you come from, but out here we don't talk about womenfolk like that."

A trickle of blood ran from the bartender's nose and his eyes were blazing. He reached up and grabbed Tyree's wrist in a huge right hand, squeezing hard, trying to loosen Tyree's grip.

For a few moments, the two men wrestled in silence. Benny, a strong, powerful man, was using his right against Tyree's left, but he could not budge the younger man's fist clenched in his shirt, feeling the steel in him.

The bartender's face slowly changed, the color draining from his cheeks as he realized he was badly overmatched. Finally he dropped his hand, and Tyree pushed the man away from him, sending Benny sprawling backward into the bar, glasses and bottles crashing to the floor.

The two Laytham men had watched the whole thing with a growing interest, but neither made an attempt to intervene. The one in the duster grinned and said to the bartender, "How's it feel to come off second best, huh, Benny boy?"

"You shut your trap," Benny said, his face surly.

"If you see Miss Brennan, tell her I'm looking for her," Tyree said. He smiled. "Benny boy."

He turned and walked to the door. He'd only taken a couple of steps when a gun blasted and a bullet crashed into his back. Tyree spun on his heel, drawing at the same time, and saw Benny standing behind the bar, a smoking Colt held at eye-level in his right hand.

Both men fired at the same instant and Tyree felt a bullet burn across the side of his head. Tyree's shot smashed Benny against the bar. He fired again, his second bullet following the first, dead center in the bartender's chest. Tyree watched the man fall. Then, all the strength suddenly gone from his legs, he was falling himself, plunging headlong into darkness. . . .

He should be dead, but he wasn't, and that puzzled him.

Tyree opened his eyes and saw a sky full of stars. But were they really stars, or holes in a tin roof? He reached up and tried to grab them, but the stars stayed well away from him. He let his hand drop, disappointed.

He'd been dreaming. In his restless sleep he'd wandered through a shifting gray fog of gunsmoke, streaked scarlet by the flare of guns. He had seen men die, men he'd known, men he'd killed, men with their mouths wide open in screams, angry at the manner and the timing of their deaths. Wes Hardin had come to him in the night, berating him for a pilgrim, telling him he'd forgotten everything he'd ever learned, and a lot more besides. Only a damn hick would turn his back on armed men and allow himself to get shot by a bartender. Then Luther Darcy had stepped beside Wes and they'd looked down at him and laughed, pointing, telling each other that Chance Tyree was an object of pity, a poor, hunted thing who couldn't even get a woman to love him.

He remembered his dream, and awareness slowly returned to him. He'd been shot in the back, then grazed by another of the bartender's bullets at Bradley's. Yet he found himself able to sit up and take stock of his wounds.

He shrugged his shoulders, feeling a sharp pain in the center of his back. Reaching around with his right hand, he probed for the wound. His fingers touched jagged metal. It was the steel ring that held his suspenders together, and it felt like it was digging into the muscle of his back near the spine.

When he looked at his hand, his fingers were covered in blood.

It was dark where he was, and cold. Tyree quickly undid his suspenders. He reached into his pocket, found a match and thumbed it into flame. By the guttering orange light he examined the damaged ring. Benny's bullet had hit the ring and had been deflected. But the lead had burst the metal apart, and it looked like a fair-sized chunk of the ring was missing.

Was that piece still in his back?

Still, he counted himself lucky. An inch to either

side, and Benny's bullet would have killed him. His hand strayed to the wound at the side of his head. He had only been creased, but the bullet had hit hard enough to draw blood and knock him unconscious.

Tyree looked around him. Where was he? And how had he gotten here?

He tried to get to his feet, but his legs felt like rubber and went out from under him. He sat down hard, his breaths coming in short, agonized gasps.

Was the missing chunk of the metal ring wedged very close to his spine? Had it done something to his legs?

A panic rising in him, Tyree found another match and flamed the red tip. He held the match high and looked around. The pale light shone on rock walls on either side of him, so close he could have reached out and touched them.

Who had brought him here? Was it someone who had thought him dead and dumped him in a slot canyon?

The match flared and burned out. Tyree was again plunged into darkness.

He reached down and massaged his legs, but they were numb and he couldn't get them to move. He tried desperately to get to his feet, beads of sweat standing out on his forehead—but it was no good. He was paralyzed from the hips down.

Bit by bit, weak from pain and loss of blood, he dragged himself closer to the canyon wall and fetched his back up against the rock.

Only then did he feel for his gun, and to his surprise it was thonged down in the holster. Maybe somebody with the poetry of the Auld Country in his soul had decided to lay him to rest with his weapons. If that was the case, he owed that man a favor.

Tyree closed his eyes, suddenly angry at his own weakness. In his present state he could die in this canyon. How long did it take a man to die of thirst? He couldn't remember exactly. But it was a matter of days, and from all he'd heard, it was a slow, agonizing death.

He had to find water. A few of the canyons had trickles along their sandy bottoms and sometimes water was trapped in rock tanks in the walls. Come first light he'd make a search, even if he had to crawl along on his belly.

Tyree drifted off into an uneasy sleep, waking now and then only to shiver from the night cold. He woke again when the dawn touched the canyon with pale light, his entire body raw with pain.

He heard footsteps.

Someone was walking through the canyon toward him, taking short, fast steps as though in a great hurry. Tyree slid his gun from the holster and thumbed back the hammer. He waited, his mouth dry, his red-rimmed eyes burning like fire.

The footsteps came closer and peering through the uncertain light, Tyree saw a small, slight man in an oversized hat coming toward him, a rifle in his hands.

"Stop right there or I'll drop you," Tyree croaked.

"Don't shoot, Chance," a woman's voice said. "It's me. It's Sally Brennan."

"Sally?" Tyree couldn't believe his ears. "But how? I mean—"

"It's a long story," Sally interrupted. "How do you feel?"

"Like hell."

"I'd say feeling like hell is still pretty good for a dead man."

Sally kneeled beside him, her face concerned. "And for a while there I did think you were dead."

She put a canteen to Tyree's mouth and he drank deep. "Hungry?" she asked.

Tyree nodded and the girl reached into her pocket. "It's only antelope jerky, but right now it's all I've got."

Tyree took a bite of the jerky and chewed. "It's good," he lied. He drank again, then shifted his position against the canyon wall. "Did you bring me here?"

"I had help," Sally said. "Don't go looking in your pocket for money—you don't have any. Good help doesn't come cheap."

"What happened, Sally?" Tyree asked. "Tell me from the beginning."

"You recollect getting shot?"

Tyree nodded. "A man tends to remember when that happens to him."

"Well, that was the beginning." Sally looked tired, dark shadows under her eyes, and Tyree's heart went out to her. "I rode into town about an hour after you killed that bartender at Bradley's."

"Benny."

"Yes, him. Sheriff Tobin told me Benny had also done for you. He said both of you were over to J. J. Ransom's funeral parlor and if I wanted to pay my last respects I should head on over there." Sally managed a small smile. "Hard to tell what he thinks behind those dark glasses, but Tobin didn't seem in the least bit put out that you were dead."

"I'm sure he didn't," Tyree said. "Then what happened?"

"Then I went over to Ransom's and you were laid out as nice as you please alongside Benny." The girl touched the back of Tyree's hand with the tips of her fingers. "Chance, I have to tell you this—you made a much more handsome corpse than he did."

Despite his pain, Tyree grinned. "Thanks. That makes me feel a whole heap better."

"Well, I shed a tear or two—"

"For me or Benny?"

"For you, silly. And I was about to leave when I thought I saw your eyelids flutter. I leaned over you and put my hand on your chest, and sure enough, I felt you breathing. I don't know what happened after you were shot, but it might be you were paralyzed from the bullet and Tobin thought you were dead."

Sally let Tyree drink again, then said, "I couldn't tell Tobin you were still alive because he would have shot you again for sure. Anyway, I knew I had no choice—I had to get you out of there."

"And you got help from somewhere?"

"Yes, first I took all the money in your pockets—"

"Thirty-seven dollars and change."

"Right. Do you always keep close track of your money like that?"

"Only when I'm down to my last few bucks."

"Well, I asked an old man who works around the livery stable to help me."

"I met him," Tyree said. "He's a watcher."

"Is that what he is?" Sally asked, puzzled. "Well, anyway, he agreed to help for the money, though it really didn't seem to interest him that much. We waited until dark and he helped me get you out of the funeral parlor and onto your horse. Got your gun, too. J. J. Ransom had it in his desk drawer. The old man rode out with me and the two of us carried you into this canyon."

Sally shrugged apologetically. "I couldn't stay with you for fear we might have been followed, so I stood guard at the canyon mouth all night."

"Thank you, Sally," Tyree said. "You saved my life. Tobin would have had J. J. Ransom bury me alive." He looked around him. "Where are we?"

"Across the Colorado, about fifty miles east of the Henry Mountains. I knew Tobin would search for you, so the old man and me crossed the river at the head of Glen Canyon and brought you here."

Sally put her hand on Tyree's shoulder and pulled him away from the wall. "Do you have a bullet in you?"

"No," Tyree answered. He showed her the mangled ring on his suspenders. "Benny's bullet was deflected by this, but I think a piece of the ring was driven into my back close to my spine. I reckon it's still in there and that's why I can't move my legs. Maybe my whole body was paralyzed after I was shot and that's why Tobin thought I was dead."

This was bad news and Sally did not try to hide her feelings. "Chance, you can't ride?"

Tyree shook his head. "I can't even stand on my own two feet."

The girl was silent for a moment, lost in thought.

Then she said, "We'll just have to stay put until you can walk again. I'm guessing that Tobin has already accused you of murdering the Bradley's bartender and the alarm is out. The way you are now, try to leave and you'd be a sitting duck for Laytham or Luther Darcy or anybody else who wants to take a shot at you."

"We can't stay here," Tyree protested. "We have no food and maybe no water."

"Yes, we can," Sally said, her little chin set in a determined way. "We'll find a way."

Chapter 16

A week drifted slowly by. During that time Sally found water farther into the canyon and shot a deer, bringing in armloads of firewood to cook the meat. She harvested prickly pear fruit, passed the pods through the open flame of the fire to burn off the spines, then cut them open to get at the sweet, juicy pulp. She foraged for wild onions to use in thick broths with deer meat and dandelion root, assuring Tyree the soup would give him strength.

But Tyree was not growing stronger. The very opposite was happening—his strength was waning fast. He tried a few faltering steps, but always ended up falling flat on his face, his legs suddenly giving way from under him. The pain in his back grew worse, though the wound itself seemed to be healing well.

All this Sally watched with growing concern. At the end of the first week she told Tyree to strip off his shirt and carefully examined his back.

After a few minutes of painful probing, she finally said, "I think there is a piece of metal in there, and it's digging right into your spine. Chance, I need to get you medical help."

"Medical help?" Tyree echoed. "There's a doctor at Crooked Creek, but if you're right about Tobin accusing me of murder, the doc could tell him and lead a posse right to us."

"There's another doctor—the old man who helped bring you here."

"The watcher is a qualified physician?" Tyree asked, surprised.

"No, not really, but he was a mule doctor during the War Between the States. Maybe he can get that chunk of steel out of your back."

"Or paralyze me permanently," Tyree said.

"I know, but that's a chance we're going to have to take. You can't ride, and we can't stay here much longer."

"Can you trust that old man?"

Sally thought for a few moments. "I've trusted him this far." Then she seemed to make up her mind about something and shook her head. "No, I really don't know if I can completely trust him. But trust or not, right now he's our only hope."

Tyree sat in silence, weighing his options. They were few. Sally was right. They couldn't remain in the canyon, leaving Quirt Laytham to grow in power and become even more entrenched. And what of Lorena? If Laytham took it into his head to put range before romance and decided to move his herds farther north, both she and her father could be in danger.

Of more immediate concern, the strain was begin-

ning to tell on Sally. She looked exhausted, the rough
food and constant wakefulness draining her.

"Get the old man, Sally," Tyree said finally, his
decision made. "But make sure you're not seen."

"I'll be careful." The girl smiled. She kneeled be-
side Tyree and lightly kissed his unshaven cheek.
"Now I have to be on my way if I hope to reach
Crooked Creek before nightfall."

"People ain't that much different from mules," the
old man said. "They're as stubborn and just as or-
nery. Leastways, that's been my experience."

He kneeled beside Tyree, groaning slightly as his
frosted joints creaked in protest. "One thing I learned
about doctoring, mules or humans, is that the art of
medicine is to amuse the patient while nature cures
the disease." He studied Tyree's face in the flickering
firelight. "Now I'll amuse you by telling you about
my days with the First Missouri Confederate Brigade
while I take a look at that back of your'n."

"Why are you helping me?" Tyree asked. "You
could have gone to Sheriff Tobin, told him where
I was."

The old man nodded. "I could have at that. But
me, I kinda enjoy just setting in the shade and watching things unfold. If I went to Tobin I'd be interfering
in the natural course of events, wouldn't I now?"
He smiled under his beard. "Like I'm not interfering
enough already by coming here."

"I never got your name," Tyree said.

"That's because I never told it to you. Anyhoo, it's
Zebulon Thomas Pettigrew, but most folks call me
Zeb, when they ain't calling me 'Hey, you.' "

"Well, Zeb, I'm beholden to you," Tyree said.

"Save all that until I take a look at your back, young feller. When it comes to doctoring, there's some things I can do and some things I can't."

Tyree stripped off his shirt and Pettigrew studied the wound, all the while talking of great battles won and a cause lost. Darkness had reached into the canyon and the only light came from the fire. Sally sat closer to Tyree and took his hand in hers.

"It will be all right, Chance," she said. "I know it will."

His examination over, Pettigrew shook his head and muttered something under his breath that Tyree couldn't hear.

"Zeb, is it bad?" he asked.

"Bad? It couldn't be much worse. You have a piece of metal pressing right up against your backbone and that's what's giving you them dead legs. It's deep, boy, real deep and hard to get at."

"Can you cut it out of there?" Tyree asked, a formless panic rising in him.

Pettigrew glanced at Sally, giving her a look that conveyed his misgivings, then turned to Tyree. "Boy, one time, right after First Manassas, I seen a Yankee captain with a musket ball in his back, same place where you got that chunk of iron. A doctor—unlike me, a real doctor—dug the ball out of there but it didn't do that Yankee officer any good. He ended up paralyzed, couldn't even move his little finger. After that he lasted for two, three days. Then he died."

Pettigrew looked into Tyree's eyes. "To answer your question, yeah, I can cut that metal out of there, but I can't guarantee you'll ever walk again."

"Maybe I can get a real doctor," Sally suggested, a worried frown creasing her forehead. "Take a chance on the one at Crooked Creek."

"Sam Neary?" Pettigrew spat. "He's a butcher. He's a butcher when he's sober and worse when he's drunk—and he's drunk most of the time. Let him be, girl. He can't help here."

"Zeb," Tyree said, "cut the damn thing out of there. Do it now."

He heard Sally's sharp intake of breath and saw the fear in her face. He held her hand tighter. "I'll be all right, Sally. Maybe that Yankee captain was just unlucky."

Zeb grinned. "You got that right, boy. Luck's got a lot to do with it."

The old man took a pocketknife from his overalls, opened the blade and passed the knife to Sally. "Burn that blade real good in the flames, girl," he said. "And don't worry none about the soot, it won't do any harm."

When Pettigrew deemed the knife was ready, Tyree turned his back to him and the old mule doctor went to work. The tip of the blade dug deep and Tyree felt Pettigrew working it this way and that as he dug for the shard of steel.

The pain was intense, and Tyree breathed hard between clenched teeth. Despite the coolness of the night, sweat covered his face and stained his shirt. Sally held his hand, her face pale and drawn in the yellow firelight.

"Damn, but it's deep," Pettigrew muttered. "Real deep." He placed a hand on Tyree's shoulder and spoke into his ear. "I can see the metal, boy. It ain't no longer than a match head, but it's got a jagged end to it. Trick is to get it out o' there without nicking your spinal cord."

"Do what the hell you have to do," Tyree said, a harsh, irritated edge to his voice. Then, surprised at his own angry tone, he said, softer this time, "Zeb, just . . . just get it over with."

"Doing the best I can," the old man said. "But I could sure use some more light in here."

The knife blade dug deep again. "Just gonna ease the iron away from the backbone," Pettigrew muttered, more to himself than anyone else. "Nice and easy . . . real nice . . . and easy . . ."

Tyree felt the knife scrape bone to the right of his spine. Then again. And again.

He gritted his teeth against the pain, wanting to cry out, to yell at Pettigrew to stop, but he knew there was no going back from this. It had to be done.

To add to the light, Sally threw another branch on the fire, and flames flared up, shot through with dancing red sparks. Out among the mesas hungry coyotes were complaining to the night and a haloed moon dominated the rectangle of sky that could be seen high above the canyon walls. The still air around Tyree smelled of wood smoke, blood and man sweat, and when he looked over at Sally he saw that his suffering had become a physical force that was pressing down on the girl like a mailed fist.

He took Sally's hand again and tried a weak smile as Pettigrew's knife scraped and skidded in his raw flesh. But the smile quickly died on his lips and he closed his eyes tight against the hurt.

"Got it!" the old man yelled after what seemed

like an eternity. "And I was right. Damn thing's as sharp as a mesquite thorn."

Pettigrew rose and stepped in front of Tyree. He took the younger man's hand and dropped a tiny piece of the steel ring into his palm. "That little thing was what caused all the trouble. Hard to believe, ain't it?"

Sally also rose to her feet. "Zeb, is his spine . . . I mean . . ."

"It's too early to tell," Pettigrew said. "If the surgery was a success, he'll be able to take some steps in a day or two. If it wasn't . . . well, we'll see." He handed his bloody knife to Sally. "Heat that blade until it's red-hot. I have to cauterize the wound real good. I can't risk an infection getting started so close to the backbone."

Sally did as she was told, and Pettigrew got behind Tyree again, the red-hot blade held upright in his hand. "This is gonna hurt like the dickens, boy."

Without waiting for a reply, Pettigrew instantly plunged the glowing knife into the open wound. Tyree heard his flesh sizzle and almost fainted from the searing, hammering agony of it.

"It's done," Pettigrew said. He eased Tyree against the wall of the canyon. "Now you rest up, boy. Gather your strength." The old man turned to Sally. "I'll try to come back in a day or two and see how he's doing. In the meantime, don't let him attempt too much. His legs will be weak for a while, so he'll have to take it one step at a time."

Sally was effusive in her thanks, but the old man waved them away with a dismissive hand. "Hell, girl," he said, "I'd a done it for a sick mule."

After Pettigrew left, Sally sat beside Tyree and held him in her arms, listening to his soft breathing as he slept.

Beyond their canyon, out in the vastness of the night, the coyotes were still calling, and the fire crackled and snapped, bathing them both in a shifting scarlet light.

Chapter 17

Within a couple of days, Sally helping to support him, Tyree was taking half a dozen steps at a time, struggling mightily to keep moving, the devil of impatience riding him. At the end of his second week he was walking almost normally and most of his strength had returned. He left the canyon, shot another deer and gathered wood to cook it, his back giving him little trouble.

A little more than two weeks after he'd been wounded, he rose at first light and saddled the steeldust. It was time to leave.

Tyree and Sally rode in the direction of the Colorado where it flowed through Glen Canyon, turning their backs to the rawboned peaks of the Henry Mountains. The river was low at this time of the year, flowing between large sandbanks; salt cedar, willows and tall reeds grew close to the water's edge. They splashed across the river without difficulty then headed east, riding through wild and lonely country across miles of untamed land. Wherever possible they kept to the flat, but occasionally climbed benches of reddish brown-and-orange rock onto eroded mesas where junipers stirred and offered their thin shade.

It was in Tyree's mind to loop north along Hatch Wash and ride directly to Luke Boyd's cabin. When he voiced his plan to Sally the girl offered no objection.

They topped a mesa streaked with wide swaths of blue-black, the result of leeching mineral deposits, and rode through stands of thriving juniper. Ahead of them the sky was cloudless, a flock of buzzards gliding in lazy circles against a natural canvas of pale blue.

Tyree watched the scavengers as they gradually dropped lower, unhurried and patient, knowing their time would come. Beyond the mesa something was dead or dying.

The mesa ended abruptly and below them lay a wide, open valley, green with grass and spruce, a thick stand of aspen along its eastern side. The path down wound from bench to bench. None of the slopes were steep, and the swings and switchback trails were easy for the horses to negotiate.

When Tyree and Sally reached the flat, a rabbit bounded away from them, then made a quick left turn around a saddled bay mustang that had moved out from behind a wide spruce a hundred yards away. The horse lifted its head to look at them, then unconcernedly began to crop grass.

Tyree had seen that ugly hammerhead before—it was Steve Lassiter's horse.

"Wait, Sally," he said, reining up the steeldust. He studied the land around him, but nothing moved in the stifling heat of the afternoon, only the serene, circling buzzards.

"Is it a stray?" Sally asked, her eyes on the mustang.

Tyree shook his head. "No, I recognize the horse and it couldn't have strayed this far from its home range."

He kneed the steeldust into motion and rode toward the bay. The pony lifted its head again and studied the approaching riders with mild interest, then went back to grazing.

Steve Lassiter lay about twenty yards from his mount. He was lying on his belly, and when Tyree swung out of the saddle and pulled the man over on his back he counted three bullet holes in the rancher's chest.

"Is he dead?" Sally asked, kneeling beside him.

Tyree nodded. "Been dead awhile—since late yesterday, I'd say."

"Do you recognize him, Chance?"

"Yes. His name is Steve Lassiter. He has a ranch north of here. He was forever running out of tobacco, and his wife got testy when he came home late for supper. That's all I know about him." His eyes bleak, he added, "Isn't much of an epitaph for a man."

"Who could have done this?" Sally asked. "A rustler maybe?"

Tyree shook his head at her. "No, this is the work of somebody Lassiter knew and trusted. He was shot at close range, judging by the powder burns on his coat. Out here a man doesn't get that close to someone he doesn't know."

Tyree scouted the area but found nothing. The

killer of Steve Lassiter had left no clues behind. The rancher had not been robbed. He still had a wrapped plug of tobacco in his pocket and a small package of colored ribbons, no doubt intended for his wife.

Tyree was worried. By all accounts Quirt Laytham was not a patient man. Was he already moving against the other ranchers? Was the murder of Lassiter the first move in the deadly chess game that would eventually win him all the available grazing land between his ranch and the Moab settlement?

And what about Lorena? How did she fit into all this? Was she still seeing Laytham and did she approve of his plans? Did she approve of Lassiter's murder? That hardly seemed likely and Tyree was ashamed that he'd even given thought to the possibility. But in a land where every man's hand was turned against him, he realized it was easy to see enemies behind every tree.

A sense of impending danger nagging at him, Tyree turned to Sally. "We'll take Lassiter to Luke Boyd's place. I don't know where the man's ranch is located and in any case, his wife has never met us and she'll need words of comfort from a friend."

With Sally's help, Tyree got the dead man across the saddle of the bay, the mustang dancing nervously at the scent of blood.

They rode east to the wash then swung north, arriving at the Boyd cabin just before noon. Luke must have seen them coming from a distance because he was already at the door when Sally and Tyree reined up in the yard.

"It's Steve Lassiter, Luke," Tyree said, dropping the reins of the mustang. "He's dead."

Boyd's face looked like it had been carved from a block of granite. "How did it happen?"

Tyree shrugged. "Sometime yesterday he was shot three times at close range. Sally and me found him just west of the Hatch Wash. He had a new plug of tobacco in his pocket and some ribbons for his wife, so chances are he was riding back from Crooked Creek when he was murdered."

"Steve had been losing cattle, told me so," Boyd said. "Then, about a week ago, his barn was set on fire. He got the horses out, but the barn itself burned to the ground. Nothing left but ashes." Boyd looked uncomfortable. "Quirt Laytham offered to take the place off his hands, told Steve that more and more rustlers were coming down from Moab and out of the Disappointment Creek country in the Colorado Territory and that pretty soon they'd pick him clean. Laytham mentioned a good price but Steve refused." Boyd's face was suddenly old. "And now this."

"Luke, do you think Laytham's behind Steve Lassiter's murder?" Tyree asked.

The old rancher shook his head. "Chance, I don't know what to think anymore." He waved a hand toward the cabin. "Lorena moved out. She's staying at Laytham's place. Now they're talking about getting hitched come the fall."

This last was like a punch in the gut to Tyree. For a few moments he sat his saddle stunned, unable to believe his own ears. Lorena was living at the Rafter-L and planned to marry Laytham. It didn't make any sense. Couldn't she see past the man's flashy exterior to the rot underneath?

"Chance, step down and set, and you too, Sally,"

Boyd said. "There's a good beef stew on the stove and a fresh-baked loaf of sourdough bread. You two he'p yourself while I take Steve home to his missus." Boyd looked hard at Tyree. "And when I get back, you can tell me where the hell you've been for the past two weeks."

Darkness was falling around the cabin when Luke Boyd returned. He stomped inside and immediately asked, "Did you two eat? I swear you're both as skinny as bed slats."

Tyree smiled. "Yeah, Luke, we ate, and it was good. Hope we left enough for you."

Boyd waved a hand. "Don't matter none. I haven't got much of an appetite. Poor Jean Lassiter took her husband's death hard and then we had a burying to do, the two of us." The old rancher cast around in his mind for the right words, then said, "When I left her, she was sitting alone in the dark grieving. She'd traveled to a place I couldn't reach and she no longer heard a word I said."

"Luke, I'll ride out there tomorrow morning," Sally said. "You can tell me the way. Maybe being close to another woman will help."

Boyd nodded. "Maybe so." He turned haunted eyes to the girl. "Yes, Sally, maybe that will help right enough."

Tyree rose from the table and poured coffee for the rancher. Then he found the jug and added a generous shot of whiskey. "Drink this, Luke," he said. "Make you feel better."

The old man nodded his thanks and drank. After a few minutes the color began to return to his cheeks.

"Now tell me what's been happening since I saw you last."

Tyree told Boyd about his search for Sally and his shoot-out with the bartender at Bradley's. He described how Sally had brought him to a canyon and Zeb Pettigrew had removed the chunk of steel from his back.

"My suspenders were ruined and since then I've had a time holding up my britches." Tyree smiled, trying to lighten the mood around the table.

"Got me a spare set, Army canvas like you was wearing," Boyd said. "You can have them." The old man reached for the jug and splashed more whiskey into his cup. "Chance, about a week or so ago, Steve Lassiter was talking about you, stuff he'd heard. He said you were wanted dead or alive for the murder of Benny Cowan at Bradley's saloon. Said a couple of Laytham punchers swore you drew down on Cowan and gunned him while he was a-squealing like a pig for mercy." Boyd sipped his whiskey. "Son, it almost seems like every man in the territory is against you and your life isn't worth a plug nickel. My advice to you is to get out of the canyon country while you still can."

Tyree's eyes hardened. "Luke, you know I can't do that, not while I still have a score to settle with Quirt Laytham."

Boyd shifted in his chair, uneasy about what he had to say. "Chance, I like you. I like you a lot. But you're talking about the man my daughter intends to marry." He hesitated, then added, "If it comes right down to it, I may have to take a side."

Tyree nodded. "You do what you have to, Luke. I believe you are an honorable man and you'll do what you believe is right."

"I'll make that decision when the time comes, if it comes," Boyd said. "No hard feelings, Chance. You see how it is with me."

"No hard feelings," Tyree said, a lost, lonely ache inside him.

Sally left early in the morning to bring what comfort she could to Jean Lassiter, and after breakfast Tyree helped Boyd with chores around the ranch.

The sun had reached its highest point in the sky when Boyd straightened up from the wagon wheel he was greasing and looked toward the creek, shading his eyes with his open hand.

"Riders coming, Chance. Three of them. Maybe best you stay out of sight."

As the riders splashed across the creek, Tyree faded back to the bunkhouse and partially closed the door behind him, leaving it open a crack to watch what was happening. He drew his gun and waited.

Boyd had stepped into the yard and the three men reined up opposite him. "What can I do for you boys?" the old rancher asked. "Starting to get right hot already."

One of the riders—the tall man in the duster who had been in Bradley's saloon when Tyree shot Benny Cowan—put both hands on the saddle horn and leaned forward. "We're scouting the canyon country, looking for murdering scum who calls himself Chance Tyree," he said. "You seen him?"

Boyd shook his head. "Not in a coon's age. Spoke to a man by that name maybe a month ago, but he was just passing through."

One of the riders had split away from the others and had headed toward the barn. Now he returned. "There's a big steeldust in a stall back there, Chet," he said to the man in the duster. "Looks powerful like the horse Tyree was riding."

The man called Chet said, "Well, do tell." He looked down at Boyd, a thin smile on his lips. "Now, Mr. Boyd, we know your daughter and our boss are planning to get hitched soon, so we don't want to cause you no trouble, you being almost kin, like. But I'll ask you one more time—is Chance Tyree here?"

The old rancher shook his head. "I haven't seen him, so you boys just ride on out of here."

Chet nodded, his smile slipping slightly. "Well, if'n that's the case you won't have no objections to us taking a look around."

The man was about to swing out of the saddle when Tyree's voice stopped him cold. "You looking for me?" he asked.

Tyree was standing outside the bunkhouse, his gun hanging loose in his hand. He was relaxed, but there was nothing careless about his posture. He was alert and ready, and by the wary look in the eyes of the three Laytham riders, they knew it.

Caught flat-footed, Chet eased back into the saddle and tried a bluff. "Tyree, Sheriff Tobin swore us three in as deputies, and we're here to arrest you for the murder of Benny Cowan."

Tyree's mouth was a grim line. "You were there.

You saw what happened. It was self-defense. That lowlife back-shot me."

"Well, now, as it happens, maybe I got a different opinion on that. So I guess you'll just have to state your case to the judge."

Tyree laughed. "Judge? Why, you lying tinhorn, you'd never let me reach Crooked Creek alive."

"Harsh talk, Tyree," Chet said, his blue eyes hardening. "Mighty harsh and insulting. And me, I never take an insult from nobody."

The man reached for his gun—and Tyree shot him.

For a few moments Chet stretched to his full height in the stirrups. Then his gun dropped from his hand, and he looked at Tyree, a puzzled frown on his face, as though he was trying to understand the awful fact of his dying. His eyes glazed and he fell from his horse, thudding onto the hard-packed dirt of the yard.

"His play, not mine," one of the other riders said quickly as Tyree swung his smoking Colt on him. The rider turned to the man beside him. "Ain't that right, Lloyd?"

The man nodded, his face stiff. "Chet called it."

"Then load him on his horse and get him out of here," Tyree said, anger riding him. "And tell Tobin if he wants to arrest me for murder, come himself next time."

"Mister," Lloyd said, "next time we come there will be a lot more of us, and we'll come a-shooting."

"So be it," Tyree said. "I'll be waiting."

Sally Brennan returned to the cabin as the day was shading into evening. She looked tired, as though

Jean Lassiter's grief had used her up and drained her vitality.

"How is she?" Boyd asked the girl.

Sally's face was pale, strain etched deep in her eyes. "Jean Lassiter grieves for her husband, and without him, she no longer wants to live," she said. "She refuses to eat, she won't sleep and very soon she'll die. Whoever pulled the trigger on Steve Lassiter murdered two people."

Boyd looked like he'd been struck. "There's been so much death," he said. "Too much dying." He took a step toward Sally, shaking his head. "We had another killing here today."

"What happened?" the girl asked, her eyes slanting to Tyree, knowing he would be the one to answer her question.

"Tobin made three of Laytham's men deputies," Tyree said. "They came looking for me and one of them went for his gun."

Sally looked at Boyd, then back to Tyree. "I have to be on my way," she said. "Things are moving so fast and I've still got to do what I came here to do."

"Stay here, Sally," Boyd said. "Lorena left out the dresses you liked. She said you'd come back for them. You can have Lorena's room."

Sally shook her head, blond curls bouncing around her face. "Thank you, Luke. Maybe there will be a time for pretty dresses after I kill Luther Darcy. Or I'll be dead and will have no need for dresses."

Tyree made up his mind. "I'm coming with you, Sally." He turned to Boyd. "Luke, I can't stay here any longer. If I do, I'll only bring Tobin and his men down on you."

The old rancher opened his mouth to object, then came a dawning awareness of the logic of Tyree's statement. "I'll sack you up some grub," he said. He glanced at Sally, who was dressed in her shabby men's clothes and looked very young and vulnerable. "Girl, you wouldn't care to step away from this Luther Darcy thing? Just let it go."

"No," Sally said. "I can't step away from it. If I did, the fact of my brother being dead and his killer still walking the earth would haunt me like a gray ghost for the rest of my life."

A sadness shaded Boyd's eyes. "Both of you are obsessed with revenge. In the end you might destroy those you hate, but in the process you could destroy yourselves." The old rancher stepped to his desk and took a wooden box from a shelf. He opened it and showed the contents to Tyree and Sally. "There's almost two hundred dollars in there—money I was saving for Lorena. Take it and ride east into Colorado. Get away from here. Leave your hate behind before it devours both of you and strips you clean to the bone."

Sally leaned over and kissed Boyd on his hairy cheek. "Thanks for the offer, Luke. I know it was kindly meant, but I have to be riding now."

"I guess that goes for me too," Tyree said. He stuck out his hand. "You're a fine man, Luke Boyd."

The old rancher took Tyree's hand and searched the younger man's eyes. "I don't know how this will all play out," he said, "but I hope I never have to choose my side."

"That goes for me, too," Tyree said, again feeling a hurt in him. He smiled.

"Buena suerte, mi amigo."

"Good luck to you, too," Boyd said. He hesitated a fraction of a second, then added, "My friend."

Under a wide starlit sky, Sally and Tyree rode east toward the La Sal Mountains, then swung south along the west bank of Hatch Wash. There was no possibility that they were being followed, yet both turned often and checked their back trail, the night falling behind them full of phantoms.

The darkness crowding around them, they made camp among tumbled rocks in a stand of cottonwoods and built a fire that was barely big enough to boil their coffee and fry some of the bacon and sourdough bread Boyd had packed for them. When they'd eaten, Tyree threw the last of the coffee on the coals. It was unlikely Tobin and his deputies would ride at night, but now was not the time to take chances.

At first light they saddled up and rode out. They angled away from the wash and headed into the wild broken country of the canyons, leaving little trail.

After an hour the two riders followed a game and cattle trail into some scattered juniper and sage, the land around them patchy desert and high sandrock. They emerged at the base of a vast tableland that rose in gradual steps to a height of well over a thousand feet. Tyree leading the way, they climbed, taking a steep, switchback route up the slope.

As the sun climbed directly overhead, Sally and Tyree stopped on a high, flat plateau of pink rock scattered with huge boulders and stunted spruce where they could overlook miles of country.

Less than thirty minutes later, they saw punchers driving a herd north along the wash, followed a few minutes after that by a group of ten riders heading in the same direction. The posse, if that's what it was, kicked up so much dust it was impossible to pick out individual riders. But Tyree had no doubt that Tobin was among them, and likely Laytham and Luther Darcy.

Tyree turned to Sally, a smile on his lips. "Well, as of right now it, looks like I'm still being hunted, so where do we go from here?"

"Do you think Darcy is down there among those riders?" Sally asked.

"It's likely. After I told Laytham he had to get out of the territory or be destroyed, he wants me dead real bad. Darcy is his man, his finger looking for a trigger."

Sally was silent for a few moments, deep in thought. Then she said, "Chance, when they don't find you they'll probably go back to Crooked Creek and head for the saloon. That's where Darcy will be, and that's where I'm going."

Tyree was aware of the dangers that awaited him in Crooked Creek, but he could not step back and allow Sally to go there by herself.

Now he put his thoughts into words. "Then I'm going with you," he said. "You could get your damn fool little head blown off if I'm not around to help."

Sally's temper flared. "You think I'm a child, don't you?"

Before Tyree could answer, she stood on tiptoe, threw her arms around him and her mouth reached hungrily for his. They melted into each other, Tyree surprised at the depth and sudden, white-hot heat of his passion.

But Sally pulled away from him, panting, her high, firm breasts rising and falling under her gingham shirt. "Did that feel like a child's kiss?"

Utterly lost, trying desperately to stem that dam of desire that had broken inside him, Tyree said, "No . . ." His voice was husky, and he cleared his throat and tried again. "No, it wasn't," he managed. "It was a grown woman's kiss."

Sally tossed her head, her curls bobbing. "Then stop treating me like a child."

"I won't," Tyree said sincerely. "I won't ever again."

He reached for the girl, but she stepped beyond his outstretched arms. "Later, Chance, when all this is over. I can't give myself to you or any other man until then."

Tyree fought himself, fought to douse the fire in his belly, and when the flames finally flickered and died, the woman smell of the girl no longer making his head swim, he managed a weak grin. "But grown woman's kiss or no, I'm not letting you ride into Crooked Creek alone."

"I never for a single moment thought you would," Sally said.

Chapter 18

Crooked Creek slumbered in the drowsy afternoon heat as Sally and Tyree rode across the brush flats, then scouted the town from near the livery stable.

There were no horses at the hitching rail outside Bradley's, and few people on the street. A mule-drawn wagon was being loaded with supplies at A. K. Dunn's general store, a couple of miners throwing bags of flour, salt and dried fruit into the bed. There was no placer mining in the canyonlands, but a few hardy prospectors panned for gold in the creeks, most of them making grub money and little else besides.

Over at the church building, a woman in a faded blue dress was polishing a brass doorknob and a bald man in a broadcloth suit stepped out of the bank, glanced up at the sun, checked his watch, then went back inside again.

A stray breeze lifted a thin veil of dust, throwing it against the legs of Tyree's horse as he and Sally swung out of their saddles at the door to the livery stable, nodding to Zeb Pettigrew, who was sitting on the bench outside, smoking a reeking pipe.

The old man ran his eyes over Tyree, then, more appreciatively over Sally, and said, "Glad to see you're on your feet, Tyree. I never did get a chance to ride back to the canyon but anyhow you healed up all on your own."

"Like I told you, Zeb, I'm beholden to you," Tyree said, "if you ever need a favor."

The man nodded. "I'll bear that in mind." A smile touched his lips under his beard. "I don't know if you're aware of it, but you two ain't exactly welcome hereabouts. Nick Tobin swears he's going to hang you for gunning the town's best bartender, that is, if Luther Darcy doesn't shoot you down first."

"Where is Tobin?" Tyree asked.

Pettigrew waved a negligent hand. "Out there somewheres, hunting, you I suppose."

Tyree and Sally led their horses into the stable, stripped off the saddles and fed them a scoop of oats. Tyree threw hay into the stalls then brushed stray straws from his jeans. "How do you plan to play this, Sally?" he asked, knowing what the answer would be and dreading it. The girl's immediate reply didn't disappoint him.

"Wait until Darcy gets here. Then brace him in the saloon."

Tyree shook his head. "Sally, Darcy is fast with a gun. You won't stand a chance against him."

"Would you?" the girl asked.

Tyree shrugged. "I don't know. Maybe. But I have a feeling I'd have to take my hits and somehow keep standing."

"I thought about bushwhacking him," Sally said, her voice matter-of-fact. "It wouldn't bother me in the least. But then I thought he might die and never know who had killed him. I want him to know it was me, and why he's dying."

For a few moments, Tyree stood silent, thinking things through. He would back up Sally when the time came, but against a skilled gunman like Darcy the outcome would be a mighty uncertain thing. Was there any other way? Tyree racked his brains, but couldn't find a solution. Sally was dead set on bracing Darcy and she'd do it with or without his help, today, tomorrow or at some other time. No matter when, the danger would be just as great.

The girl's kiss had roused something in Tyree, an all-consuming passion he'd never felt before. But in his heart of hearts did he consider Sally merely a pale substitute for Lorena, a woman he wanted but could never have? A vehement denial did not immediately spring into Tyree's mind, and that troubled him.

"You two can stay here if'n you like," Zeb Pettigrew said, walking back to where Sally and Tyree were standing. "Best you stay off the street. You can see all you want to see from here." He cocked his head to one side like a hairy, intelligent bird. "And what do you want to see?"

"Luther Darcy," Sally said without hesitation. "I plan on killing him today."

Pettigrew scratched his great belly. "Luther Darcy and his kind don't kill easy, little lady. I'd do some reconsidering on that score."

"I've considered it," Sally said. "In fact it's all I've

thought about for the past year since he murdered my brother. I've considered it time and time again, and all that reflecting has convinced me of just one thing—I have to rid the earth of Luther Darcy's shadow."

The old man grinned. "Well, I reckon your mind's made up and you'll do what you have to do. Tell you this, one good thing about getting to my age is that a man can sit in the shade, light his pipe and watch it all happen. It ain't near as dangerous thataway."

Tobin's posse rode into Crooked Creek at sundown. Luther Darcy was with them, but there was no sign of Quirt Laytham.

Tobin went directly to his office, but Darcy and the others barged through the swinging doors of Bradley's. Tyree thought they looked like a tired, dispirited bunch.

Beside him, Sally tensed. She went back to the stall, got her Winchester and levered a round into the chamber. The girl's face was ghostly pale, her lips white, but there was a hard, determined glint in her eyes and Tyree realized there would be no turning her away from what was to come.

"Wait, Sally," he said. He drew his Colt, fed a round into the empty chamber under the hammer and reholstered the gun.

"Ready?" the girl asked, the word coming strained and thin from a tight throat.

Tyree attempted a smile. "As I'll ever be."

As they stepped past Pettigrew, the man was lighting his pipe. Talking around the stem through a cloud of rank smoke, he said, "Well, good luck, you two." He smiled, shaking out a match. "I'll be watching."

Sally and Tyree walked along the town's main street, a few people on the boardwalks stopping to look at them curiously as they passed, a tall young man who wore his gun like it was part of him and a pretty, sunburned girl in men's clothing, holding a Winchester, hammer back, in her right hand.

Above them, the darkening sky was banded by streaks of white cloud, their edges trimmed with burnished gold, and the air smelled of dust, pine resin from the planking of the buildings, and the sage and rabbit bush of the brush flats.

They stopped outside Bradley's, taking stock of what awaited them. Inside someone was playing the saloon's battered piano, picking out the notes of Chopin's beautiful Nocturne no. 2 in G Major. It was an incongruous sound against the roars of whiskey-drinking men and the hard laughter of the girls who had come down from the line behind the courthouse to welcome home the posse, aware that most of them were Quirt Laytham's highly paid, free-spending riders.

Tyree adjusted the position of his gun and turned his head to look at Sally. The girl had a determined set to her chin and the knuckles of the hand that clutched her rifle were white.

She looked very young and pretty, the kind of girl who should be married, happily busy in her kitchen baking apple turnovers, not standing in a dusty street with a rifle in her hands about to confront a deadly gunman.

Suddenly Sally stepped toward the boardwalk. "Let's go do it," she said.

Tyree followed Sally into the saloon, and at first no one noticed them, every man present concentrating on his whiskey or a woman. But gradually eyes were drawn to the pair standing silent and significant at the saloon door. The chatter slowly died, laughter fleeing the painted lips of the saloon girls, the piano faltering note by note into silence.

"Luther Darcy!" Sally called out in the sudden hush. "Show yourself."

The girl's voice opened up the crowd like Moses parting the Red Sea, men and women stepping back until Darcy could be seen standing alone at the bar, a glass half-raised to his lips.

Sally held the Winchester level, pointed at the gunman's belly. "I told you I'd kill you someday, Darcy," she said. "Now turn around and look into my eyes as you die."

For a few moments Darcy didn't move, then he slowly placed his glass on the bar, staring at it all the way as though it had become a thing of consuming interest to him.

The saloon's railroad clock ticked loud in the silence, like a racing heartbeat, and Tyree could hear the short, nervous breaths of a woman standing close to him.

Without turning, Darcy said, "Tyree, I guess you're taking a hand in this play?"

Tyree nodded. "You called it."

"Damn you, Darcy!" Sally yelled. "Face me like a man instead of cowering there like a mangy yellow dog."

The gunman slowly turned and smiled at the girl. Then he moved.

Darcy dived for the floor, rolled, then came up on one knee, his guns out and spitting flame. Sally's shot splintered the wood of the bar where Darcy had been standing. But the girl was hit immediately, the Winchester spinning out of her hands. Tyree drew and fired. His bullet thudded into the pine boards of the floor. A miss. Lithe as a cat, Darcy had rolled a second time. The gunman slammed hard against the red-slippered feet of a saloon girl. The girl screamed and tried to step away, but she stumbled on high heels and fell on top of Darcy. Tyree hesitated a split second, momentarily uncertain of his target. Then something hard crashed into the back of his skull and he sank to his knees, the room spinning around him.

He tried to raise his gun, but suddenly it felt too heavy for him. He was roughly dragged to his feet, then, from out of nowhere it seemed, he saw Nick Tobin. The big lawman pulled back his fist and crashed it hard into Tyree's chin. Then the men who had been holding him stepped away and let him fall.

Chance Tyree woke with a pounding headache. He lay still until his surroundings swam into focus. He was lying on his back, and above him he saw a sagging timber ceiling, dusty gray triangles of spiderwebs gathered in the corners. He shifted his position slightly and the iron springs of the bunk under him shrieked in protest.

Tyree moved his head, looking around him. To his left was an iron door set into a redbrick wall with a barred opening less than a foot square. But, like the roof, the three remaining walls were constructed of heavy pine logs, and iron bars secured the small, narrow window high on the wall opposite his bunk.

Now came the dawning realization of where he was—he was in Nick Tobin's jail cell.

Slowly, like in a hazy dream, the events at Bradley's saloon came drifting back to him.

Sally!

Tyree rose to his feet, an effort that made his head reel. He staggered to the door, pounded on its unyielding iron and yelled through the opening, "Tobin!"

A couple of minutes passed before the sheriff opened the door to his office and stepped to the cell. The man was not wearing his hat, and his hair was snow white, falling in untidy tangles over his ears. His eyes were lost behind his dark glasses, and the sagging, pasty face was expressionless. Tyree caught the disgusting stench of the man, the odor of ancient sweat and unwashed clothes.

"Wondered when you'd wake up," Tobin said. "Been out for an hour, I'd say."

"How is Sally?" Tyree asked, a taut fear in him even as he asked the question.

The lawman shrugged. "She's over to the hotel, locked in a room, on account of how I don't have a cell for females."

"How is she?" Tyree asked again, his voice edged by anger.

"She took Luther Darcy's bullet."

"Where, Tobin? Where was she hit, damn you?"

The sheriff's pudgy white hand strayed to his left shoulder. "Here. Luther's bullet hit the chamber of her rifle, ricocheted off an' struck the lass in the shoulder." Tobin grinned. "Luther wasn't trying to kill her, just disable her Winchester, but his bullet bounced the wrong way. See, he has plans for that little gal, big plans. He isn't even pressing any charges against her. Says he'll teach her the error of her ways with a horsewhip when the time comes."

"Is Sally hurt bad?" Tyree asked, his anger bubbling to the surface. At that moment he wanted to kill Darcy in the worst way.

"Doc Neary says she'll live. Be up and around in no time at all."

Tyree rubbed the back of his neck. "Who hit me?"

"I did. Slammed the stock of my Greener into your fool head then I slugged you. And just as well I did, because ol' Luther was mad clean through and he would have killed you fer sure. Why, he wanted to put a bullet in you whilst you were lying there, all fast asleep, like. But I convinced him it was best to wait for a proper hanging."

"Hanging? I haven't even had a trial yet, Tobin," Tyree said.

"Oh, yes, you have. You had it about an hour ago while you was still asleep. John Rawlins told Judge Hay what he saw at Bradley's when you killed the bartender. Then two others told how you killed poor Chet Austin over to Luke Boyd's place, and Chet just trying to do his sworn duty by arresting you. Well, Judge Hay listened to all this, said as how you was as guilty as sin and set the hanging for noon tomorrow."

"So the judge is also in Laytham's pocket, or yours," Tyree said bitterly.

Tobin grinned. "Remember I tole you to take the thousand dollars and then scat? You should have listened to me, Tyree."

"Tobin, you go to hell," Tyree said.

The sheriff laughed. "I like you, boy. I really like you, but hell, I'm gonna hang you just the same. Hey, but don't you worry none, it won't be like the first time when those idiots Clem Daley and Len Dawson bungled it. I've got you a new rope, the best three-quarter-inch Manila hemp all the way from Salt Lake City. And I already boiled it and stretched it to get rid of all the spring, stiffness and the inclination ropes have to coil. Then I lubricated the knot and noose with melted paraffin so it will slide real easy." Tobin grinned and slapped his thigh. "Oh, I tell you, boy, you're gonna think it a real pleasure to be hung by me."

"Tobin," Tyree said, ignoring the man, "take me to see Sally. I give you my word I won't try to escape."

The sheriff shook his head. "Boy, you won't see Sally Brennan again until both of you meet in the sweet by-and-by. Besides, now she's Luther Darcy's woman and he don't cotton to her seeing other men."

Tobin turned and began to walk away. Tyree called out after him, but the sheriff waved a dismissive hand and stepped into the gloom of his office, slamming the door behind him.

Time lay heavy on Tyree. Through the window of his cell he watched the light change, shading from day to night. There was no lamp in his cell, and he lay on his bunk in the dark, wishful for a smoke but having no makings.

He rose and stepped to the window, standing on

the bunk to reach the iron bars. He pulled and pushed with all his strength, but the bars remained firm and unyielding, cemented into the heavy logs by someone who knew his business.

Tyree stretched out on the bunk again. Did he really have only hours to live? It seemed that was the case because there was no one around who could save him.

Noise reached him from Bradley's, the piano now playing dance music, the tinkling notes competing with shouting men, laughing women and the clink of bottles and glasses. Late as it was, Laytham's riders were still in town and a party was in full swing. The festivities would probably go full blast until tomorrow's hanging, always a gala occasion in the West and well attended.

A slow, dragging hour passed, then another. Tyree dozed off and on, wakening now and then as the racket from the saloon grew in volume.

"Pssst . . ."

A man's whisper at the window, loud enough to be heard above the din of Bradley's. Tyree rose quickly and stood on the bunk. He looked through the bars and saw the bearded, amused face of Zeb Pettigrew. "I'm standing on a cracker barrel, boy," he said. "And it's none too steady."

"Zeb," Tyree asked, surprised, "what are you doing here?"

The old man giggled. "Interfering when I shouldn't be interfering. But, hell, if they hang you tomorrow, the play is over and I've got nothing to watch. Tobin is over to Bradley's, and that's how come I'm here to spring you out o' this here calaboose."

Chapter 19

"Zeb," Tyree whispered urgently, "this place is built like a fortress. How are you planning to get me out of here?"

The old man shook his head. "Don't talk, boy. Listen. Your horse is saddled and ready to go at the livery stable. Your rifle is still in the scabbard and I put a Colt in your saddlebags."

"But how are you—"

"Don't talk, boy. When the time comes, jest you hightail it to your hoss and skedaddle out of town."

"Zeb, listen to me—"

"Don't talk anymore, boy."

"But I have something to say. How are you planning to—"

"No more talk, Tyree."

"Damn it, why not?"

"Because"—Pettigrew looked down at the ground—"judging by the fuse on the dynamite I put against the wall, this whole place will go sky-high in . . . oh . . . less than ten seconds."

The old man quickly faded into the night, and

Tyree frantically ripped the mattress off the bunk, ran to the far wall and covered himself up as best he could.

A few seconds ticked by, followed by an earsplitting roar and a blinding flash. For a while Tyree was blinded by dust, but after his eyes cleared, he saw the devastating effect of the blast. Contrary to what Zeb had expected, the building still stood, but a hole several feet wide had been blown in the logs of the opposite wall and the roof was tilting dangerously.

Tyree rose to his feet and dashed through the opening. Then he was running for his life through the darkness toward the livery stable.

Behind him, Tyree heard men shout and guns bang, but not a single bullet came his way. It was wild shooting by some of the drunken revelers at Bradley's, confused about what was happening.

There was no sign of Pettigrew when Tyree reached the livery. But, as the old man had promised, the steeldust was saddled and ready in a stall. Tyree reached into his saddlebags and found the Colt and a box of ammunition. The gun was a .44-.40 and brand-new, the slick browning of the frame, barrel and the walnut handle showing no wear. He spun the cylinder and checked the loads, then stuck the revolver in the waistband of his jeans.

Tyree led his horse to the entrance of the stable and swung into the saddle. A bullet chipped wood from a beam near his head, followed by a man yelling: "I got him! He's here!"

Tyree kicked the steeldust into motion and left the stable at a lope. Off to his left a man in a vest decorated with bright silver conchas threw a rifle to his

shoulder and took aim. Tyree's Colt blasted and the
man sprawled on the ground.

At a fast gallop, Tyree rounded the side of the
livery barn and headed for the open brush flats. Behind him guns hammered, and a bullet split the air
close to his head. A few moments later, he reached
the flats and the moon-streaked darkness swallowed him.

The galloping steeldust kicked up a thick cloud of
yellow dust that could be seen from a long distance,
but Tyree did not slacken his pace. Once he reached
the wild, broken country of the canyons he could
lose himself among the high rock ridges and shelter-
ing arroyos.

When Tyree glanced over his shoulder he saw a
rising billow of dust coming on fast behind him.
Tobin had managed to mount a posse. Every now
and then a gun flared, but the riders were shooting
wild at shadows.

Tyree grinned to himself. The men following him
were full of whiskey bravery, the smell of scented
women still on them, and maybe they'd discourage
easy. He reined in his horse, yanked the Winchester
from the boot under his knee and threw the rifle to
his shoulder.

He cranked off three fast rounds into the following
dust cloud, and immediately the posse split apart,
the cloud breaking into a dozen separate whirling
dust devils.

Tyree fired a couple more shots. In the dark he
had no chance of hitting anything, but he figured his
bullets would serve to keep his pursuers honest.

The devil of mischief riding him, his grin widened

as he swung the steeldust toward the milling horsemen, firing rapidly from the shoulder at a fast gallop.

He saw a man go down with his horse, then roll free from under its kicking hooves. Another was hit and reeled in the saddle, a revolver spinning from his hand.

Now Tyree was almost among them. He shoved the rifle back into the boot and pulled the Colt from his waistband. He rode through the cursing, angry horsemen, many of them fighting frightened, plunging horses. A man swung into Tyree's view, his gun coming up fast. Tyree fired and the rider went backward out of the saddle. He had no time to see the man fall, because now he was through the riders, emptying his Colt as he went.

Behind him, the members of Tobin's posse were sobering up fast. They had thought this would be a lark, a dozen of them running down one man and either shooting him to doll rags or dragging him back to be hanged. But they had seriously underestimated Tyree and his gun skills, a mistake those who survived would be wary of making ever again.

As Tyree galloped toward town, then looped back toward the canyonlands, no one was following him. Tobin and his men had obviously decided they'd had enough for one night.

The events of the past few minutes had lifted Tyree to recklessness and it felt good to have fought back and won. As he slowed the steeldust to a steady lope, he threw back his head and laughed, all the tension that had been in him draining away as he rode into the moonlit canyons and became one with the night.

*   *   *

Over the next several days, Tyree watched from vantage points on top of mesas and high rock ridges as posses hunted for him. Once he saw Tobin and Luther Darcy together, but no sign of Quirt Laytham.

Where was the man? Tyree wondered if he had lost interest, leaving it to Tobin and Darcy to hunt him down. Or was he spending his time at his ranch in sweet dalliance with Lorena, the woman's stunning beauty making him forget, at least for now, all his soaring ambitions?

As long as he was alive, Tyree knew he was a thorn in Laytham's side. Surely the big rancher would soon take a hand in hunting him. Or would he do that only if Tobin and Darcy failed?

Time would answer that question, but for now, a more immediate concern was Sally. Somehow Tyree had to get the girl out of the clutches of Luther Darcy. But that meant riding into Crooked Creek, a risky course of action he did not relish. Still, since there was no other way, he would do it.

First he would have to find food. The strips of beef jerky that Zeb had thoughtfully stuffed into his saddlebags were gone and with posses hunting him Tyree could not risk a rifle shot at a deer. He was hungry and getting hungrier, and the only place he could find something to eat was at Luke Boyd's cabin.

But did he dare risk getting Luke involved with Tobin and Luther Darcy? Not if he waited until nightfall when the chances of him being seen were slight. He'd be risking Luke's Spencer, but that was a chance he'd have to take.

Tyree spent the remainder of an oppressively hot day in a slot canyon north of the Abajo Mountains, dozing off and on until the light changed and darkness began to gather around him.

He led the steeldust from the canyon, then swung into the saddle and headed north toward Luke's ranch. If all went well, he could eat, then make a night ride for Crooked Creek. It would still be dark when he reached town and, if luck was on his side, he could get Sally out of the hotel. He had no doubt the girl was guarded, but he would deal with that when the time came.

The sky was scattered with stars and the night air was soft and warm as Tyree headed up Hatch Wash then swung in the direction of Luke's cabin.

After an hour he rode west along the creek leading to the Boyd place, passing cattle grazing on both banks, relieved that all of them bore the old rancher's brand. As he got closer, a slight breeze stirred, rustling the slender reeds by the creekbank, carrying the smell of sage and juniper . . . and something else. The sharp, tangy odor of wood smoke.

Worry nagging at him, Tyree kneed his horse into a lope. The moon was up and riding high. The coyotes were yammering among the shadowed canyons and the night birds were calling out to each other.

The glow of the cabin lamps should have been in sight as Tyree rounded a bend in the creek, his eyes scanning the darkness ahead of him. But there were no lights, just the dark, looming bulk of the mesa behind the cabin and above that the vast purple arch of the starry sky.

Tyree reined in his horse, his instinct for danger

clamoring at him. His eyes probed the gloom and gradually he made out the vague shape of the cabin. But the shape was all wrong, the contours of the building distorted. The roof was no longer there and the sturdy walls were broken down; in the moonlight, a spar of scorched timber was visible behind what was once a window frame.

His eyes moved beyond the cabin to the corral. A section of the fence was down, pulled over by a rope thrown around a post. It was an old trick that, and in the past he'd seen it done to many a nester and sheepherder.

Warily, Tyree rode to the front of the cabin. Most of the base of the porch and the wall behind still stood, but the door had been burned away and all the glass panes in the windows were shattered. The roof had collapsed, a few wisps of smoke drifting up from inside, and a feeble flame fluttered on the side of a fallen beam like a scarlet moth.

Tyree swung out of the saddle and walked around to the rear of the cabin—and found Luke Boyd.

The old rancher was lying on his back, his body from the waist down buried under a pile of charred, fallen timbers. His voice was weak, but Boyd managed a smile when he saw Tyree emerge from the darkness. "How you doing, boy? Good to see you again."

"Luke," Tyree said, kneeling beside the old rancher, the odor of scorched flesh in his nostrils, "what happened?"

Boyd's face looked like it had been chipped from marble. "They hit me late this afternoon. I was over to the barn when they rode in and I made a run for my Spencer. Then this feller, one of them fancy two-gun shootists we hear about all the time, cut loose at me and I fell right here. After they set the cabin on fire, the wall came right down on top of me. Been lying here since. Mighty thirsty though."

Tyree looked around and found a tin cup that had escaped the flames. He walked to the creek, rinsed out the cup, then filled it with water. When he got back he held the old man's head and put the water to his lips.

Boyd drank a few sips, then nodded. "That was good, Chance. Real good." He swallowed hard. "They burned my fiddle, boy. Burned the old cabin where Lorena grew up and my fiddle with it. Now why would they do a thing like that to a man? Tell me why, Chance?"

Tyree shook his head. "I don't know, Luke. I only know evil exists and it's continually at war with all of God's creation. Maybe someday a preacher will tell me the why of it."

Tyree gently laid Boyd's head back on the ground. "The man with two guns. Was his name Luther Darcy?"

"I seem to recollect that's what they called him. Of course, I'd heard the name before. He's a bad one, Chance. As bad as they come."

"Recognize any of the others?"

Boyd shook his head. "No. It all happened so fast, I didn't get a good look at any of them."

"Think, Luke," Tyree said. "Was Quirt Laytham with them?"

"Didn't see him, Chance. I don't think Quirt had a hand in this."

Tyree let that go. "Luke, I've got to get you to a doctor."

"Too late for that, boy," the old man said. His fevered eyes sought Tyree's in the gloom. "Listen, Chance, I've been lying here thinking and it's good you came along when you did. When I'm gone, I want you to have this place. I'm giving it to you. I once thought Lorena would live on here, but that ain't likely now she's getting hitched to Quirt Laytham." Boyd reached up a smoke-blackened hand and clutched the front of Tyree's shirt. "Ranch this place and make a go of it, son," he said. "I think them who burned me out want to have it for themselves, but don't let them. Hang on to it, Chance, fight for it if you must, and don't let anybody take it from you."

Tyree smiled and shook his head. "Luke, this will be Lorena's ranch. She's your daughter and it's hers by right."

"No, Chance. Lorena will have all of Quirt's lands and cattle. She doesn't need this place, but you do." The old rancher took a couple of tortured, shuddering breaths as waves of pain swept over him. "In the cabin. Look for it now. A steel box. The flames won't have touched it." Boyd saw Tyree's hesitation and said, "Go, boy, get it now."

Tyree walked into the smoking cabin and after a few minutes searching found a large metal box. The steel was scorched and blackened, but the box itself was intact. He carried it out to Boyd and the old man said, "Open it."

Tyree opened the box and took out the items one

by one, a deed to Boyd's ranch, a couple of double eagles and a gold medal on a colored ribbon.

The rancher smiled. "I was given that by old General Winfield Scott after the battle of Contreras in the Mexican war. I'd been with him since Vera Cruz and stood at his side when he took the Mexican surrender at Mexico City on September fourteenth, eighteen and forty-seven." Boyd looked up at Tyree, shaking his head. "Hell, it seems like just yesterday, but it was sure a long time ago."

Boyd's hand reached to his shirt pocket and took out a stub of pencil. "Bring that deed close to me, Chance. I'm signing this ranch over to you."

"Luke, I don't think—"

"Don't argue, boy. I was thinking of doing this for a spell and not just tonight. In fact right after you met that pretty Sally gal. You two will make this a proper ranch, and you'll have children to bring life to the place." Boyd scribbled on the deed, and handed it back to Tyree. "There, it's done. I've signed the ranch over to you and it's yours."

Again Tyree opened his mouth to object, but Boyd waved a hand and hushed him into silence. "Now, boy, there's something you can do for me," he said. "Chance," he whispered, his voice hoarse with pain, "I'm burned away from the waist down. Nothing left of my legs but ash. I'm in so much pain I can hardly stand it and it's getting worse by the minute. There's no hope for me, but I don't want to linger like this. I wouldn't allow an animal to suffer like I'm suffering right now."

Boyd again clutched Tyree's shirt. "Make it a clean

shot, son." His pleading eyes sought those of Tyree's in the darkness. "Do this much for me, boy. Help an old man."

Tyree eased a fallen timber off Boyd's legs and he was shocked by what he saw. Luke was right—both his limbs were incinerated, burned to a mass of blackened, melted flesh, spikes of white bone showing here and there. Luke Boyd must have been in agony, and so far only the old rancher's stubborn courage had prevented him from screaming.

The terrible sight of Boyd's legs made Tyree's decision for him. He turned the old man's head in the direction of the western sky where a million stars shimmered. "Watch the stars, Luke," he said. "Watch the stars and remember your life. Remember how it was, every single moment of it."

The old man nodded and the night sky was reflected in his eyes. His face settled into repose, smiling, a man at peace with himself and his death.

Tyree thumbed back the hammer of his Colt. "Remember how it was, Luke," he whispered. "Remember how it was, my friend." The sound of a gunshot echoed loud through the canyons, then faded away like the beat of a distant drum.

Tyree laid Luke Boyd to rest at the base of the mesa. He dug the grave deep, and when the old man was covered with earth, he piled the spot high with talus rocks so that it would be seen and be safe from animals. Then he fashioned a cross from a couple of the burned timbers from the cabin and set it up among the rocks.

Hat in hand, Tyree stood at the graveside for long

hours as the moon dropped in the sky and a deeper darkness fell around him. The coyotes sang Luke's lonely funeral dirge while the breeze sighed and whispered a eulogy to the listening night.

When the dawn came, Chance Tyree finally turned away from the grave and allowed his grief to be replaced with a savage anger.

He looked up at the brightening sky, his face a mask of pain and hate, and made a vow . . . to visit a hundred different kinds of hell on the canyon country.

Chapter 20

Tyree searched among the ruins of the cabin and found several cans of food. The labels were burned away and he had no idea what the cans contained. But he was lucky. There were beans in the first can he opened, peaches in the second, the contents of both scorched but edible.

He ate hastily, then swung into the saddle. His first task was to rescue Sally. No matter the odds, he was determined to free the girl and bring her back here—home to his ranch.

Tyree rode through the remainder of the night, chasing the dawn, and the morning sun was just beginning its climb into the sky when he rode into Crooked Creek and reined up outside the Regal Hotel. A few people were walking briskly along the boardwalks and several cow ponies stood three-legged at the hitching rail of the restaurant, but at this early hour the town was quiet.

Tyree stepped out of the saddle, yanked his Winchester from the scabbard and levered a round into the chamber. He jumped onto the boardwalk and slammed through the hotel door. The clerk at the desk—a small, round man wearing an eyeshade, muttonchop whiskers bookending a cherubic face—looked up from the ledger he'd been studying, his eyes alarmed.

Giving the man no chance to talk, Tyree snapped, "Sally Brennan's room?"

"Top floor, number twenty-six," the clerk answered. "But, hey, you've got no right to—"

Tyree didn't wait to hear the rest. He was already taking the stairs two at a time.

At the end of the hallway, a couple of men with deputy's stars pinned to their shirts, shotguns in their laps, were sitting on chairs outside the door. One was Len Dawson, the other a tall, sour looking man Tyree didn't know. The two immediately sprang to their feet, and Dawson shouted, "Tyree! What the hell are you doing here?"

"Move back from the door, Dawson," Tyree said, making his point with his waving rifle. "I'm here for Sally."

"The hell you are!" the man with Dawson yelled. He swung the scattergun in Tyree's direction. Tyree fired, levered the Winchester and fired again. Hit twice, the deputy slammed against the wall, then slid to the floor, a trail of blood smearing the flowered wallpaper behind him.

Dawson made no attempt to level his shotgun. But he was eyeing Tyree, a hard, angry scowl betraying the fact that he was thinking about making a play.

"Don't even try it, Dawson," Tyree said. "I'm all through talking. From now on I'll let my guns do all the speechifying for me."

Dawson was bucking a stacked deck and he knew it. He let the shotgun remain right where it was, the man sitting still as a marble statue. Tyree stepped up to the deputy, wrenched the gun from his hands, broke it open and removed the loads. "Inside," he said. "And please, Dawson, give me an excuse to drill you."

Wordlessly, his face suddenly gray, the deputy opened the door to Sally's room and Tyree followed him inside. The girl was sitting up in bed, a bandage around her shoulder, her eyebrows raised in shocked surprise.

"Chance, I heard the shooting and—"

"Get dressed, Sally," Tyree interrupted. "I'm taking you out of here."

Sally needed no further encouragement. She was wearing a plain white shift that someone had given her, and she swung out of bed, showing a deal of shapely leg. "You two turn around until I get dressed," she ordered.

"You heard what the lady said, Dawson. Turn around," Tyree said.

The deputy did as he was told and when Sally was dressed she stepped beside Tyree and said, "I think my horse is at the livery."

Tyree shook his head. "No time for that," he said. "My shots will have attracted a crowd." He extended an open palm to Dawson. "Key."

Dawson dug in his pocket and came up with the room key. "You'll never get out of Crooked Creek alive," he said. "You know that, don't you?"

It was an empty threat, the last resort of a vexed,

angry man and Tyree did not answer. He stripped
the deputy of his gun belt, then locked him inside
the room. He removed Dawson's Colt from its holster, filled his pockets with ammunition from the
loops, and hung the belt on the door handle. "Take
this," he told Sally, handing her his Winchester. "If
you have to, favor your shoulder and shoot from
the hip."

"Chance," Sally said, a mild exasperation in her
voice, "my left shoulder took Darcy's bullet. I shoot
off my right."

Tyree grinned. "Shows you how observant I am."

The girl followed Tyree downstairs to the lobby of
the hotel and the frightened clerk cringed against the
wall as Tyree turned and glared at him.

Tyree crooked a finger in the man's direction.
"You," he said, "come over here."

"Mister, I've got a wife and kids," the clerk
whined. "Don't kill me."

"Step out the door and take a look," Tyree said.
"Tell me what you see."

"Sure, sure, mister, anything you say."

The clerk opened the door, stuck his head outside
and hesitated for a few moments. Then he threw the
door open wide and ran into the street, hollering,
"Murder! Murder!"

Tyree cursed under his breath and stepped
through the door, a gun in each hand. But, as it happened, luck was with him.

A small crowd of curious townspeople had gathered on the boardwalk opposite the hotel, but neither
Tobin nor the Laytham punchers were in sight.

Tyree smiled grimly to himself. Tobin, Darcy and the rest were probably still out hunting him, leaving Crooked Creek wide-open but for the inept Dawson.

He didn't plan on staying around to push his luck, but there was time to get Sally's pony. He stepped to his horse and swung into the saddle, then helped Sally get up in front of him. Tyree swung the steeldust around and loped toward the livery stable.

Zeb Pettigrew stepped out of the stable, leading the paint, grinning from ear to ear. "You know I'm a watching man, Tyree, so I saw you ride in to town. I guessed why you were here. Then I heard the shooting and knowed for sure why you were here." He jerked a thumb over his shoulder. "The young lady's mare is saddled and ready to go."

Tyree nodded his thanks and waited until Sally stepped into the saddle. "Once again, Zeb," he said, smiling, "thanks for your help. And once again, I'm beholden to you."

"No trouble, Tyree," the old man said. "But it seems like everything I do to help you shortens the play." He grinned. "But what the hell? It's not the length of the performance that counts. It's the excellence of the actors." He shook his head. "And you two are excellent."

"Then stick around for the last act," Tyree said. "It's coming soon."

The old man lifted a hand. "Hell, I wouldn't miss that for the world."

A cloud of dust roiled around the steeldust and the paint as they stretched their necks and hit the flats at a fast gallop. Behind him Tyree suddenly heard the sharp, spiteful bark of a wheel gun. He turned and saw the little hotel clerk standing in the middle of the street, a raging, arm-waving Dawson beside him. The clerk held a small pepperbox revolver at eye level in his right hand and he fired again and again, his shots flying wild.

Tyree grinned and shook his head at Sally. "For a married man, that hombre sure likes to live dangerously."

Because of Tobin's posses, Tyree and Sally again kept to the rugged canyonlands well away from Hatch Wash. As they rode, Tyree told the girl about Luke Boyd's death.

"So Luther Darcy has another killing to answer for," Sally said, tears springing into her eyes.

Tyree nodded, his face grim. "Darcy will answer to me for that one."

Just as the sun was setting they rode over a saddleback ridge between the sloped bases of high, twin mesas and then down into a small meadow covered with wildflowers, long streaks of blue columbine, white wild orchids and scarlet monkeyflower.

"Let's stop here for a while," Sally said. "I want to gather some of those."

Tyree helped the girl from the saddle and watched as she collected a bunch of the wildflowers, all of them fresh and blooming, watered by underground seeps from the mesas.

They mounted again and fetched up to Boyd's ruined cabin as the darkness fell around them and the night birds began to peck at the first stars.

Sally walked to the old rancher's grave and laid

the flowers on top of the piled rocks, her cheeks wet with tears. After a while she returned to Tyree's side and looked around her. "I can't believe he's gone," she said. "I keep expecting him to step out of the barn and wave and give me that big grin the way he always did."

Tyree nodded. "He was a good man, a fine man, and I'll miss him."

He led the steeldust into the barn and forked the horse some hay, then gathered wood along the creek and built a fire. After that he again foraged in the cabin, finding a few more cans of food and the still intact whiskey jug.

As he and Sally sat by the fire, they shared a can of meat and some canned tomatoes, then each had a drink from the jug, the strong liquor helping to quiet some of the clamor inside them.

"How is the shoulder?" Tyree asked.

The girl shrugged. "Darcy's bullet just grazed me, but it was enough to knock me off my feet. Well, it was that or shock maybe, because I sure enough fainted." She lifted a corner of the bandage and looked at her injury in the firelight. "I'll have a nice little scar there, but the wound itself is healing well."

"I've got something to show you," Tyree said.

The firelight bronzing his face, he took the deed to Boyd's ranch from his shirt pocket and wordlessly passed it to Sally. The girl read what the old man had written and looked at Tyree in surprise.

Tyree shrugged. "Luke wanted me to have the place. By rights, it belongs to Lorena. If she cares to claim it, then I'll hand it back to her."

For a few moments, Sally sat in silence. Then she

said, "Lorena may not want the place, but Quirt Laytham surely does. And when he and Lorena get married, he can claim it legally through his new wife."

"It seems he doesn't want to wait that long," Tyree said. "That's why he had Darcy kill Luke."

Sally shook her head. "But, Chance, that just doesn't make any sense. Why would Laytham murder the father of the woman he intends to wed?" The girl looked at Tyree, red flames dancing in her dark eyes. "Chance, I think someone else has taken cards in this game—the same person who killed Steve Lassiter and then ordered Darcy to murder Luke. There's another player, a mystery man who wants all the same things Laytham does, especially wealth, and the power that goes with it."

"Who?" Tyree asked, skepticism heavy in his voice.

Sally shook her head. "I don't know."

"Luther Darcy?"

"Maybe. But Darcy isn't the kind to settle in one place for long. Whoever killed Steve Lassiter and Luke Boyd wants to put down roots, dig them deep and found a dynasty."

"Describes Quirt Laytham to a tee," Tyree said. "Seems to me your mystery man is no mystery."

"No, Chance, it's not him. It's someone else, someone who shares all of Laytham's ambitions."

"Do you have a single shred of proof for all this, Sally?" Tyree asked.

Again the girl shook her head. "No." She hesitated a few moments, then added, "Just call it woman's intuition."

Tyree laughed. "Well, does your woman's intuition tell you it's time we were heading for our blankets?"

"You're making fun of me again, aren't you?" Sally asked, her cheeks reddening.

"No, no, I'm not." Tyree smiled. "I'll think about what you said. But I doubt it will change my mind about Laytham. He was behind the killing of Owen Fowler, and now Steve and Luke. There's no mystery man, Sally. It's still only Quirt Laytham."

"Think what you want, Chance Tyree," the girl said, her back stiffening. "But I know I am right."

They bedded down in the barn that night, but Tyree stayed awake for a long time, listening to Sally's gentle breathing beside him. Could she be right about another player? Was he perhaps Tobin's mysterious "party of the third" who had offered him a thousand dollars to leave the territory?

In the darkness Tyree shook his head. All the signs pointed to Laytham, no one else. Come morning he planned to make his first move against the big rancher, to let him know the reckoning was about to start.

After a while Tyree closed his eyes, lulled to sleep by the echoing cries of the calling coyotes and the warm closeness of the woman lying beside him.

Tyree and Sally were awake at first light. They shared a can of tomatoes for breakfast, Tyree grieving over the fact of having neither coffee nor tobacco and being fervently wishful for both.

After they'd eaten, Tyree said, "I plan on moving Laytham's cows out of Owen Fowler's canyon this morning. Then I aim to check on Mrs. Lassiter."

"I'll come with you," Sally said. "I want to see how she's holding up."

"It might be safer if you stay here, Sally," Tyree said. "Luther Darcy did what he came to do when he shot Luke. I doubt he'll be back anytime soon."

An eyebrow arched high on the girl's forehead and an amused smile played around her lips. "Chance, think about it. When was the last time you punched cows?"

Tyree thought the question through and admitted to himself that he'd forgotten just about all he'd ever learned about cowboying over the years. Those skills had left him a long time before, round about the time he'd bought his first Colt, and his knowledge of the ways of cattle was blunted.

Sally saw the doubt in the young man's face and she smiled. "I've worked cattle all my life, Chance, and did it until recently. Believe me, you'll need my help to get Laytham's herd out of the canyon."

Tyree saw the logic in Sally's suggestion and he grinned. "You're right. Maybe it's best you come along."

Before they left, Tyree fashioned a sign from scraps of pine board he found in the barn. There was some leftover white paint from one of Boyd's projects and he hurriedly blocked out some words using a discarded brush he'd also discovered.

Satisfied with his efforts, he carried the sign to his horse, ready to ride.

He and Sally mounted up and they traveled east through the brightening light of the early morning. After the shrouding darkness of night, the silent wilderness of rock around them was again touched with color, the pink, red and yellow of the mesas and ridges and the occasional green of grass and trees.

Once they saw a small herd of bighorn sheep mount the almost vertical slope of a mesa, and behind them a flash of molten gold as a hunting cougar bounded with fluid grace from rock to rock.

They reached Fowler's canyon without incident, seeing no sign of Tobin's posses. Tyree told Sally she was now the boss since she knew much more about hazing cows out of a canyon than he did.

Sally shook out a loop and for the next couple of hours she and Tyree moved cattle off Fowler's grass to the east bank of the wash. Sally was an excellent puncher who made the hot, dusty work look effortless. Tyree helped by turning back the occasional stubborn maverick that didn't want to leave, at first showing more enthusiasm than skill, until the remembered ways slowly came back to him.

"You know, Sally, a man could get used to this again." He grinned as they stopped in the shade for a while and shared a canteen. "Especially if he was working his own cattle on his own place."

In the end they moved more than two hundred head, and when it was over Tyree stuck his sign into the ground at the mouth of the canyon.

KEEP OUT
PRIVATE PROPERTY

Sally sat her paint and looked down in amusement at Tyree's handiwork. "Of course, it could be argued that Laytham has as much right to the canyon as Fowler did," she said. "I doubt this is deeded land."

Tyree nodded. "That's true, except that Owen was

here first. As far as I'm concerned he staked his claim to the place."

"Do you think that sign will keep Laytham from moving his cows back?"

"No," Tyree answered. "But it will tell him that he's been notified."

Sally looked around her. "Well, where do we go from here?"

"We ride north," Tyree said. "I want to check on Mrs. Lassiter. I don't want the same thing to happen to her as happened to Luke."

The Lassiter ranch lay five miles northwest of the La Sal Mountains, a scattering of buildings and corrals alongside a winding, narrow creek with plentiful grazing on both banks. Cattle lay in the shade of the cottonwoods lining the banks or stood belly high in the cool creek water. A red sandstone cliff, all of eight hundred feet high, was an impassible barrier to the north. To the east and west, beyond the creek, the land stretched away level, tufted with sparse grass, in the distance a few dark junipers and after those the sheer, towering walls of flat-topped mesas and rawboned ridges of craggy rock. The wind blew steadily here, coming off the high mountains, carrying with it the smell of sagebrush and pine.

Tyree reined up in the shade of a cottonwood, his eyes scanning the Lassiter ranch and the wild, broken land around him. Nothing moved but the wind that got tangled up in Sally's hair, blowing shining curls across her cheeks.

Kicking the horse into motion, Tyree checked the

brands on the cattle he passed. Most bore the Lassiter Lazy-S, but a few were marked with Quirt Laytham's Rafter-L.

Tyree rode into the yard in front of the cabin. "Hello the house!" he yelled. His voice echoed away in the distance and the following dead silence mocked him. The cabin windows turned blank eyes to him and Sally, revealing nothing of what lay inside.

There was a feeling of death and danger in the air, an atmosphere so strong Tyree felt it reach out to him, unsettling him enough that he pulled his Colt from his waistband, grateful for its reassuring heft.

He waited a few moments, his restless eyes scanning the cabin and what he could see of the other buildings. The place was still, lifeless, and in the waning day shadows clung to walls and corrals, dark, mysterious and fraught with menace. Tyree swung out of the saddle. He let the reins of the steeldust trail then turned and looked up at the girl. "I'm going into the cabin." He smiled, attempting to make light of what he was about to say. "Just be ready to hightail it out of here if anything real bad happens."

The girl nodded, and gathered up the paint's reins. She slid Tyree's rifle out of the scabbard on his horse and laid it across the saddle horn. "I'll be ready, Chance," she said. "But I'm not hightailing it anywhere."

Stepping to the door, Tyree knocked hard a few times. Nothing stirred inside. He pushed on the door and it swung open on oiled hinges. He stepped into the cabin, his gun up and ready.

After the bright sunlight, the place was dark. He

walked into its different rooms and finally checked
the bedroom. But the cabin was deserted. A coffeepot
on the stove was still warm, though the fire had
burned down to a few red coals, and the remains of
breakfast were still on the table. Two people had sat
there to eat, but hadn't finished their food—scraps
of salt pork and congealed, greasy eggs still lay on
the plates.

Tyree searched further and found a metal box, like
the one Boyd had kept at his cabin. The lock had
been forced and the box was empty. Was this where
Steve Lassiter had kept the deed to his ranch—or
his money?

Stepping outside again, Tyree motioned Sally to
follow. He walked around the back of the cabin, and
found the first dead man. The puncher was sprawled
facedown in the dirt, the back of his shirt covered in
blood, fat blue flies already buzzing around his body.

Tyree turned the man over and recognized a face
he'd seen in Bradley's when Sally had braced Luther
Darcy. He was one of Laytham's riders and he'd apparently been shot in the back while trying to make
a run for it.

The second Laytham puncher was in the barn.
There were signs he'd tried to fight off his assailants,
five .45 caliber shells scattered around him. He'd had
time to reload his gun before he was killed. This man
had been shredded by bullets, the last one between
his eyes, the muzzle of the gun so close, black grains
of unburned powder had been driven into his nose
and forehead.

Where was Mrs. Lassiter?

Puzzled, Tyree scouted the area around the cabin.

After a few minutes he found two graves dug side by side well away from the house, toward the cliff. One held the remains of Steve Lassiter, a rough wooden marker bearing only his name. The other was fresher and unmarked. It could only be Jean's last resting place.

Short of opening the grave, there was no way of telling if the woman had died a violent death or had passed away from grief. The two Laytham punchers might have known, but they were beyond questioning.

Tyree was aware of Sally stepping beside him. The girl looked down at the grave, a sadness in her eyes. "She was a real nice lady," Sally said. "She deserved better than this."

Turning to Sally, Tyree asked, "Who would gun Laytham's punchers? Something here doesn't set right with me. As far as I know the man has no enemies but me."

"It makes sense if there's another party involved," the girl said.

"The party of the third," Tyree whispered, deep in thought.

"What was that?"

Tyree shook his head. "Oh, nothing. I'm just repeating something Nick Tobin said to me."

"Maybe it was rustlers," Sally offered. "Laytham said he was losing cattle and he blamed Owen Fowler. We know Owen wasn't stealing his cows, so it had to be someone else."

"No, Sally, not rustlers," Tyree said. "Look around you. There are Lassiter and Laytham cows everywhere. If it had been rustlers the whole herd would be gone."

"Then who?" the girl asked.

"I don't know," Tyree said. "But whoever he is, he took the deed to this land from a box in the cabin after he killed the punchers. I'd say he's a dangerous man, with as much ambition as Laytham, and maybe more." He took the girl's arm and together they began to walk away from the grave.

Sally had been right all along: Someone else had taken cards in the game. But it didn't change anything. As far as Tyree was concerned, Quirt Laytham was still the enemy.

The question was, how would Tyree get at him?

Chapter 21

Over the next couple of days, Tyree and Sally began the task of salvaging what they could from the Boyd cabin, especially the heavy logs, expensive and hard to come by in the canyon country. Tyree planned to rebuild one day, and the logs would be a start.

He shot a deer and a brace of sage hens and they ate well, helped along with the coffee, flour and salt they'd found at the Lassiter cabin.

When Tyree checked on Fowler's canyon, he discovered that Laytham's cattle were back, his sign broken and trampled into the dust. There were plenty of horse tracks along the wash, and he guessed the rancher was hunting him, no doubt blaming him for the deaths of his two riders.

It was now only a matter of time before Laytham swung by Boyd's cabin. If Luther Darcy had indeed been acting on someone else's orders, the chances were Laytham didn't even know the old man was dead. And, Tyree realized with a pang of regret, neither did Lorena.

Tyree had thought to take the fight to Quirt Laytham, but it seemed likely that the man would soon bring the fight to him. Tyree would make his stand on his own ground, and he decided to try and even the odds.

Using heavy talus rocks, he spent a morning building a stone parapet at the base of the mesa behind the cabin where he and Sally could hold off an attack. The steep slope behind the rock wall was of soft, weathered sandstone, unlikely to cause ricochets, and the base of the mesa stretched away straight on both sides, providing no cover to anyone trying to flank their position.

Tyree gathered up several canteens from the barn and bunkhouse and filled them at the creek. He placed the water in a shady spot behind his stone breastwork and figured he and Sally were as ready as they'd ever be to repel an assault.

They had only one rifle, and this he gave to Sally, trusting to his Colts.

Now all they could do was wait.

A day passed, then another. Tyree spent most of his time on the summit of the mesa, scanning the land around him. Once he thought he saw dust rise far to the west across the Colorado, but it was fleeting and brief, and soon disappeared.

Where was Laytham? Had the man given up the hunt and returned to his ranch?

But why hadn't he come here to Luke's cabin? Or had Lorena put him off the scent, maybe telling Laytham that her father had long ago ordered Chance Tyree off his property?

It was possible, Tyree decided. But somehow he

didn't think it likely. Lorena's first loyalty must be to her future husband and it would stand to reason she'd help him any way she could.

On the morning of the third day, just as he returned to his position atop the mesa, Tyree spotted dust to the south, the lifting cloud laced red by the rays of the rising sun. He waited for long moments, making sure his eyes had not been deceiving him. But he was not mistaken. The dust was getting closer, kicked up by many riders, coming on hard. And there was no doubt where they were headed—right for him.

The fight with Laytham had come and Tyree felt something akin to joy rise in him. He had waited long for this moment, and now, his heart pounding, it was getting nearer at a gallop.

Tyree scrambled down from the mesa and shouted a warning to Sally. The girl grabbed her rifle and ran to the rock wall where Tyree joined her, a gun in each hand.

"Laytham?" Sally asked, her eyes wide.

Tyree nodded. "Him and what looks like a passel of others."

But Quirt Laytham was not among the seven men who rode up to the cabin and sat their horses in the yard. Five of them, all wearing deputy's stars, Tyree didn't know. But he recognized the huge, arrogant bulk of Clem Daley. The man was sitting astride a prancing black, holding upright a Winchester, the butt resting on his right thigh. Beside him was Len Dawson, looking old and tired, aged not by his years but by the violent events of the past weeks.

Daley said something over his shoulder to one of

his men. The deputy rode to the barn and checked inside. "His horse is here all right, Clem!" he yelled from the open doorway. "Big steeldust, like you said."

Daley rode to the side of the cabin, looking warily around him. He cupped a hand to his mouth and called out, "Tyree, show yourself. We need to talk."

Tyree knew his position would be discovered sooner or later, so he stood and hollered, "Say what you came to say, Daley. Then light a shuck out of here."

The big deputy's bloodshot eyes scanned the base of the mesa and stopped when they lighted on Tyree. He kicked his horse forward twenty or so yards then reined up. "Tyree," he said, "I want you to come with us. You have a date with the hangman, boy, and best you get it over and done with." He waited a few moments, letting that sink in, then added, "Now you surrender or we'll mosey on over there after you. I see you got that little Brennan gal with you. Just remember, when we start shooting, our guns won't make no never mind between a man and a woman."

"Where's your boss, Daley?" Tyree asked, an anger rising in him. "Too yellow to do his own dirty work?"

Daley looked perplexed for a moment, then said, "You talking about Sheriff Tobin?"

"Hell, no, I'm talking about Quirt Laytham, and you know it."

To Tyree's surprise, Daley threw back his head and laughed. Then he wiped tears from his eyes and yelled, "You are a one, Tyree, funny as a three-legged

mule trying to pull a buggy. You know Laytham is
dead, on account of how you were the one that
plugged him just yes'tidy."

Tyree felt like he'd been slapped. Quirt Laytham
was dead? That hardly seemed possible. Or was
Daley, for dark reasons of his own, lying?

Voicing his doubt, Tyree said, "You're a liar,
Daley. I didn't kill Quirt Laytham and neither did
anybody else."

"Suit yourself," Daley said. He turned in the saddle and called to Dawson, ordering the man to join
him. When the deputy reined up alongside him,
Daley said, loud enough for Tyree to hear, "Tell
Tyree what happened to Mr. Laytham yes'tidy
morning."

"Hell," Dawson growled, "he knows already."

"Tell him anyway. Make this official, like."

Dawson shook his head at the pointlessness of the
task, then, looking right at Tyree, he said, "Mr. Laytham stepped out the door to go to the cookhouse
for his coffee like he done every morning. Only yesterday morning was different because he hadn't took
but three steps when you cut him down with a rifle
bullet, Tyree." Dawson's fingers strayed to his temple. "Got him right here and he was dead when he
hit the ground." The deputy's lips twisted into a bitter smile. "Mighty good shootin'."

There was no doubting Dawson's sincerity. Someone had murdered Quirt Laytham, gunned him
down in cold blood from ambush. But who?

Tyree had no time to ponder the question because
Daley was asking, "Now will you get out from them
rocks, or do we come in after you?"

Turning to Sally, Tyree said, "Maybe I can get Daley to give you a safe conduct away from here. How does that set with you?"

The girl shook her head, her face determined. "I'll stick, Chance. You need my help. I'm not going anywhere."

"I was hoping you'd say that." Tyree grinned. He looked over at Daley and yelled, "I'm not making it easy for you, Daley. You want me, come and get me."

The big deputy shrugged, a cold grin on his fleshy lips. "Your funeral. But we'll try not to shoot up the girl too much. We'll want her all in one piece later."

He and Dawson swung their horses around and loped back to their waiting men where they immediately engaged in a heated conversation, heads now and then swiveling to look at Tyree.

There were seven of them against two, one of them just a slip of a girl, but it was obvious that Daley's deputized riders didn't relish the idea of attacking across a hundred yards of open ground where there was not a scrap of cover. These would be Laytham's men, hired guns anxious to avenge their dead boss, but with his death their wages would stop and the loyalty of their kind only stretched so far.

Judging by Daley's flushed, angry face, the five were ready to pull out and wait for another time when the odds would be more in their favor.

In the end, Tyree never knew how Daley convinced them. Maybe he appealed to their dubious loyalty, but more likely he offered money, a bonus in double eagles, like the one paid to the Arapaho Kid for killing Owen Fowler.

Whatever it was, Daley's argument swayed his deputies. The huddle of riders broke up and shook out into a loose line, the big deputy in the middle. A few pulled rifles from the boots under their knees, the rest drew their Colts.

"It's coming, Sally," Tyree said, his voice tense. "Don't try to rush it. Just draw a firm bead and shoot nice and steady."

The girl nodded, laying her cheek on the rifle stock. Tyree saw fear in Sally's eyes, but he didn't blame her any. He was scared himself.

Daley let out a wild whoop, and the line of riders spurred their mounts into a gallop, charging fast across the open ground.

Tyree rose to his feet and cut loose, both six-guns hammering. Beside him he heard the flat, emphatic statement of Sally's rifle. A horse screamed and leaped into the air, throwing its rider. The man scrambled to his feet and managed to get off a wild shot from his rifle before Tyree cut him down. A second man, clutching a bloody chest, lost his balance and fell. His horse, a big, rangy sorrel, swung to its right and careened into a bearded rider. Both the bearded man's mount and the sorrel crashed to the ground in a tangle of flying hooves and billowing dust.

Seeing three of their number go down in just a couple of hell firing seconds was enough for the remaining two Laytham riders, neither of them very committed to the wild charge in the first place. The surviving attackers, Daley included, scattered. A man ran his horse into the barn, while a second headed for the bunkhouse. Daley and Len Dawson rode around the cabin and vanished from sight.

The bearded man who'd gone down with his horse suddenly staggered to his feet. He'd lost his rifle, but he pulled his belt gun and snapped a fast shot at Tyree, the bullet whapping into the sandstone inches from his head. No mercy in him, Tyree fired both his guns at the same instant and the man staggered, then fell flat on his face.

Tyree reloaded quickly, and, ignoring Sally's frantic yell to stop, he leaped over the rock wall and ran for the cabin. His blood was up and he was full of fight, determined to end it. It was time to smash Daley and those who'd come with him so that he'd never have to see their shadows foul the earth again.

The rider who'd sought refuge in the barn dropped to one knee and fired at Tyree from the door. Without slackening his pace, Tyree again triggered both Colts and, hit hard twice, the man slumped to the ground.

Off to his left, Tyree heard pounding hoofbeats as a frightened rider cut and ran, a man who had just experienced enough of gunfighting to last him a lifetime.

That left only Clem Daley and Len Dawson. And to Tyree, thinking back to when he first entered the canyonlands and ran afoul of those two, it seemed his life had come full circle.

Tyree slowed his pace as he reached the corner of the ruined cabin. He eased down the hammer on one of his Colts and stuck the gun into his waistband. On cat feet, he moved to the front of the cabin. He stepped out into the yard, his gun ready, but saw only Daley's horse, its head hanging, reins trailing.

A bullet thudded into the cabin wall and Tyree dived for the ground and rolled into the crawl space under the cabin porch. Another shot kicked up a plume of dust in front of his face, and a second slammed into a supporting timber, splintering slivers of pine.

Tyree spotted a drift of smoke rise from the creek. He aimed low into the tufted grass along the bank, thumbed off a shot and was rewarded by a yelp of surprise and pain as a man was hit.

Immediately, answering bullets slammed around him, spurting angry Vs of dirt inches from where he lay, others chewing into the wood boards above his head. It was time to move. If he stayed where he was he could be shot to pieces.

There was less than a foot of crawl space, but it was enough for Tyree to work his way toward his left where the porch ended. Squirming on his belly, he dislodged an old pack rat's nest built close to a supporting beam, sending up a small veil of dust. After what seemed like an eternity he reached the end of the porch. He rolled clear from the crawl space, sprang to his feet and headed for the rear of the cabin at a run, bullets thudding venomously around his feet.

Tyree was gambling that Daley and Dawson would expect him to head back to the shelter of the rock wall. But, a wild recklessness in him, he intended no such thing. He kept on running, rounded the front of the cabin again and vaulted into the saddle of Daley's black.

Swinging the horse around, Tyree ignored the bullets whistling past him and galloped to the stone breastwork where Sally was standing, the Winchester in her hands.

Without slackening his pace, Tyree yelled, "Rifle!"

The girl threw the gun and Tyree caught it deftly in one hand. He rode parallel to the base of the mesa for a hundred yards, then swung toward the creek. The big black hit the water at a flat run. Tyree stood in the stirrups, wrenched the horse's head around and splashed along the shallows toward Daley's position on the bank.

The black's hammering hooves churned up cascading columns of water as it closed quickly on Daley. The big deputy jumped to his feet and threw his rifle to his shoulder. He fired. A miss. Tyree fired and Daley staggered a step back, his face stricken, blood staining the front of his shirt just above the belt buckle. Levering his Winchester from the shoulder, Tyree fired again, and Daley was hit a second time. The big man rose on tiptoe, did a half turn and splashed facedown into the water.

Dawson had left the creekbank. He fired his rifle from the hip and Tyree heard the bullet buzz past his ear like an angry hornet. Tyree swung the black away from the creek, riding straight at Dawson. The man tried to work his rifle, then looked down in panic at the gun as the lever jammed halfway on a round. He threw the rifle aside and went for his Colt. Tyree was so close, he held his Winchester in one hand, pushing the rifle out in front of him like a pistol. He fired at Dawson and then charged past him. The black, unnerved by the gunfire, got the bit in its teeth and galloped another fifty or sixty yards before Tyree managed to rein it in, the horse slamming hard onto its haunches before coming to a skidding stop.

Tyree swung out of the saddle and looked across at Dawson, his gun ready. But the man lay flat on his back, his body spread-eagled, back arched against what appeared to be agonizing seizures of pain.

Stepping to the fallen deputy, Tyree looked down at Dawson but saw no sign of a wound. The man's face was ashen and his breathing was short and painful, hissing through tightly clenched teeth.

Dawson's frightened eyes lifted to Tyree. "Something is broke inside me," he said. "It's like a rock is crushing my chest and my left arm is hurting like hell."

Kneeling beside the fallen deputy, Tyree nodded. "Dawson, you weren't hit by a bullet. I think your pump is giving out. Seen it once before in a man."

"Then it's all up with me?"

Choosing the truth over a lie, Tyree said, "I'd say it is. And soon."

Tyree looked up as Sally stepped to his side. He tapped his chest. "He's hurting. In there."

"Hurting all over, boy," Dawson said. "Maybe my conscience most of all." He reached out and grabbed Tyree's arm. "We never should've hung you, me and Clem. That was a hell of a thing to do to a man."

"I was only passing through," Tyree said. "You and Daley should have let me be."

Age had faded Dawson's eyes, and now approaching death was shadowing them further. "Tell me, Tyree. Was it really you who done for Laytham? I figured it had to be you."

Tyree shook his head. "I didn't kill him. I didn't even know the man was dead until you told me."

"Well, it don't make no never mind because ol' Quirt done for his share his ownself, and Owen Fowler was sure enough one of them." Dawson managed a thin smile. "It was Laytham who killed Deacon John Kent, you know." He tried to raise his head, but the struggle was too much for him and he let it sink back to the ground. "I want to die clean, boy. Tell you how it was."

"Then let's hear it. Get that weight off your chest, old man."

Dawson nodded, battling pain, his back arching like he was slowly being crushed by the claws of an iron crab. "See, Laytham wanted Fowler's canyon, but the man had already staked his claim and the rumor was he'd soon get it all deeded and proper. Maybe Quirt could have taken it to court, I don't know, but he didn't have the patience for that. He wanted to get big and do it all at once, fast, like. Well, one day Laytham happened on Deacon Kent on the trail near the canyon. The two talked and after he said so long, ol' Quirt turned and put a bullet into the preacher's back. Me, I helped him dump the body near Fowler's cabin. Then Quirt give me and Clem the preacher's watch and money, told us how we should say we found them in the cabin on the table."

The death shadows were gathering dark gray in Dawson's eye sockets and cheekbones. He gasped as

a new wave of pain slammed him, then after a few
moments whispered, "Laytham figured he'd move
his cows into the canyon after Fowler was hung. He
didn't count on him getting a prison sentence. Still,
he did for him in the end, and he paid the Arapaho
Kid well for doing it."

The deputy shook his head, as though he was trying to erase bad memories. "Tyree, I ain't proud of
what I done. But Laytham said he'd get me fired
from my lawman's job and then he'd run me out of
the territory if'n I didn't help him. Me, I was too old
for cowboyin' and too proud to beg, so I done like
he told me."

"Dawson," Tyree asked, "who ordered the mur-
ders of Luke Boyd and Steve Lassiter? Was that more
of Laytham's doing?"

The deputy shook his head. "Quirt had no hand
in that." Dawson felt death crowding him and he
knew his time was short. He clutched Tyree by the
front of his shirt. "Listen, there's somebody else . . .
somebody who wants respect, admiration maybe,
and on top of that, he wants Quirt's woman real bad.
Crazy bad. He plans on being the biggest man in the
territory and the only way he can do that is by
money and power. He . . . he . . ."

Dawson was slipping away. Tyree leaned closer to
him, whispering in his ear. "Who is he, Dawson?
Who is that man?"

The old deputy opened his mouth to speak, but
the words fled his tongue as his heart faltered to
a stop.

Len Dawson was dead.

Chapter 22

Six dead men were scattered around the ranch, and Tyree and Sally spent the rest of that day burying them. It was hard, grueling work that involved dragging the bodies well away from the cabin and digging graves deep enough to discourage coyotes.

One horse was dead, and Tyree dragged the carcass behind the powerful black to the mouth of a canyon where he left it to be taken care of by scavengers. On the plus side, he and Sally had acquired five good horses and enought weapons and ammunition to start a small war. Tyree also relieved two of the dead of their tobacco and papers, necessity overcoming any squeamishness he might have felt on the matter.

Later, as the day died around them, he and Sally sat by the fire drinking coffee, lost in their own thoughts.

The men on whom Tyree had planned to take his revenge were now all dead, and their passing had left a void inside him that he had no idea how to fill. As he sat and watched the firelight play in Sally's hair, touching each curl with burnished gold, he

made a vow—as long as he lived, he would never
hate another man. To hate a man as he had hated
Quirt Laytham was to walk in darkness, never again
to see the light. He had lived long with his hate and
the older it got, the tighter it became until it gripped
his gut like a fist holding a stick.

Now Laytham was gone, but Tyree found he could
take no joy in his death.

But perhaps there was a path to the light, a way
to remove the emptiness inside him . . . replace the
hate he'd felt with another, more tender emotion.

He reached out and ran the back of his forefinger
down Sally's cheek. The girl smiled and inclined her
head, trapping Tyree's hand between her neck and
shoulder. They sat that way for a long while as the
coyotes called in the distance and the guttering fire
made its small sound in the gathering darkness.

At first light, Tyree rose from his bed in the barn
and filled the coffeepot with water from the creek.
He built up the fire and placed the pot on the coals
to boil.

Sally had heard him stir, and now she stepped
beside him, looking impossibly fresh and pretty, despite the few stray straws in her hair.

Anticipating her question, Tyree said, "I'm riding
to the Rafter-L. I have to tell Lorena about her father." He hesitated a few moments, then added,
"And hear what she has to say about Quirt Laytham's murder."

"Do you think she'll accuse you?" Sally asked.

Tyree shrugged. "I don't know. I hope she was
around me long enough to realize that I'm not a

bushwhacker. But there's no telling how she'll react. Could be when I tell her what Len Dawson said she'll change her mind about Laytham, although I'm not counting on it. What is a lowlife like Dawson's word to Lorena, or anybody else come to that?"

"He was dying when he told us about Laytham killing the preacher," Sally pointed out. "Don't dying men always tell the truth?"

His face bleak, Tyree said, "I've heard dying men lie, right up until they took their last breath. Lorena will have no reason to believe me, but I've got to try."

"I'll come with you," Sally said. "I like Lorena and I think she likes me. I'm sure she'll listen when I tell her you'd nothing to do with her intended's death."

Tyree nodded. "I'm hoping she will. As it is, she'll take the news about Luke real hard and coming on top of what happened to Laytham. . . . Well, who knows how she's going to react."

The girl hesitated, thinking about what she had to say, then managed finally, "Chance, Luther Darcy could be at the ranch."

"I thought about that, Sally. But if he is, let me deal with him. Him and me, we're in the same business—the gunfighting business—and it's only a question of who between us learned his trade better."

"Chance," Sally said, "I'll take a shot at Darcy if I can. I haven't let go of a thing."

There was no point in arguing and Tyree knew it. He took the pot from the fire. "Ready for coffee?" he asked.

The night shadows were washing out of the canyons, and the mesas and ridges stood out sharp and clear in the morning light as Sally and Tyree rode away from the cabin toward the Laytham ranch, following a route Lorena had once described to him.

They rode for most of the morning through the wild country. Around them lay a vast, endless maze of winding canyons, craggy ridges and red-and-yellow mesas, one layer of rock piled on another, each a little smaller than the one before, like a tiered wedding cake. The air of the new day, still free of dust, smelled fresh and clean. They rode by a couple of deer, then a small herd of pronghorn antelope grazing under a cottonwood by a slow-moving creek, their heads buried to the ears in dark green grass.

The sun was almost directly overhead in a cloudless sky when Sally and Tyree topped a low lava ridge and saw the Rafter-L spread out in a wide valley below them.

The ranch was dominated by a white-painted, two-story frame house with a veranda wrapped around three sides and a spectacular backyard view of a towering mesa. To the right and left of the main house were stables, a blacksmith's forge and other buildings, including an extensive bunkhouse, all of them well maintained. A couple of roofed artesian wells, shaded by trees, provided cool water, adding a reliable supply to the rushing spring that ran just to the north of the property.

Whatever Quirt Laytham had been, he knew ranching and he hadn't stinted on hard work, as his place testified.

Tyree rode down the slope of the ridge, Sally following close behind. They reined up in the yard in front of the house, the eerie silence of the place enveloping them. Nothing stirred, not even the wind, and the door to the bunkhouse stood open, some scattered scraps of clothing lying in the dirt outside as though the occupants had left in a hurry.

"Hello the house!" Tyree called out.

He was answered with a hushed, uneasy quiet.

"There's nobody to home," Sally said, her voice sounding very small in the oppressive silence. "Maybe they're all attending Laytham's funeral."

"Could be," Tyree agreed. He looked around him, wondering what to do next. He was an uninvited stranger here and couldn't very well go barging into the house.

Then he and Sally heard it at the same time . . . the slow, steady beat of a muffled drum. The noise seemed to come from the cookhouse, a small cabin with an iron chimney built for convenience sake near the bunkhouse. But no smoke rose from the stove inside, and, like the one to the bunkhouse, the door stood ajar.

The drumming stopped for a few moments, then started up again, a slow, cadenced *Thud! Thud! Thud!*

"Wait here, Sally," Tyree said. "I'm going to take a look-see."

He felt no sense of impending danger, but he eased the Colt in his waistband, bringing it closer to hand should he have to draw in a hurry.

Tyree walked his horse to the cookhouse, looking around him. No one was in sight, and this at a time when the ranch should have been bustling with activity, the smith's hammer clanging, riders coming and going, the ranch cook busily preparing the hands' lunchtime beef and beans.

And where was Lorena?

As he swung out of the saddle, the drumming, which had stopped momentarily, began again. But this time there were only a few beats, then the drum fell once again into silence.

As Tyree remembered, ranch cooks were often a bad-tempered bunch, notoriously touchy about anyone entering their domain uninvited. He stopped outside the door and asked, "Anybody to home?"

A second or two passed; then a weak voice from inside whispered, "I'm in here."

Tyree stepped inside, and once his eyes became accustomed to the gloom, he saw a man lying on his back on the floor. Blood was congealed on the pine boards around the fallen cook, the white apron around his waist stained a rusty red. What looked to be a wooden washtub had fallen at the man's left foot, and he hit it with the toe of his shoe. The tub gave off a dull thud. "Knew if I kept this up long enough, somebody would eventually come looking," he said.

Kneeling beside the cook, Tyree asked: "What happened?"

"Hell, that's easy to see, even for a puncher," the cook snapped. "I've been shot through and through."

"Who shot you?" Tyree asked.

"Is it bad?" the cook asked, ignoring Tyree's question.

Quickly Tyree untied the man's apron and looked at his wound.

"Well, is it bad?"

Tyree nodded. "Yeah, as bad as it gets. You've been gut-shot."

"Thought so," the cook muttered. "Paining me considerable." His eyes sought those of Tyree in the dimness of the cabin. "Been bad around here recently. Luther Darcy showed up real early this morning before first light. Killed one of the hands who stood up to him and ran the rest off. Miss Lorena, she came down wearing only her nightgown and tried to get them boys to stay, but they lit out just the same, said she couldn't pay them enough to face Darcy." The cook coughed, a rush of blood staining his lips. "Can't say as I blame them."

"Darcy do this to you?" Tyree asked.

The man shook his head. "Nah, even Luther Darcy knows good cooks are hard to replace. He had me pour him some coffee after the killing, but he didn't offer me no harm. He stayed awhile, back-talked Miss Lorena, and then rode out of here."

"Then who—"

"Nick Tobin."

Tyree was stunned. "Sheriff Tobin shot you?"

"After Darcy left, maybe an hour before you showed up, he stepped in here and asked me who was to home. I said only me and Miss Lorena, and as soon as I got the words out, without even a howdy-do, he shucked his pistol and shot me. Then he walked away mighty fast toward the house."

Alarm clamoring at him, Tyree asked, "Where is Lorena?"

"Still at the house I guess," the cook said. "Leastways she didn't come a-running after she heard the shot that's done killed me."

Tyree rose to his feet. "Stay here," he said. "I'll be back."

"Hell, I ain't goin' no place," the cook said.

Tyree sprinted for the house, ignored Sally's shouted question and bounded up the stairs of the veranda to the front door. He tried the handle, but it had been locked from the outside.

Fear sliding into his belly like a knife blade, he raised his boot and kicked the door. Once, twice, then it crashed inward, splintering wood from around the lock. Behind him he heard Sally's bewildered yell, "Chance, what are you doing?"

But he didn't take time to answer. He ran into the house and called out, "Lorena, where are you?"

The house was silent, but for the slow, stately tick of a grandfather clock standing in the hallway.

There were several rooms opening off the hall, and Tyree entered all of them. One was a parlor, another a dining room, both expensively and ornately furnished in the accepted mode of the time, but Tyree took no time to admire the decor.

Lorena had to be upstairs, maybe hurt.

Taking the steps two at a time, Tyree ran up the winding staircase and when he reached the landing he hollered again, "Lorena!"

There was no answer.

Tyree tried a bedroom. It was a man's room, no doubt Laytham's, but it was empty. He tried another room off the long hallway. That too was empty. The door to the remaining room was slightly ajar. Tyree pulled his Colt and walked on cat feet to the door, the gun upraised and ready. He pushed the door wide, slamming it hard against the wall, then stepped inside—into a scene of unimaginable horror.

Chapter 23

Lorena was sprawled across the top of her bed. She was naked, torn scraps of her nightgown scattered around the floor, a look of terror mixed with outrage frozen on her dead white face.

Tyree willed himself to step closer, trying desperately to grapple with the stark reality his eyes were revealing to him. The woman had been used like a line-shack whore and then strangled, deep purple bruises marring the smooth skin of her throat.

Her assailant had been a powerful man, with strong hands, bringing to Tyree's mind's eye the thick shoulders and heavy arms of the massive Nick Tobin.

Lorena had fought like a tiger, both for her life and her virtue. Under the nails of one outflung hand, Tyree noticed shards of skin and a few hairs—long, white hairs.

On the dresser lay a stack of currency. Numb, scarcely aware of his actions, Tyree picked it up and riffled through the bills with his thumb. There was all of a thousand dollars there—and now came the dawning realization of who had put up the money to bribe him to leave the territory.

He had no way of knowing how and where it had happened, but Lorena must have finally decided she loved Quirt Laytham and wanted to get rid of the man who had vowed to do him harm. That was why she had given Tobin the money and told him to make the offer.

After the death of Laytham, Tobin had made returning the bribe an excuse to visit the ranch. He'd shot the cook, then, blinded by lust, the lawman had thrown himself on Lorena. But she'd fought him, and in the end Tobin had murdered her.

Afterward, no doubt horrified by the enormity of what he'd done, the man had fled in a panic, leaving the money behind.

Tyree realized it must also have been Lorena who had told Luther Darcy to warn him out of town. That was why the gunman had not pushed a gunfight at the livery stable.

Lorena had done what she thought was right, and Tyree could not find it in his heart to blame her. Whatever she'd felt or believed was now in the past, and Tyree would not dwell on it. He knew by bitter experience that in the carriages of the past, a man can't go anywhere.

He stepped back to the bed.

He shouldn't be seeing Lorena like this, nor should anyone else. Gently, he closed her eyes, crossed her arms over her breasts, then covered her with the calico quilt that had dropped to the floor during the struggle.

Footsteps sounded on the stairs and Sally called out, "Chance, where are you?"

"In here," Tyree said, aware of the strange, hollow echo of his voice.

Sally stepped into the room and her eyes widened in horror when she saw the still figure on the bed. "Lorena?" she asked.

Tyree nodded. "She was murdered. Strangled." Then he said, "Nick Tobin." He saw in Sally's eyes that he had no need to elaborate further.

"Chance, was she . . . was she . . . ?"

"Yes," Tyree said. "She was." He stepped to the girl and took her in his arms. "Now just let it go. Don't think about it."

Sally laid her head on Tyree's shoulder and sobbed, her shoulders heaving. After a few minutes, Tyree led her from the bedroom and out of the house and into the bright light of the day.

He left Sally sitting head bowed on the steps to the veranda and went back to check on the cook. The man was dead.

Tyree had vowed to never hate another man, but his loathing of Nick Tobin went deep, and with it came a killing fury. He knew exactly what he was going to do—ride to Crooked Creek, gun the fat albino and leave him dead in the street.

That was to come. But first he had a burying to do.

Tyree went back to the Lorena's bedroom, wrapped her up tightly in the quilt and carried her downstairs. With Sally at his side, he walked with the dead woman in his arms until he found a shady spot surrounded by trees a ways from the house.

He went back and got a shovel and buried Lorena in the dry earth, then Sally read words from a Bible she'd found in the house.

"The Lord is my shepherd; I shall not want. He maketh me to lie down in green pastures; He leadeth me beside the still waters. He restoreth my soul . . ."

After she'd finished reading, Sally closed the Bible. She and Tyree stood in silence by the graveside for a long time, then turned away, their faces like stone, and walked back to the ranch.

The dead cook was a complete stranger to Tyree, but he would not leave him to the coyotes. No matter what he was, what kind of a man he'd been, he deserved to be decently laid to rest. Tyree was there, so he had it to do. The cook's dying had ceased to be his own affair and had become a matter for the living.

There were still a couple of hours of daylight left after Sally and Tyree buried the ranch cook and swung into the saddle and headed for Crooked Creek. Neither of them felt much like talking until they reached the brush flats just as the sun was dropping in the sky and the first lamps were being lit in the town.

"I'm going to Tobin's office. If he's not there, I'll try the saloon," Tyree told the girl. "Sally, maybe you should wait at the livery stable until I deal with Tobin."

The girl shook her head. "I plan to be with you every step of the way," she said. "Lorena was my friend."

Tyree saw by the stubborn set of Sally's chin that

he could not talk her out of going with him. "All right, but just make sure you take every step of the way real careful."

The sky had turned a dark scarlet to the horizon, banded by thin, violet clouds as they cleared the flats and rode into town. Lamps glowed pale orange in the houses and businesses along the main street and the bright lights of Bradley's splashed a rectangle of yellow on the boardwalk.

As Sally and Tyree rode past the livery, Zeb Pettigrew hailed Tyree, and waved him over.

"If'n you're looking for Luther Darcy you're a spell too late," the old man said, looking up at Tyree sitting tall and grim in the saddle.

"Him," Tyree said. "And Nick Tobin."

Pettigrew scratched under his beard. "Tobin's gone too. Rode in here late this morning with his face all clawed up, like he'd had an argument with a cougar, then him and Darcy talked and left in a hurry."

"Which way were they headed?" Tyree asked, disappointment tugging at him. He'd badly wanted Tobin to be in town. And Darcy too, come to that.

"North," Pettigrew said. "Maybe hunting you."

Tyree glanced around him, at the crowding darkness, and knew there could be no going after Tobin until sunup.

Pettigrew read Tyree's grim face, and asked: "You got something to tell me, boy, seein' as how I'm what you might call an interested party?"

Tyree nodded, and the old man said, "Let's step into my office. We can talk there."

Tyree swung out of the saddle and so did Sally.

They walked their horses to the barn, then left them inside while they stepped into Pettigrew's tiny office by the door of the stable.

The old man poured coffee for them both. "Here," he said, handing them each a steaming tin cup, "you two look like you could use this."

Pettigrew sat back in his creaking chair while Sally and Tyree perched on his desk. "Well, tell me all," the old man said, smiling under his beard. "Let the play begin."

Tyree rolled a smoke, thumbed a match into flame and lit the cigarette. While he smoked he began by telling Pettigrew about his fight with Clem Daley and Len Dawson.

The old man nodded his approval. "The world's a sight better off without them two," he said. "An' that's a natural fact."

Then, his face strained, Tyree told about the events of the morning.

Pettigrew looked like he'd been struck. "So that's why Tobin's face was all tore up." He shook his head. "I remember Lorena when she was just a skinny kid in pigtails," he said. "She rode this old paint mare, half the time without a saddle, and she explored just about every corner of the whole territory."

Swallowing hard, Pettigrew rubbed his eyes with the palm of his hand. "I just can't believe Lorena is gone. She was such a beautiful girl."

"Now you know why I want to find Tobin," Tyree said.

"He won't come back here," Pettigrew said. "After I spread the word around town, if he shows his face in Crooked Creek again, he'll be lynched and I'll haul on the rope my ownself."

"Why would a man, any man, do a thing like that?" Sally asked, her voice faltering a little.

Pettigrew's grin was bitter. "Girl, I've known Nick Tobin for a long time, and he isn't a man—he's a freak. He doesn't think like other men. One time he told me all his plans are long-term, years from now, and that he'd be a big man in the territory one day and walk a wide path. In the meantime he was happy to sit there in his office with them pink eyes of his shut and dream his big dreams, biding his time. I figure he only went along with Quirt Laytham because he wanted all the things Quirt had: a big ranch, a beautiful woman, money and power. Tyree, I'm a watching man, but I'm also a thinking man, and I always reckoned Tobin planned on someday taking them all away from him."

"Zeb, do you think Tobin killed Laytham?" Tyree asked.

The old man nodded. "Could be he got tired of waiting. If he didn't kill Laytham his ownself, he had somebody else do it for him."

"Lorena's father is dead, killed by Luther Darcy, and so is Steve Lassiter," Tyree said. "And I found a couple of Laytham's punchers murdered at Lassiter's ranch."

"And Jean?" Pettigrew asked, his faded eyes troubled.

"Found her grave," Tyree said. "I don't know how she died."

The old man sat deep in thought for a few moments, then said, "Son, you surely do have a tiger by the tail. I think Tobin had already made his move to take over the Laytham's place and every other ranch between here and Moab.

"Killing Luke Boyd and Steve Lassiter was the beginning. Then he got rid of Quirt Laytham and the way was wide open for him.

"Only trouble was, his big dreams ended when he rode into Laytham's ranch this morning with a woman's body on his mind. Now all he can do is leave the territory, but I reckon he'll try to get even with you afore he does." Pettigrew shrugged. "You've been a big part of his downfall."

"I'll be waiting for him," Tyree said. "I'm heading back to—" He realized he was about to say, "Luke Boyd's place," but corrected himself and said, "My place. I'll make myself an inviting target."

The reference was not lost on Pettigrew. "You've staked yourself out a spread?"

Tyree nodded. "You could say that. Luke Boyd signed his ranch over to me just before he died. I intended to ask Lorena if she wanted it"—he hesitated, his face bleak—"but that's not going to happen now."

Rising to his feet, Tyree said, "Well, I'm riding, Zeb. I want to be at my cabin come first light. Thanks for everything you've done for me." He nodded to Sally. "And take care of my best girl while I'm gone."

"Zeb, there's no need to do that," Sally said. "I won't be staying in Crooked Creek."

"Sally," Tyree snapped, exasperation edging his voice, "I aim to put myself in harm's way. No point in us both getting killed."

"And that's exactly why I'm going with you,

Chance," the girl said stubbornly, "to see you don't get killed."

Tyree threw out his arms and turned to Pettigrew. "Zeb, make her see reason."

The old man grinned. "Tyree, when love comes in the door, reason flies out the window. And there's an end to it."

"And I do love you, Chance Tyree, and that's why I want to be at your side," Sally said. "I want to be at your side always, through the good times and bad." Her eyes searched Tyree's face. "Can you understand that?"

For a few moments, Tyree was speechless. Then came the dawning realization that this pretty, brave and wonderful girl had just said she loved him. He took Sally in his arms. "I understand perfectly. Then I guess it's you and me."

The girl nodded. "You and me, Chance, together, for now and for always."

"For now and for always," Tyree repeated, liking the sound of it.

Pettigrew sniffed. "Damn it all," he said, "if them wasn't the purtiest words I ever did hear. Now you two get out of here afore I start to caterwaul."

Sally and Tyree swung into their saddles and rode out of the barn, turning their horses toward the north.

"You two be careful," Pettigrew called out after them. "And come back in one piece."

The two young riders loped onto the brush flats, the lights of Crooked Creek falling behind them. Ahead lay a hidden trail and the dangerous dark of the night.

Chapter 24

The moon swung into the sky and the land around them was bathed in pale light as Sally and Tyree entered the canyonlands and rode north along the bank of Hatch Wash. Around them lay a vast country of deep shadows and brooding silences, the mesas and ridges standing like ghostly sentinels, guarding the troubled night.

As the two riders looped east toward the cabin, an owl urgently questioned the darkness as they passed, its call carrying no echo, a lost and lonely sound that went unanswered.

Sally and Tyree left the yelps of the coyotes behind them as they reached the creek under a roof of stars and rode toward the cabin. There was no wind, as though the land was holding its breath, waiting for what was to come.

Ahead of them, Tyree saw a dull, red glow in the sky that puzzled him. It was only a faint smear of scarlet against the brighter light of the stars, but Sally saw it too. She turned to him in the saddle. "Trees on fire maybe? Or grass?"

Tyree shook his head. "I don't think so. I reckon it's a campfire, a mighty big one at that."

"Tobin?" the girl asked.

"Could be," Tyree answered. "He's a pale, bloodless creature and he might be feeling the night chill."

As they drew closer to the ruined cabin, the reason for the glow in the sky gradually became apparent. A huge bonfire burned in the yard, fed by wood scavenged from the ruin, a few heavy logs flaming at its base.

Tyree reined up and slid the Winchester from the scabbard. He swung out of the saddle and told Sally to do the same. The girl dismounted and stepped beside him. "I . . . I don't understand, Chance. Why this?"

"It's a beacon, Sally. To bring us here. They knew we'd see it and wonder at it."

"Like moths to a flame," the girl said, her face revealing her unease.

"Something like that," Tyree said. "And I'd say Tobin and Darcy already know we're here."

They left their horses where they were and walked toward the bunkhouse and cabin. There was no one in sight, the only movement the flickering flames of the fire, the only sound the crackle and snap of the burning logs. As they reached the sidewall of the bunkhouse, a log at the center of the fire fell under its own weight, sending up a cascade of bright red sparks that danced into the darkness.

Where were Tobin and Darcy?

Tyree, his senses tuned to the danger, felt their presence, as though even now they were watching him, waiting before they moved in for the kill.

Sally was right behind him, close enough that he could hear her fast little breaths. His mouth dry, Tyree transferred his rifle to his left hand and wiped a sweaty palm on his jeans before again taking the gun in his right.

Tyree stepped around the corner of the bunkhouse, pushed the door open with the barrel of the Winchester and stepped quickly inside. The glare of the bonfire bathed the place in a shifting scarlet-and-orange light. It was empty.

Closing the door behind him, Tyree motioned Sally to follow and they walked on cat feet toward the corral. He had repaired the pulled-down fence and all the horses were still there, standing around quietly, without any show of alarm.

Slowly, Tyree worked his way past the corral toward the barn. A single cloud drifted across the face of the moon, deepening the shadows around them, and something big jumped in the creek, its splash loud in the silence.

Tyree stopped in midstride and studied the barn. The doors were open and the building was shrouded in shadows, an angled wedge of moonlight falling across the dirt floor. The tin rooster at the peak of the roof caught a brief passing breeze and swung, creaking, in Tyree's direction, as though annoyed by his intrusion.

Turning to Sally, Tyree whispered, "Stay here. I'm going to check out the barn."

The girl's eyes were scared. "Be careful, Chance," she said. "I don't like it here."

Tyree managed a weak grin. "That makes two of us."

He stepped toward the barn door, trying his best to keep to the shadows. At the entrance he stopped and levered a round into the chamber of the Winchester, an intimidating *chink-chunk*! he hoped might unnerve anyone hiding inside.

He heard a horse stomp its foot and blow through its nose somewhere in the dark interior. All the horses Tyree had taken after his fight with Daley and his men were in the corral. That had to be Tobin's mount, or Darcy's.

Quietly, Tyree took a step into the darkness of the barn, his rifle up and ready. He took another, his eyes desperately trying to penetrate the gloom.

But he never saw until too late the loop that dropped from above him and settled around his upper body and arms. The loop tightened, pinning his arms to his side. Then, from somewhere over his head, Luther Darcy yelled, "I got him, Tobin!"

Tyree struggled against the imprisoning noose, but Darcy yanked it tighter. From out of the darkness Tobin's face swung into view. The man had no need for dark glasses at night, and his staring, pink eyes looked strangely lifeless, without expression.

Tobin drew back his first and crashed it into Tyree's unprotected chin. Tyree took a step backward under the force of the blow, then sank to his knees, his head reeling. He desperately tried to free his arms, but the big sheriff now had the rope and he looped it again and again around Tyree, trussing him into immobility.

"Darcy, get down from there," Tobin said, looking up at the gunman. "I've got him knotted up as tight as Dick's hatband."

Darcy, who'd been standing on a crossbeam just inside the barn door, dropped to the ground and with amazing agility and grace landed lightly on his feet.

"Let's take him outside," Tobin said. "I want to watch his face when I start to burn him."

"Where's the girl?" Darcy asked Tyree.

Tyree tried to kick out at the gunman, but Darcy stepped back, easily evading the swinging boot, then slammed the back of his right hand across Tyree's face, the loud crack making a horse snort and stamp uneasily.

"Where is she, Tyree?" Darcy asked again. "I've got big plans for that little whore."

The smoky taste of blood in his mouth, Tyree said through split lips, "You go to hell."

Darcy smiled, his teeth flashing white under his mustache. "It doesn't make no never mind. She hasn't gone far. I'll find her."

The gunman yanked the Colt from Tyree's waistband then stooped and picked up the fallen Winchester.

"I'll take him out by the fire," Tobin said, his pink eyes, white skin and the deep furrows Lorena's nails had left on his cheek making him look like he was wearing a grotesque mask. "Maybe I'll have some fun with him afore I finally burn him up."

The sheriff grabbed Tyree by the rope around his chest and dragged him out of the barn. Darcy followed, carefully looking around at the surrounding darkness as he stepped after Tobin.

Tobin pulled Tyree close to the fire, so close Chance could feel the burning heat on his face. Tyree turned to Darcy, desperately trying to drive a wedge between the gunman and the sheriff, knowing it was his only hope and a slender one at that. "Darcy, you know Tobin is finished in Crooked Creek, don't you?" he asked. "The word about what he did to Lorena Boyd got around fast, and I'm betting there's already a lynch mob hunting him."

The gunman shrugged. "Hell, he didn't do anything to her that ol' Quirt hadn't done already. Who misses an extry slice when the pie has already been cut?"

"He murdered her, Darcy. Did he tell you that?"

The gunman was startled. "No, he didn't tell me that." He turned to the sweating lawman. "Tobin, did you kill that gal?"

Tobin's eyes captured and held the firelight, glittering like rubies. "She struggled agin' me, Luther," he said, his voice rising in a thin whine. "She called me names, bad names, and I slapped her around a time or two but she wouldn't let up. Then I took her by the throat. Hell, it was like when you strangle a bird. Just a little squeeze, and the next thing she was dead."

Fighting down his revulsion, Tyree tried to hold his voice steady as he said, "It was all for nothing, Tobin. You murdered Luke Boyd and Steve Lassiter for their spreads. And once you'd done that you decided to go for broke and had to get rid of the one man who had everything you wanted so you could take it all for yourself." Tyree turned to Darcy again. "He had you lay for Quirt Laytham and kill him, didn't he?"

"It was easy." Darcy smiled. "An aimed rifle shot

at two hundred yards is no big thing. Of course, it was a traitorous act, my killing my boss like that, but the sheriff paid me well and that does sway a man."

"Enough of this talk," Tobin said to Darcy. "Let's burn him now."

"You've lost, Tobin," Tyree said. "You can't show your ugly face in Crooked Creek again without getting hanged, so all you can do now is make a run for it."

The big sheriff thought that through, the heat spreading his vile stench around him. His pink eyes suddenly scared, Tobin touched his tongue to his dry top lip and said, "He's right, Luther. After we kill Tyree, we got to get the hell out of the territory."

Darcy laughed without a trace of humor. "What's this 'we,' fat man?"

"You and me, Luther, like we planned."

The gunman shook his head. "It's you they want to hang in Crooked Creek, Tobin, not me. You don't really think I killed Laytham for your benefit, do you? I was setting back, letting you do all my work for me, knowing I could pin the blame on you and Tyree later. Now I can claim the Rafter-L and the other ranches. Think about it, Tobin. Who is there around to stop me?"

"But . . . but . . . that's not how it's going to be, Luther," Tobin protested. "We can go somewhere else, the Colorado Territory maybe, and start all over again."

"With you, Tobin?" Darcy's lips curled into contemptuous smile. "Do you think I want to live with your foul stink around me, those pink eyes always looking at me, you biding your time until you can put a bullet in my back? Tyree is right. You're through, fat man. Your day is done."

Tobin let out an enraged cry that was almost a scream. He bent over, grabbed a thick, blazing brand from the fire and shoved it close to Tyree's face. "You did this!" he shrieked. "You poisoned Darcy's mind, turned him against me." The flames came closer, licking Tyree's skin. "Now I'm going to burn that pretty face right off'n you, boy. See what it's like to be ugly like me, so ugly no woman would ever want you."

Tobin drew back his arm, preparing to shove the flaming brand into Tyree's face, but a gun roared and the side of the man's head disappeared in a sudden fountain of blood and bone.

The sheriff staggered to his right, the brand dropping at his feet, then his knees collapsed and he fell headfirst into the heart of the blazing bonfire, flames and showering sparks hungrily embracing his body.

"Just let him lay there," Darcy said, smiling as he reloaded his smoking Remington. "His fat will feed the fire." The gunman stepped in front of Tyree and shook his head, his smile widening to a grin. "At this very moment ol' Nick Tobin is burning in two places, right here and in hell. Makes a man think, doesn't it?"

"What are you going to do with me, Darcy?" Tyree asked. "By now there are too many people who know you were involved with Tobin. Your only chance is to hightail it out of here and never come back."

The gunman shook his head. "Too thin, Tyree, way too thin. See, the way I figure it, there's no one who can stand up to me in Crooked Creek. I plan to make myself sheriff, take over Laytham's spread and all the other ranches between here and Moab and live high on the hog." He smiled. "And I aim to tame that little Brennan girl. She'll be my woman for a spell until I tire of her; then I'll send her up on the line. Hell, I just thought of it. I'll make money out of her too."

Tyree spat in Darcy's face. "You are scum, Darcy," he said. "A piece of low-life trash."

The gunman wiped the spittle off with the back of his hand, his face black with anger. "I was going to give you an even break, Tyree," he said. "See if you are as good as you think you are." He drew a gun with flashing speed and jammed the muzzle against Tyree's head. "Now I think I'll just scatter your damn brains."

"I always took you for a yellow tinhorn, Darcy," Tyree said. "Now I know you are."

Darcy thumbed back the hammer of his gun. The firelight chased crimson shadows across his face and the air smelled of Tobin's burning flesh. For a few moments he stood like a living statue; then he took a single step back, smiling.

"Ah, what the hell?" the gunman said. "I forgot all about professional courtesy. Mind you, Tyree, your manners are so wanting you really don't deserve it." He holstered his gun, reached into his pocket and unfolded a case knife. Then he drew Tyree's Colt from his waistband and held it aimed at the bound man's head while he cut away the ropes.

As the ends of rope fell around Tyree's feet, Darcy stepped back until fifteen feet of open ground stretched between them. He threw Tyree's gun into the dirt at his feet, then said: "All you have to do is pick it up and start shooting." The man smiled. "Of course, I don't believe for one minute you'll make it that far. And I guess neither do you."

Behind Tyree the fire roared and sputtered, fed by Tobin's bubbling fat. The stench of the man had been bad when he was alive; now, in death, it was almost unbearable.

"Well, Tyree, go for it." Darcy grinned. "If you show yellow, then I'll just gun you where you stand."

The gunman stood easy and relaxed, his hands at waist level, steady and open, the long fingers slightly curled.

Tyree had to bend, pick up the Colt, then fire. Darcy was lightning fast and Tyree knew he wouldn't make it. But he had to try, at least go down fighting. It was better than dying a dog's death like Tobin.

He tensed, getting ready. Darcy noted Tyree's slight movement and his hands lifted, closer to the Remingtons.

"Do it, Tyree," he yelled. "Do it!"

A rock flew out of the darkness.

Thrown with considerable force and skill, the rock slammed into Darcy's right temple with a sickening thud. The gunman's head jerked and, shocked, he took a single step back.

Tyree dived for the gun at his feet.

Darcy's Remingtons flared, bullets splitting the air where Tyree had been standing a moment before. But Tyree had already dropped to his knees, scooping up the Colt before he threw himself flat on his belly.

He fired at Darcy, fired again. Hit hard, the gunman staggered, his guns coming up. Darcy's guns roared as Tyree rolled to his right, two bullets kicking up dirt just inches away from him. Tyree fired, thumbed back the hammer and shot a second time.

Under his brocaded vest, Darcy's white shirt was scarlet with blood. The man backpedaled until he tripped on the cabin porch and toppled backward, his arms sprawling at his sides, convulsively triggering his revolvers until the hammer clicked on spent rounds.

Warily, Tyree rose to his feet and walked toward the fallen gunman. He was aware of Sally emerging from the shadows, another rock in her hand.

Darcy was still conscious, but the grayness of death was on his face. He looked up at Tyree and smiled. "You got lucky," he said. "You'd never have beaten me in a fair fight." He grimaced against a wave of pain, and asked, "What the hell hit me?"

"A God apple," Tyree said.

"A what?"

"A rock, you eejit. God left them around to help us poor cowboys."

Darcy shook his head, his eyes unbelieving. Then he rattled deep in his throat and suddenly all the life that was in him was gone.

Tyree turned as Sally stepped to his side. "Who taught you to throw like that?" he asked, grinning.

The girl smiled. "When you grow up as poor as I did, that's how you hunt prairie chickens," she said. "We didn't have money for shotgun cartridges, and

I soon learned not to throw like a girl. Hunger is an excellent teacher.''

Tyree took Sally in his arms and kissed her hard and long. After a few moments, he heard the God apple drop at her feet.

Epilogue

Four months later Sally Brennan and Chance Tyree were married in the church at Crooked Creek. Zeb Pettigrew stood as best man.

Just about everybody in town attended the wedding, and all agreed bride and groom made a handsome couple and were surely destined for a long, happy life together.

Afterward, at a reception organized by the stalwarts of the fire department, Pettigrew stepped beside Tyree, a glass of champagne in his hand. Zeb had scrubbed up for the occasion and wore a black suit and collarless white shirt.

"First time I ever seen you without a gun, boy," he said.

Tyree nodded. "It's back to home at the cabin, Zeb, hanging on a nail." He smiled at the old man. "The play is over, watcher."

Pettigrew shook his head. "The old play is ended, maybe so, but a new drama begins."

"Not for me," Tyree said. "I'm all through with

guns and gunfighting. Soon I hope to be a family man and be known only as a respectable rancher."

"Who said anything about guns?" Pettigrew said, looking mildly offended. "I'm talking about seeing those young'uns of yours grow up, the girls as pretty as their ma and the boys as tall and straight as their pa."

The old man sipped his champagne and smiled. "I'll be watching. . . ."

GRITTY HISTORICAL ACTION FROM
USA TODAY BESTSELLING AUTHOR

RALPH
COTTON